CARDINAL CABIN

ALSO BY JOANNE DEMAIO

Wintry Novels
Snow Deer and Cocoa Cheer
Snowflakes and Coffee Cakes

The Seaside Saga
The Beach Inn
Beach Breeze
Beach Blues
The Denim Blue Sea
Blue Jeans and Coffee Beans

Countryside New England Novels
True Blend
Whole Latte Life

cardinal
cabin

A NOVEL

JOANNE DEMAIO

Copyright © 2017 Joanne DeMaio
All rights reserved.
ISBN: 1548161713
ISBN 13: 9781548161712

www.joannedemaio.com

To Glastonbury, Connecticut

*My New England hometown
filled with holiday heart.
This one's for you.*

one

"WHAT'S IT ALL FOR, ANYWAY?" Frank Lombardo asks. With a wool cap on his head, and his tan canvas jacket zipped up tight against the chill wind coming off the river, he lifts a string of twinkling lights. The question was meant only for himself, standing on the top rung of a ladder perched against the roofline. But of course, his hovering sister picked up every dismal syllable.

"What do you mean?" Gina asks from down below while giving him yet another string of lights.

"All this fussing and decorating." His gloved hand motions to the grand two-story Addison Boathouse, with its vast deck and, on the roof, a white cupola with paned windows. The boathouse rises from the banks of the river, and his ladder's been propped against the building for hours. "All these lights. And wreaths. And ornaments. For what, really?"

"Frank. We just finished a two-year, gut-to-glory renovation of this place," his sister reminds him. "The mayor even called it the crown jewel of Addison. So string those lights like a spotlight on this riverside beacon."

From his elevated vantage point, the Connecticut River is a silver flowing ribbon, visible through the snow-laced tree branches. There couldn't be a better location for their historic boathouse; it's obvious by the view alone. Apparently the town of Addison agrees, because just about every one of the interior boat racks—row upon row—is stacked with residents' kayaks, canoes and rowboats. They're all secured for winter storage, until that first warm spring day arrives. Then, the frenzy. Throngs of locals, wearing shorts and leather boat shoes, race to launch their small vessels into the winding river from the boathouse's private ramps.

But in the meantime, it's winter-wedding and Christmas-party season in this premier waterfront venue. That the boathouse serves a dual purpose keeps Frank and his sister plenty busy year-round. Above the building's lower-level boat storage, the banquet hall's windows and observation deck are strung with more white lights. Inside, swags of faux snow-tipped green garland loop across the reception room's vaulted, beamed ceiling, and a tall, sparkling Christmas tree anchors the center of the room.

Weeks of decorating work have been undertaken, culminating with these final twinkling touches this cold morning.

"And don't forget," Gina tells him. "You're really doing all this for Dad. He kept this landmark going for decades before turning it over to us."

Frank loops the string of lights on the roof's edge. "Dad. Right. Who is now one of your built-in elves, helping you and Josh with everything since moving into that in-law apartment at your place."

"Mom, too. She loves being a grandma! And you should be thanking me. Because you won't have to worry about them

2

There's a pause then, one long enough to prompt Frank to look down below at his sister, bundled deep into her puffy jacket.

"Well," she says with a tip of her pom-pommed head, "who do you ever expect to meet out in the woods?"

❧

Penny Hart's never ridden on a snowtorcycle before. But apparently it's the easiest way to get through Addison's snowy woods to her rented cabin. She has to admit it was a little surprising to see this odd taxi-like vehicle waiting for her Friday afternoon—a squat motorcycle with its fat, studded snow tires idle, its engine quietly chugging.

Even more surprising is Gus, the driver: a heavyset man in his seventies, at least, with bushy white eyebrows and a wise, serious expression. When he removes his hat, Penny sees that he's nearly bald, except for a fringe of white on the sides and back of his head. Saying few words, Gus helps her settle into the snowtorcycle's sidecar. It's attached to the motorcycle, has a big snow tire with a curved fender, and the whole car is polished to a low shine. There's a windshield, safety bar and comfortable padded seat, too, with enough room for herself and a few pieces of luggage—her mittened hands nervously folded over one small suitcase on her lap.

With nary a nod of his head then, Gus mounts the snowtorcycle and off they go. The vehicle putt-putts along the wide trail through sweeping pines and tall maples, their branches heavy with fresh snow. Wide black-and-silver fenders over the snowtorcycle's studded tires keep that snow from flying back at them as Penny takes in the wintry view. This short sojourn from home certainly draws her into a magical new world, one all white and glistening. Occasionally they pass piles of chopped wood stacked trailside, and random stone benches, too.

Finally, the snowtorcycle slows and stops before a wooden footbridge.

"This is where you get off," Gus tells her over the sound of the sputtering engine.

Penny looks past the bridge to where she barely makes out scattered cabins in sloping, snowy yards, then looks to Gus. "Here?"

He nods. "Can't cross that narrow bridge with this vehicle." He turns the throttle and gives the engine a light rev. "Out you go. You'll find your way." With that, he climbs off the snowtorcycle and sets her luggage at the start of the footbridge. "Cardinal Cabin's just around the first curve, past the pines."

Penny considers the pines surrounding her, okay, for seemingly miles.

"You can't miss it," Gus says as he climbs back on his vehicle, gives a nod of his head and zooms off on his snazzy snow-bike.

"Well, I'll be," Penny whispers. She hikes a heavy tote up on her shoulder and steps through the soft snow. She can bet, well, every last *penny*, that she's already missing her apartment in the refurbished mill factory right in town. Misses her gas fireplace, glowing with the flick of a switch. Misses her kitchen island with its granite countertop. And, oh yes, misses looking *out* her frosted, paned windows to the snowy scene beyond.

Instead of standing practically knee-deep in it.

After one last glance over her shoulder at the diminishing sputter of the snowtorcycle, she tugs her thick scarf tighter, lifts her suitcases and crosses the rickety footbridge. With each cautious step, she looks first this way, then that. Beneath the gently arched bridge, a brook babbles along over large snow-covered rocks. Once she gets across and takes a turn on the hushed trail, a peaceful vista rises from the wooded landscape.

Ahead, just like Gus promised, a dozen or so wood cabins—some A-frames, some bungalows—surround a secluded lake. They're seasonal homes nestled among the trees, little getaways from the hustle and bustle of everyday life. Windowpanes are aglow with lamplight; fresh-fallen snow blankets rooftops; an old sled leans against the front porch railing of one cabin; a pair of ice skates hangs by its laces on the wooden door of another.

What it all looks like is a pretty painting ... on a Christmas card. Yes, a greeting card sprinkled with glitter and penned with pleasant salutations to friends and neighbors. A greeting card she'd normally be sending from the comfort of her warm, lamp-lit office nook, at home!

Penny takes another few reluctant steps, her booted feet sinking in the powdery snow, then stops. She squints at the cabins while reaching into her parka pocket for the tiny ad clipped from the *Addison Weekly*, the ad she begrudgingly answered to arrange a two-week stay on this Snowflake Lake, imagining a picturesque place in Vermont, maybe. Or New Hampshire.

Not right here in the heart of Addison, Connecticut! She's still surprised by the sight. But being new to the area, she'd never heard of the town's lakeside hideaway. It's no wonder, the way it's concealed in the small forest along the end of winding Old Willow Road, and accessible only by trail or a narrow one-lane road on the far side of the lake. From what she's gathered, it's a well-kept secret, much treasured by those familiar with it.

As much as she treasures her own cozy apartment—left behind for now, she thinks with a longing look over her shoulder. But that only makes her miss it more, so she turns back to the task at hand.

"Let's see," she reads. "Cardinal Cabin, with its bright red berry wreath welcoming you."

When she scrutinizes the wood-framed bungalows and A-frames, she can't miss it. The owner must've gotten the place ready for her stay, as smoke curls from the chimney of the cabin with the red wreath hanging on the planked door. So she lifts her luggage once more and follows the wintry path around Snowflake Lake. Two squirrels tumble in the snow ahead of her, and a white-tailed deer stands on the far side of the lake, near the trees. On the cabin's front porch, sprigs of pine branches with delicate green needles rise from a silver metal milk can set atop a plaid blanket, just like she was told. Pulling off her mittens, she tips the milk can and finds the door key hidden beneath it.

With everything familiar gone now—far, far beyond the lake—she inserts the key in the door, then stops. Before turning the key, she manages a small smile at the doorknocker mounted beside the entryway: a carved woodpecker perched front-and-center on a barked slab of wood.

Okay, so it's time to make the best of things. She playfully tugs the doorknocker's pull-string, and *rat-a-tat-tat-tat* ... she has arrived.

Inside, little Cardinal Cabin is decorated for Christmas. Clusters of red berries dot the swag of evergreen reaching across the rough-hewn mantel. More berries, and snowcapped pinecones, are tucked into the branches of a Christmas tree wrapped in white twinkling lights beside the fireplace, where logs are burning and snapping in the flames. Hooked-wool pillows and warm throws cover the sofa and upholstered chairs.

Behind those, on a small, round dining table, a lantern glimmers beside a crystal bowl spilling with pinecones and cinnamon sticks.

Penny hesitantly turns around, feeling like she's stepped into a woodland fairy tale. Berry wreaths and sprigs of Scotch pine hang from the wood-planked walls. Vintage Mason jars etched with cardinal motifs sit on end tables. And beside a floor vase filled with white birch branchlets, a whittled deer stands sentry.

So she takes off her parka and hangs it on a coatrack shaped like deer antlers, no less, then hooks her scarf and mittens there, too. All while glancing around at the paneled walls and frosted, paned windows.

What it does, all of it—from the crackling fire in the stone fireplace to the twinkling tree lights setting the wood walls aglow—is this: It begins, just *begins*, to melt away any doubts she had brought with her through Cardinal Cabin's rustic front door.

two

By SUNDAY MORNING, PENNY'S STILL getting herself settled into cabin life on Snowflake Lake. Wearing her blue parka, she heads outside thinking the lake is actually more of a pond. It's small, easily walked around, and frozen solid. With a fringed blanket over her arm, she carries a leather journal in one hand, a travel mug of hot cocoa in the other. Her booted feet crunch on the snow, and it's the only sound in this hushed place—which makes her take even softer steps.

"And hum," she whispers, before humming a low tune as melodic as the birdsong coming from a snowy pine. A stone bench sits beside the lake, and it's right where she's headed. Beneath the sunlight breaking through the tree branches, the frosted edges of the lake look like lace tatted along the banks. It's thoughts like that which she hopes to jot in her journal during her brief assigned stay, one taking a little time getting used to. Though there's no place like home, roughing it in the woods will certainly have her cherish home—even her tiny apartment in the old mill factory—all the more.

While cautiously walking with her hands full along the snowy path, she notices a flash of red color. It must be one of the many cardinals she sees everywhere here, flitting from tree branch to tree branch, with gentle swoops to the bird feeders, too. So she turns to glance at the pretty red bird, only to discover it's not a bird at all. It's a man in a red-and-black plaid coat, off in the distance, splitting wood logs on a tree-stump chopping block.

"A lumberjack!" Penny declares under her breath. As she does, she hears the distant thud of the axe hitting a log. "Imagine that. Just like in an old-fashioned movie. Or on a nostalgic, wintry postcard."

Yes, that's how she'd describe this place: nostalgic. Smoke rises from the cabin chimneys; a white-tailed deer stands on the outskirts of Snowflake Lake; a toboggan leans against a split-rail fence; and a genuine lumberjack chops wood. She gives another once-over to the man swinging an axe.

"And a handsome man, at that," she whispers, seeing that he's tall, with a shadow of whiskers on his face. Brown hair curls from the edges of his wool cap, and leather gloves cover his strong hands. But the wonder of this whole woodland scene— especially the lumberjack—is that it prompts something: a slow smile. Something she's surprisingly been doing since arriving here as a resistant tenant.

Until suddenly everything is flying out of her hands as her feet slip out from under her. The cocoa travel mug goes in one direction, the leather journal in another, while her blanket soars straight up in the chilly air, right behind her snow-booted feet, getting her to exclaim one shrill, "Eeep!"

༄

All weekend, Frank couldn't get it out of his head. Like a broken record, his sister's words stuck, playing over and over again.

Take a chance! Of course, it didn't help the way she nudged him to ask any available bridesmaid for a dance at the boathouse wedding yesterday.

Which is exactly why he took this part-time lumberjack gig—for a peaceful escape from family. It's a loving one, but intrusive nonetheless.

So he comes out to the lake and chops. And whacks. And splits wood for all the woodstoves and stone fireplaces in the lakeside cabins and A-frames. Each one—from Chickadee Shanty to Meadowlark Manor to Sparrow Suite—needs a small split-log stack at the ready out here. The problem today is that with every thud of his axe blade into a log, he hears Gina's snappy retort: *Take a chance!* And with each creak of the axe being pulled from the wood, there it is: *Be spontaneous!*

As if Gina knows. As soon as his little sister got her college business degree, she went and married her high-school sweetheart, Joshua. Two years later, right on predictable schedule, along came baby Dante. And, once convincing their parents to move into the in-law apartment in her colonial in the old apple-orchard development, she had built-in daycare, to boot. So who's his sister to talk about spontaneity?

Is he really even that unadventurous? So he prefers things a certain way, but does that make him inflexible? More likely, he simply knows himself well and does what suits him. Things like this: spending time at serene Snowflake Lake, helping out old Gus with the cabin chores. And finding an hour or two of wintry bliss away from nagging sisters and romantic weddings, where it seems like everyone in town is paired up. Everyone except for himself and a few random wedding guests.

"There's one," Gina said yesterday, nodding at a tall blonde wearing a sequined bridesmaid gown. His sister nudged him closer and closer to the dance floor as he stood, arms crossed, monitoring the wedding reception from the back wall.

And for every bridesmaid Gina pointed out, Frank instead confirmed that the coat-check closet wasn't overstuffed, or that the caterer found the kitchen satisfactory. Or he turned on the spotlights out on the upper-level deck for an evening snow dance overlooking the river, like he does for every Christmastime wedding.

Maybe Gina isn't so off her nut. Because, yes, that's Frank Lombardo, all right: regular and routine, standing in the shadows at every boathouse wedding and business holiday party, every December weekend, making sure each festive event goes off without a hitch. That perfect photos are had, appetites satiated, smiles spread.

Now, with each axe chop, he hears it … *Be spontaneous!* Chop … *Take a chance!*

Frank picks up a split log and turns to add it to his fresh-cut stack when a blur of motion near the lake catches his eye.

A fur-lined navy parka is suddenly propelled into the cold, misty air, preceded by two silver lace-up boots as a woman takes a fall on the snowy path.

So he carefully puts down the axe, lodging the blade firmly into his tree-stump cutting station, then whips off his leather gloves and hurries over to the slippery path. The path he *promised* Gus was next on his to-do list: chop wood, *then* chop ice.

"Hello!" he calls out to the woman. "Are you okay?"

With a gasp, she props herself up on her elbows from where she's sunk in the snow, then lightly laughs. As Frank hurries over, his work boots clumping along the troublesome path, she brushes off her arms and legs. Which is when her furry hood falls off, and her copper locks glint in the sunshine. But that's not all Frank notices. There's also a pretty face with rosy cheeks that were hidden by that parka hood, a gentle face with a bit of flying snow having dusted her eyelashes.

"I was just heading to that bench near the lake," she says as she sits further up, "when my feet suddenly went skyward!"

"I've been meaning to clear that icy patch." Frank stands close now, not once having taken his eyes off her. "Are you hurt?"

"Let me see." Though still breathless, this young woman with the copper hair tests out her limbs, stretching one, flexing another. "I think I'm okay. Just got the winter wind knocked out of me. But this nice snowbank cushioned my fall."

"Well, here." Frank bends low while extending his hand. "I'm Frank. Frank Lombardo. Let me help you up."

"Thanks." From her prone position nestled in the white snow, she extends her hand. "I'm Penny."

Penny. That one word gets Frank to pause, then smile, before leaning lower to take her hand in his—all while a catchy phrase comes to mind. As his hand wraps around hers, he says it. "See a penny, pick it up."

Which he does. He pulls her up—carefully, just in case she's broken a bone, or pulled a muscle. Then he slips his two hands beneath her jacketed arms and hoists her out of the snowbank while saying, "And all day, you'll have ..."

As he sets Penny on her snowy, booted feet and holds her until she gets her balance, he doesn't finish the happy rhyme. Instead, he leans in close to those rosy cheeks, snow-dusted copper hair, twinkling eyes, and ... what? Even he's stunned, but he does it anyway.

He kisses her.

Yes, his hands rise to cradle her face as he lengthens and deepens the kiss, just for two seconds. Okay, maybe three, before suddenly pulling away and stepping back. Frank only touches her shoulder to be certain she's steady on her feet after that fall.

"So, you're okay, Penny?" he asks while backing up.

"Well." Penny looks behind her at the frozen lake. "I *think* so." She glances at him, then quickly away.

Not knowing what else to do other than salvage his reputation, Frank does the gentlemanly thing and scoops up her fallen blanket, then reaches for her cocoa travel mug at the very same second she does, awkwardly apparent by the way their hands bump. And so they're eye-to-eye once more, which is when she blushes. Or is it merely the cold snow flushing her face? He can't tell as he hesitantly gives her the cocoa cup.

"Okay," Frank stammers. "I'm glad you're fine."

When Penny only nods, he looks at his arm as though checking his watch buried beneath his plaid jacket sleeve, then instinctively extends a hand when she takes an unsteady step in the snow.

But he pulls right back, mostly because of what happened the *last* time he gave her his hand, which was about fifty-four seconds ago. *This* time, he turns up those hands that got him into spontaneous—yes, there's that word—trouble, then rubs them on his jeans. All the while, Penny fusses with her snow-covered blanket and the cocoa cup.

"About that," Frank begins. "Before ... you know," he says with a shake of his head. What he wants to do is straighten the strand of hair clinging to her cheek, or adjust her hood, crooked from the fall. But he can't, and when her gray eyes meet his, he simply freezes. "Okay, you take care now," he says, rather than risk any more embarrassment.

That's it. Some lame rambling and a quick exit as he hurries off in the snow. Just like that, as suddenly as he came upon her, he leaves.

So there you go. Frank Lombardo's first foray into spontaneity ends with him rushing away down that darn icy path, his feet slipping and a-sliding beneath him.

"Seriously, dude?" he asks himself. "See a penny, pick it up? And all day, you'll ... what? And all day you'll feel like a *heel*, is what." He glances over his shoulder as he makes his way toward the one-lane road where his pickup truck is parked, then pulls off his wool cap and shoves it in his jacket pocket.

Really? He *kissed* her? Is she married? Single? Maybe a mother to little children? What *ever* came over him? He doesn't even know a thing about her, except that her name's Penny. A name the same color as her silky hair sprinkled with snow.

That's all he knows. That she's Penny, who fell in the snow.

It isn't until he sits in his truck and starts the engine that he gets his flustered self calmed down. A few long breaths do it as he unzips his jacket, now that his heart's stopped pounding from that chopping and snow-walking.

Oh, who's he kidding? It's more like a snow-kiss that did it.

Before driving off, Frank adjusts the rearview mirror to get a glance at the stone bench beside the lake.

A glance at this pretty Penny he found in the woods.

three

P ENNY HART DIDN'T GET A thing done the day after
that snow-tumble. Not one thing. No travelogue notes written
in her new leather journal; no photographs taken of the lovely,
crystallized winter scenes. She only hopes her boss won't mind.

"It's just that, well," she whispers, "a sudden *kiss* … set
everything amiss!"

Monday evening, she turns around and bumps into Cardinal
Cabin's dining table, set behind the living room area. The little
cabin's open floor plan is certainly cozy, but tiny, too—leaving
her colliding with cushioned chairs and sidestepping blanketed
sofas as she makes her way to the stone fireplace. She checks
the embers, thankful for the thermostat on the wall freeing her
from stoking a fire all night.

Cramped quarters, chopped wood, fireplaces, outdoor hikes
… Getting used to cabin living will take time, that's for sure.
And by the time she's settled in and comfortable, it'll likely be
time to leave. With a shrug of her shoulders, she walks down the
hallway to her bedroom and removes her earrings at her dresser.

"But that kiss!" she says to her reflection. Even though
it distracted her from her work assignment, she tried getting

things done. "I did!" she insists, thinking of how she walked outside the charming bird-themed cabins all afternoon, each one adorned with its own whimsical woodpecker doorknocker. She passed little Finch Farmhouse and a quaint A-frame named Robin Residence before coming upon Blue Jay Bungalow, Gus' place. His snowtorcycle was parked alongside that cabin, and she waved to him as he filled a bird feeder in the backyard. Though she can't be sure he waved back.

Still … throughout the entire day, no matter where she looked, there were no photo ops to be found at the edge of the woods, or near the pretty lake. By the end of the afternoon, every snowy nook and cranny had met her critical gaze.

"Oh, who am I kidding?" Penny admits to her reflection. "I was searching for that red-plaid coat. A red-plaid coat filled with two strong arms."

Alas, nothing. There were no signs of red other than the flitting cardinals swooping from snow-covered branch to bird feeder to porch railing. So now she walks to her bedroom window and presses the lace-edged burlap curtain aside. Moonlight shines on the snow and illuminates the lake with a pale glow. Lights are on in neighboring cabins, their paned windows glowing yellow. And the air is filled with the scent of burning woodstoves.

Is Frank in one of those cabins? Stoking a fireplace, maybe? His buffalo-plaid coat hung on a wall hook near a woodstove?

"What am I doing?" Penny asks herself again. "Looking out my window for a mystery man!" Wearing her snowflake-patterned thermal pajamas, she touches her hair, wondering if any of it even happened.

After a moment, she drops the curtain, turns to her bed and folds down the patchwork quilt. Each patch is covered with

"That's cool, help Pete deliver the mail. Hey, tell your father I just put his whittled deer out on my mantel, too."

"That right? He'll like that. Listen, send him a photo through his website, Near and Deer. My dad loves posting that stuff on his social media."

"Will do, when I get a free minute," Frank adds. "Busy with reception-planning for a certain wedding, man. You and Jane ready for the big day?"

"Absolutely. Your sister's working out final details with Jane, then it's our first married Christmas together."

"Gina will take good care of things at the boathouse. Only the best for you two."

"Appreciate that, Frank. Seriously," Wes says as he turns to a crate of separated mail beside him and thumbs through a handful of envelopes.

A blustery wind hasn't let up since last night, so Frank bounces in place, blowing into his cold hands while waiting for his mail. "You running late today?"

"Oh, man." Wes holds up a newspaper. "It's the annual Christmas edition of the *Addison Weekly*. Damn truck's weighed down with the papers, *and* its holiday calendar, *and* the coupons and bargain-sale flyers. Slowing me, big time." He hands Frank his mail, including the town newspaper folded over it all.

But it's not the newspaper's calendar and coupons that catch Frank's eye as he slip-slides back to his house. It's the surprising front-page photograph of a copper-haired beauty.

A woman the caption calls Penny.

A *familiar* Penny he recognizes from her fall in the snow. According to the paper, she's a local celebrity now ... Penny Hart.

And Frank can't get back inside his mostly undecorated English Tudor fast enough to read the article.

To devour it, actually, riveted to its every word.

Guess Travel Agent's Holiday Hideaway for a Chance to Win the Getaway

A local travel agent at Addison's Suitcase Escapes has packed her own suitcase for a merry mystery. Penny Hart, 33, is kicking off a fun holiday program for the travel agency called "Where in New England is Penny?"

Ms. Hart has traveled to a New England destination undisclosed to even her coworkers. For the next two weeks, she'll share clues from her secret whereabouts. Her photos and riddles will be posted daily in the front window of Suitcase Escapes, located on Main Street across from the town green. Residents are encouraged to join in the mystery-merriment and cast their "Where's Penny?" vote in the ballot box inside the travel agency. With each guess, a donation in the form of a new, unwrapped toy for Addison's Toy Drive is appreciated, to ensure all the town's children will experience the joy of the season.

On Christmas Eve, one lucky entrant will be drawn to win an all-expense-paid weekend getaway at Hart's secret New England locale. Tune in to chief meteorologist Leo Sterling's morning weather forecast on December 24th, as he will host Penny Hart's special holiday-hideaway big reveal.

'Tis the season for adventure and Yuletide surprises!

༄

As Penny puts on her fluffy earmuffs, she looks out her window for a flash of color. Okay, for a flash of red plaid. But ... nothing.

Good. That means no more distractions. No more flitting away the hours like one of the pretty little cardinals flitting about in the snow. Because it's finally Tuesday—newspaper delivery day—so there's no escaping her mystery notoriety now. Everyone knows that if you want anything nicely broadcast to the entire town, one article in the *Addison Weekly* will do it.

So Penny fastens the toggles on her camel peacoat and steps outside in search of a photo op to email to Suitcase Escapes. Her boss, Ross, *has* to be waiting for the very first clue to hang in the front window of the travel agency—especially after the way she'd resisted partaking in this promotion. Ever the reluctant travel agent, she's happiest at home and sending *others* around the world.

But since she never cashed in last year's Christmas-bonus voucher for a free getaway of her choosing, Ross turned it into this work assignment. Now it's up to Penny, and Penny alone, to supply clues—because no one else knows where she is.

No one knows she's tucked herself away in the heart of Addison at its secluded Snowflake Lake, accessible only by wooded trail, and one single-lane road. No one. Not her best friend and coworker, Chloe. Not her boss, Ross. Not her friends and family.

Well, no one except for maybe one person.

"Why, oh why, did I ever say my name to that Frank Lombardo?" she asks a red cardinal sitting on a low pine branch beside the front porch. "Surely he'll see my photograph in that paper and put the pieces together." She brushes snow from the railing and leans closer to the bird on the branch. "Frank will enter the contest guessing the right destination, and the competition will be over before it even has a chance to begin! Tsk!" she exclaims with a stamp of her booted foot.

To make matters even worse, her distress prompts the curious cardinal to fly off in a chirpy huff. "Sorry," Penny whispers as she leaves the porch and walks through the snow.

Unless … Maybe Frank's not from around here. That *is* a distinct possibility, which would help keep her secret. She hasn't seen a sign of him since he rushed off after their sudden kiss.

Okay. Convincing herself that her travel mystery still is, in fact, a mystery, Penny gets to work, *trying* to think like a worldly traveler seeing the sights. She takes a quick breath and raises her cell phone, looking through the screen for a photo-clue to snap. A fun image to send to Suitcase Escapes. A picture alluding to her New England whereabouts, without revealing she's right in everyone's backyard.

She slowly turns, seeing the morning sun glinting on the snowy tree branches; seeing the icy Snowflake Lake looking like winter lace; and seeing a wood-chopping block. A tree-stump chopping block that she passes the camera lens over, then pans right back to. Her boots sink into the snow with each step in that direction, over on the side of the lake, closer to Gus' Blue Jay Bungalow.

An idea starts taking shape for the very first photo-clue hinting at her location. As she nears the chopping block, two gloves laying on it catch Penny's eye. They're a tan leather, worn and soiled from handling wood.

Why, they must be Frank's! She figures he left them behind in his flustered departure on Sunday. So she picks them up. And turns them over. And cups them in her hands. Finally, she arranges them alongside the axe blade wedged into the tree stump that Frank used as a chopping block. The sharp blade is pierced into the stump, the axe handle sticking up, ready to chop once more.

After a little more glove-fussing, Penny steps back.

"Hmm. Nice." She raises her cell phone and snaps the picture, then types an email right there on the spot. She sends it to her boss, Ross, and copies Chloe for good measure:

Made it to my destination, safe and sound. Getting settled in. I'm sure folks are lined up in front of the agency's window looking for my first clue. So here it is, with the accompanying photo attached.

Clue One
Need lots of chopped wood ... to stay warm in this rustic neighborhood!

five

FROM THE WINDING LINE IN Whole Latte Life coffee shop that afternoon, Frank looks out the frosty windows. On the town green across the street, balsam garland wraps up the coach-light lampposts topped with festive wreaths. Beyond, the red covered bridge is outlined in white glimmering lights. When he and his sister walk outside with large coffees in hand, the green-and-gold Holly Trolley drives by with Gus Haynes at the wheel, jingling the trolley bells at folks window-shopping.

"We made it!" Gina exclaims. "The coupon in the paper this morning said only the first thirty customers get the free coffee." She raises her gingerbread latte to Frank's peppermint mocha in a toast. "So cheers to a good deal."

Frank cups his mocha and takes a sip to warm up. "Except you told me this would be a business break, so now we need to talk shop. We've got a few last-minute details hanging for Wes and Jane's wedding."

"I know," Gina answers as they stroll the cobblestone sidewalk, passing shoppers with mittened hands carrying bulging bags. "Per boathouse policy, I told Jane no glitter's allowed on the wooden deer they're bringing. And hey, did you know they're life-sized? Wes' father carved those deer."

Frank nods while taking another sip of steaming coffee. They pass the vintage bridal shop Wedding Wishes, where mannequins with fluffy white muffs wear fur capes draped over long satin gowns.

"The glitter gets everywhere and is impossible to clean up," Gina is saying.

"Okay, now how about the caterer? George Carbone from over at The Main Course. Does he have any final kitchen requirements?"

"Ooh, look!" Gina veers to a toy store window edged in faux spray-snow. "I want to stop in here on the way back and get something for Dante." She squints through the window to a toy wonderland chock-full of dollhouses and sleds and fuzzy polar bears and miniature racetracks. "Maybe that stuffed caboose!"

Frank sees the plush blue caboose with red, velvety trim and soft, pillowy tires—perfect for his young nephew. "I'll get it for him. That's a good Christmas present." When he turns away with another sip of coffee, he nods to a crowd gathered on the sidewalk. "What's going on over there?"

Gina peers out from beneath her pink pom-pom beanie and hurries closer. "That must be Suitcase Escapes! Their contest starts today, did you see it in the newspaper?"

"I glanced at it," Frank lies, when in fact, he's got the whole article practically memorized.

"What fun ... the intrigue of the traveling travel agent. Everyone has to guess where Penny is staying on her New England getaway. And at the end of her stay, one entrant wins a trip to her mystery destination! Let's go see the first clue."

"I'm busy, Gina." Frank holds back. "Have lots to do at work."

"Come on," his sister calls over her shoulder, waving him closer. "Don't be a stick in the mud. And who knows? Maybe I'll win. Josh and I could use a romantic getaway."

"Seriously?" Frank asks as he catches up to her. Okay, so he's curious, too, and wants to see what clue Penny found at Snowflake Lake. He must be the only person in town who knows her secret. "*You* need a break?" he presses his sister while eyeing the gathered crowd. "For crying out loud, you have live-in help with Mom and Dad right there under your roof."

"Exactly." Gina stops just long enough to glare up at him. "Mom and Dad, *always* there. *Always* hovering. Leaving me and Josh no privacy."

They make their way through the crowd of down parkas and wool peacoats and quilted barn jackets. Every nudge and step gets Frank closer to the large travel agency window. As he shoulders and squeezes his way through, he hears the murmurs of people studying the photo-clue: *Vermont? Is she at a ski chalet?* And, *Are those pine trees further back?* Followed by, *She sure angled that picture to not reveal too much and give it away!*

It's all Frank can do to not push through the final few townsfolk in front of him. But at last, he's there. He's at the window, with Gina standing behind him on tiptoe, squeezing a peek around his shoulder.

The problem is, he can't stop looking at Penny Hart's first clue: It's a picture of his chopping block, with his leather work gloves nicely arranged around the axe blade wedged into the tree stump. It's obvious she fussed with his things left haphazardly behind, post-kiss, and it leaves him feeling a little … exposed.

"She *didn't*," he whispers.

❦

There's only one thing for Frank Lombardo to do now: remove the evidence. So an hour later that Tuesday afternoon, he finds himself driving down the narrow, frost-heaved, one-lane road to Snowflake Lake. At least his sister didn't recognize his chopping gloves, which he'll promptly retrieve. Because look at what spontaneity got him—nearly on the front-page headlines, sharing the spotlight with Penny Hart! It'll just take a few minutes to rush out and grab those darn gloves, leaving behind not a trace of his and Penny's sudden encounter to be scrutinized, studied, photographed and logged.

Parking his truck at the end of the road, he hikes down a snowy trail and makes it to the chopping block in minutes. Apparently someone else has the same idea. As Frank pulls the axe from the tree stump, he hears Gus' snowtorcycle approaching.

"Frank!" Gus calls over the sputtering engine.

Frank turns and waves to his old friend as he shuts off the vehicle. Gus wears a thick scarf over his jacket and a tweed newsboy cap on his head.

"Just got back from my Holly Trolley shift and I noticed some low-hanging branches needing trimming," Gus tells him as he walks over. "Some behind Cardinal Cabin, some at my place."

"Blue Jay Bungalow, too?" Frank asks. "The tree on the side?"

"That's right. And at Cardinal Cabin, it's the tree with the bird feeder. Think you can get to it today, before any more snow weighs them down?"

"Today?" Frank glances up at the sky, gauging the afternoon light. "It's late, Gus. I need to finish chopping this firewood for your neighbors, before the sun goes down."

"Speaking of neighbors." Gus steps closer while lowering his voice. "Got a secret one hiding out here."

"Really?" Frank turns and glances at Wren Den first, then Cardinal Cabin—which has smoke curling from the chimney. "Which place?"

"Cardinal Cabin."

"No kidding. What's her story?"

Gus takes another step closer, this time while squinting at Frank. "*Her?*"

"What?"

"Her. You said *her*, as though you already knew ... Oh, never mind. I don't like to get involved. But I saw something in the paper this morning." Gus drops his voice to a whisper. "Thought the front-page photo looked a *little* familiar." With a wry smile, he tips his head at Frank then turns back to his snowtorcycle. "Just keep it under your hat, you hear me?" Gus asks right as he turns the key and the engine chugs and pops to life.

Frank shakes his head and waves him off, then lifts the axe to finish splitting this pile of logs. Which would take practically no time, *if* he could find his work gloves. He steps around the tree stump, glances at the snow-covered ground, looks anywhere but at that little nearby cabin with the smoke curling from the chimney. And the windows aglow with lamplight.

Until there's nowhere else to look.

So with a slight shake of his head, he walks toward Cardinal Cabin, climbs the porch steps and stops at the planked front door with the festive red berry wreath on it. Now this is something he never saw coming today. He takes off his wool cap and drags his hand through his hair, looking back toward Gus' departing snowtorcycle ... doing anything but knock on that door.

"No sudden kisses this time," he whispers while glancing at two white rocking chairs on the porch. "Keep it business."

With that, he raises his hand to knock, but stops when he sees a carved woodpecker mounted on a slab of wood beside the doorframe. After a second, he carefully tugs the pull-string, steps back and waits.

six

As SOON AS PENNY HEARS the puttering snowtorcycle engine, she rushes to the cabin window and peeks outside. Because there's some part of her still keeping an eye out for that mystery lumberjack.

"It's him!" She moves to the side of the window, barely peeking behind the swag curtain. "Frank *does* exist."

So ... now what? Well, nothing without a little fussing, first. She rushes to her bedroom dresser and brushes her hair, then loops an icy-blue scarf around her neck on her way back to the living room window, when suddenly—*rat-a-tat-tat-tat-tat!*

It surprises even herself the way she gets to that front door before the last *tat-a-tat* comes to a stop. Just as quickly, she's got the door wide open—and there he is in his red-and-black plaid jacket, shoving a wool cap into its pocket. But even if it were on his head covering that dark hair, she'd recognize that face with its shadow of whiskers; those eyes watching her right back; his slow, hesitant smile.

"Frank!"

"Penny? Penny ... Hart?"

"Ohhh! You read the article." She glances past him to be sure no one's around from the other cabins, overhearing her name. "Okay." She sizes him up, then steps aside. "Come in, and I'll tell you all about it."

Frank's shaking his head while she talks. "Thanks, Penny, but I really have to finish chopping wood for the cabins. And my gloves ... Well, you may have found them?"

She doesn't miss it then, that new twinkle in his eye letting her know he's seen more than the *Addison Weekly* article. He's seen her photo-clue, too.

"My cover's really blown with you, isn't it?"

Frank simply turns up his hands and tips his head with ... that smile.

"Listen," Penny suggests while crossing her arms in front of her against the cold air sweeping inside. "I have homemade tomato soup simmering, and was putting a grilled cheese sandwich on the griddle. Can I bribe you with a sandwich for your secrecy? Stay for dinner?"

Frank looks out at the sky, then at the tree-stump chopping block before turning back to her. "I have to chop while there's still sunlight. How about a quick bite when I'm done?"

"Deal."

"My gloves?"

"Oh, of course." Penny turns and retrieves his gloves from where they're tucked on the hearth, getting toasty near the snapping fire. "These were frozen solid out there. But they're nice and warm for you now." What she notices as she, well, okay as she *prattles*, is that Frank is silent. Watching her, but silent. Still with a twinkle in those darn brown eyes, too. "I put them near the fire ..."

With a quiet thanks, Frank gently takes the gloves and pulls them on as he heads out to split logs.

No sooner is he off the porch than Penny closes the door and turns to the cabin kitchen, where she pulls dishes from a stack of plates on an open shelf. And it's on her way to the dining area off the living room, when she hears it—the distant thud of Frank's axe chopping wood.

Turning to the simple table and straight chairs painted a distressed white, she carefully sets the table for two, hums a light tune, and lastly lights the candle in the lantern beside the bowl of pinecones and cinnamon sticks.

૦✺ာ

Frank never thought his life's story would come down to a grilled cheese sandwich. Well, two sandwiches, to be exact. Two thick, gooey, warm, melted-cheese toasted sandwiches, dunked in the best tomato soup he's ever had. A tomato soup made from the canned tomatoes Gus stocks in the cabins.

But it did.

Both his and Penny's stories spilled out between bites, and nods, and sips of hot cocoa as the candle flickered in the tabletop lantern. Behind them, burning logs snapped and popped, casting a glow from the stone fireplace. A glow falling on Penny's copper-colored hair, and her cable-knit sweater with that soft blue scarf.

Nobody knows ... My location's secret ... Travel agency promotion ... Please don't tell.

He remembers every word she said. And his words, too.

Busy with weddings and Christmas parties at the Addison Boathouse ... Arranging rack reservations for the next year ... Hundreds of kayaks and canoes.

seven

WHEN PENNY ANSWERED THE NEWSPAPER ad to rent Cardinal Cabin, she didn't give, well, two cents' thought to the line asking tenants to *cater* to the cardinals. But apparently it was intended literally, as evidenced by the scrawled checklist beneath a refrigerator magnet.

Which is precisely where Penny finds herself standing the next day. Because while sipping her coffee at the kitchen window, she was clearly reminded of her avian obligation. Only one glance outside at the empty bird feeder did it—a glance that landed on several cardinals pecking at the snow in search of seeds. Forlorn cardinals giving plaintive chirps while flitting about.

Birds she now has to feed.

"Okay, I can do this," she tries to convince herself while giving another glance out the window, then turning to the refrigerator checklist. It's a bit curt, with not much explanation: *Sliced Bananas, Chopped Apple Pieces, Black-Oil Sunflower Seeds (in shed).*

Squinting closely at the handwritten feeding instructions, she gathers a banana and an apple, chops, peels and slices, then drops the fruit pieces into a plastic bag. Once her snow boots

45

are laced and her parka zipped, she pulls up the fur-lined hood and heads out the back door with the fruit bag.

"Yup, I've got this covered," she says, feeling a little more confident about roughing it out here in the woods. She passes the hanging bird feeder, thinking it looks as cozy as her cabin. Its wood frame is weathered and rustic, the roof snowcapped, and boughs of a pine tree sweep alongside it.

First stop, though? The shed, where Penny fills an empty jug with the sunflower seeds and, on the way out, grabs a step stool near the door. Humming to herself, she sets the stool solidly in the soft snow beneath the bird feeder's snowy branch, then nods to two cardinals—one bright red, the other pale gray with red flecks and a reddish crest—perched on a nearby pine tree. An honest-to-goodness cardinal couple!

Which gives her a photo-clue idea for Suitcase Escapes' front window display. So she takes off her gloves, pulls her cell phone from her pocket, frames the two patiently waiting cardinals huddled side by side, feathers fluffed against a chilly breeze, and snaps the picture.

Humming her tune as gently as the newly falling snow-flakes, Penny types her next clue:

Branches of snow-laden pine …
Suit wintry songbirds here … just fine!

A tap of the Send button, and her photo and clue are promptly emailed to the travel agency's office. Leaving her free to step on the little stool and pour the black-oil sunflower seeds into the feeder, right to the brim. Then she spreads banana slices and apple chunks on the feeding tray, having to steady the hanging bird feeder when the drooping pine branch sways.

"Breakfast is served, my feathered friends!" she announces to the cardinals as she steps down. The birds dart from branch to branch, getting closer to their food. To Penny, they look like nature's Christmas ornaments, especially against the peaceful light snowfall dusting everything in a sparkling white. She must admit, in her few days here, the most magical part of her stay has been the hush of the woods ... soft and calm.

So it surprises her as she bends to fold up the step stool, when a loud, snapping *CRAAACK* rings through the wooded bliss.

༄

"Penny!"

While rubbing her left shoulder, Penny spins around to see Gus trotting closer with a fleece jacket zipped over his heavyset girth, unlaced snow boots on his feet.

"Shh!" she warns while looking past him to be sure no one overheard. "Don't say my name!"

All the while, Gus is hurrying to her yard. "Well, I saw that heavy branch fall! Did it hit you? Are you okay?"

Penny glances to her shoulder, gives it another rub and moves it back and forth. "I think so. The branch just clipped my shoulder, that's all. I might have weighed down the limb when I overstuffed the bird feeder."

"Oh, no. It's not your fault. I've been after my grounds-keeper to trim those dead branches." Gus picks up the bird feeder and sets it at the base of the tree. All around them, apple chunks and seeds are scattered everywhere across the snow. And that's not all: Cardinals are swooping now, and squirrels are chattering nearby, while a small deer inches closer from the edge of a thicket.

"I'll clean this up, Gus," Penny says. "There must be a broom in the shed." She steps over the snowy banana and apple pieces. "What a mess I made!"

"Nonsense." Gus straightens his tweed newsboy cap and eyes her straight on. "We have to get your shoulder checked out. I'm bringing you to the doctor."

"I can't bother you like that. And look," Penny insists while rolling her shoulder with, okay, with only a small wince.

"Uh-huh," Gus says, nodding. "And that injury will set. Then tomorrow your shoulder could be locked."

"But you don't understand, Gus," she admits. The last thing Penny can do is risk being recognized in Addison, especially when Suitcase Escapes' traveling-travel-agent promotion is getting under way. She backs up a step, moving closer to Cardinal Cabin. "I can't go into town."

"Hmm. I understand perfectly ... Miss Hart."

"Good grief!" She squints through lightly falling snowflakes just as a cardinal swoops to the scattered sunflower seeds on the ground beside her. "You know, too?"

Gus nods and says nothing for a second. "Don't worry, Penny," he finally tells her, his voice softening, his wise eyes twinkling. "Because here's my assurance, good as gold: What happens at Snowflake Lake, *stays* at Snowflake Lake. So let's get going."

Penny merely watches him as he begins the short snow-trek to Blue Jay Bungalow. Watches until he stops and looks over his shoulder at her.

"Well, I'm still not sure," she calls out. "Because I can't blow my cover, being seen in town."

A smile then, beneath Gus' bushy eyebrows and rosy cheeks. It's slight, but apparent.

"And I've got your cover *covered*, Miss Hart."

When he extends a gloved hand her way, she hesitantly takes it in hers as he leads her to his cabin. From behind, she hears snatches of his words, something about his wife's things ... and a closet full of old clothes ... and going to town incognito!

⌒❦⌒

An hour later, Penny Hart surprisingly finds herself hidden beneath a polka-dot kerchief, oversized sunglasses and a belted, cinched trench coat—with a turned-up fur collar, no less. She's also walking into a local orthopedic surgeons' office in Addison.

"Please sign in," the receptionist says with not more than a glance as she slides a lined-and-numbered sheet across the countertop in Penny's vague direction.

Which is precisely when Penny gives a worried look to Gus beside her, just as he reaches for the list.

"Allow me," Gus says while putting pen to paper. "Since your shoulder is injured."

Penny leans over to watch him scrawl the patient name: *Miss Haynes.*

So it is with welcome relief that Penny picks up a clipboard covered with medical forms and finds an empty seat in the waiting room. Most of the patients are skimming magazines, or on their cell phones, or filling in their own forms—and not paying a lick of attention to her. Here, she's nothing more than another patient in line for a doctor.

In a moment, Gus sits beside her. "One of the doctors here is a friend of mine," he explains. "Helped me out when I hurt my rotator cuff chopping wood at the cabins last winter. So I phoned in ahead and he agreed to squeeze us into his schedule." Gus removes his cap and spins it in his hands as he glances down at the clipboard forms she's been filling in.

"Miss Haynes," a woman's voice eventually says from the reception desk. After a few quiet seconds when Penny's pen checks off and itemizes and circles answers to questions relevant to insurance and health background, the voice calls out again, louder this time, "Miss Haynes!"

Gus prods her with his jacketed arm. "That's you," he whispers. "*Incognito.*"

"Oh!" Penny quickly stands and clutches the clipboard filled in with her true name and stats. "Yes. Yes, that's me."

"This way." The waiting nurse opens a door leading to a bright hallway of examining rooms with more clipboards propped on closed doors. Nurses and doctors crisscross the hall, and serious voices murmur to each other.

Nudging her large sunglasses up higher on her nose, Penny follows behind the nurse until she opens the third door on the left. Once in the room, the nurse turns to Penny with her hand extended.

"I can take that now," the nurse says.

Penny clutches her clipboard even closer, with both arms wrapped around it as she still grips her pen, too. "I'm not done," she lies with a brief smile. "I'll finish it while I wait?"

"Well ..." The nurse gives a slight squint at Penny. "Of course, then. And what did you say the problem is today?"

Penny rolls her shoulder. "An ache in my arm. A falling tree branch grazed it."

"Oh! I'll let the doctor know, and he'll be in shortly."

As soon as the door closes, Penny lowers her sunglasses and perches them on the tip of her nose as she scans the room. The quicker she's done here, the quicker she can get back to her secret hideaway and not risk being spotted. So she hoists herself up onto the examining room table as the paper crinkles beneath her. Outside the door, occasional muffled footsteps and voices pass her room, but none enter.

To stop herself from worrying, she gazes at a framed painting of a buck with full antlers, the deer emerging from a wooded thicket. All she thinks of upon seeing it is the peaceful hush of the woods around Cardinal Cabin. *"Breathe in,"* Penny whispers from beneath her kerchiefed hair. *"Breathe out."*

When she feels warm all cinched and buttoned up, she lowers her trench coat's fur collar and unties the belt wrapped tight around her. Then she slips the coat off her shoulders, wincing as she does—which prompts her to roll her hurt shoulder again. On the wall across from her, labeled skeletal diagrams are framed and mounted; hopefully, the doctor won't be pointing out any bones that may be broken on her own frame.

A sudden knock on the door is followed by the doctor walking in. He looks to be in his mid-thirties, his light brown hair is nicely combed, and his shirt and tie are visible beneath his white lab coat.

"Hi there. I'm Dr. Davis. Greg Davis." His smile is friendly, his tone easy. "And you are?" he asks as he reaches for the clipboard with its multitude of medical forms.

Which Penny snatches right up. "Wait. Before you read these," she begins, "there is doctor-patient confidentiality, right?"

This Dr. Davis studies her while leaning against a counter and crossing his arms in front of him. "Even if there wasn't, I'd make an exception for you." With that, he holds out a hand for the clipboard again. After she reluctantly turns it over, he reads the first form, lifts to the second, then looks up at her. "Penny Hart of front-page *Addison Weekly* fame?"

With a sigh, Penny removes her sunglasses and sets them on top of the trench coat on the examining table. "Guilty as charged."

"Now my day just got interesting." He reads her medical form again. "And it says here a *tree branch* fell on you?"

"Yes. Not a very big one, but heavy enough. It clipped me here," she says, pointing to her left shoulder and upper arm. "I'm okay, really."

"When did this happen?"

"Only an hour ago, early this morning."

"Any numbness or tingling?"

"No. But it's a bit sore."

When Greg steps forward and gently lifts her arm, she winces. "Penny," he begins as he lowers her arm, "can you stand please, and lift both arms as high as possible for me?"

As Penny does, he watches, and asks her to also extend her arms to the side, then reach behind her back. But he does something else, too, Penny notices. In between noting range of motion, and checking the bone along her clavicle to her left shoulder, he slips in curious questions.

"Now where are you hiding yourself away these days?" he asks as his hand presses in a circular motion on her shoulder. "Or can't you say?"

With an apologetic smile, Penny shakes her head.

Dr. Davis jots notes on the clipboard, then sets it down while stepping back, a finger to his jaw. "So, Penny—"

"Shh! Please keep your voice down," Penny says with a quick glance at the partially open door. "I'm sorry, but I'm afraid someone might put the pieces together and recognize me as Penny from the travel agency."

"Of course. I totally understand." Greg steps aside and gently closes the door then. "Now, about your injury here. Tell me how it happened, exactly, this branch that fell and hit you."

"I was filling the bird feeder at Cardinal Cabin—whoops! Oh, heck," Penny says as she sits herself on the crinkly paper on the examining table again. "I blew it."

"I *thought* I saw my friend Gus out in the waiting room. He called me earlier to squeeze in an appointment, and I figured he chopped too much wood at the lake and had some aches and pains."

"No, it's me with the ache. Gus is my neighbor and *insisted* on bringing me here when he saw the branch fall. He's my partner in crime today, and supplied me with an ensemble to camouflage my identity," Penny explains as she points to the oversized sunglasses.

"Well, your health comes first, so I'm very glad Gus brought you in." Greg clips his pen into his lab coat pocket, then lifts a printout from the countertop. "And rest assured, your secret's very safe with me. In the meantime, you'll want to follow these instructions," he advises while handing her the paper. "Your shoulder's bruised, but nothing more. Still, do these stretching exercises, so the arm doesn't get stiff."

"Thank you." Penny tucks the instructions into her purse. "How long do you think it'll be before the pain's gone?"

"It's a slight injury, so give yourself a week." Greg nods to that framed painting of a buck with full antlers. "I like to remind my patients that antlers are the fastest growing bone tissue on the planet. And, well, though your bone's not broken, you can expect your healing to be considerably slower than that deer's."

"Okay, then," Penny says as she makes a move to slip off the examining table. When she does, the doctor quickly steps closer to assist her.

"I'll have the nurse get Gus for you," he says with a friendly smile. "You can go out the back way, to preserve your identity."

"Oh, I appreciate that!" Penny puts on her trench coat and belts it tightly. "Thank you, Dr. Davis."

"Greg," he answers over his shoulder as he opens the door. "Just call me Greg."

∽

Later that Wednesday afternoon, safe and sound back at Cardinal Cabin, Penny sits in front of the fireplace. Curled up on the sofa beneath a checked throw, she takes a break from holding an ice pack on her shoulder to chat on her cell phone with Chloe.

"The travel agency is super busy now," her friend tells her. "Folks come in to guess your mystery whereabouts—and end up booking a cruise before leaving!"

"Chloe, that's wonderful. And what we all *hoped* for, bringing in new business. But it's an adjustment where I am, nothing like being home in my little apartment … with its modern conveniences. I'm really roughing it here: trekking through snow, keeping the fire going, getting creative in the kitchen, because, well, let's just say I can't get to any restaurants," Penny explains while sitting in the rustic room. "Wrapping food scraps before putting them in the bear bin."

"The what? A *bear* bin?"

"It's a fancy term for the garbage can, that's all. One that keeps out the animals."

"Oh my. You *are* roughing it."

A tin bucket of kindling wood sits on the hearth, and the Christmas tree is twinkling beside the stone fireplace. "And I had a little incident, too," she says.

"Incident?"

Penny drops her voice. "Of a *romantic* nature."

"Ooh. Do tell!"

"I can't. Everything's a secret for this two-week assignment."

"Not even a hint?"

"My only hints are *location* hints, emailed to you for posting in the office's front window. That's it." As she says it, Penny wonders if Chloe can sense her smile.

"You can't tell your best friend ... *anything?*"

"Nope. Nothing." But her resolve softens with a glance toward the paned window, where outside the sun is lowering in the December sky, and she can just imagine a lumberjack getting a few more chops in before dusk. "No hints, except for this: There may have been a secret kiss at this hideaway."

"What? A *kiss?*"

"Mm-hmm."

"You met somebody?"

"Could be. We sort of, well ... He just picked me up, is all."

Penny jumps then at the sound of a sharp *rat-a-tat-tat-tat-tat*—her woodpecker doorknocker!

"Listen, Chloe. I'm having dinner—"

"With your mystery man?"

"What? No! With a nice, elderly neighbor. A kindly gentleman. And someone's at my door," Penny says as she lifts the soft throw off her lap. "I have to go."

"Who is it? You can tell me!"

"Bye for now," Penny says as she sets down her cell phone, smoothes her hair, shoves her ice pack beneath a couch cushion, clears her throat and hurries to the door. All with the hope that it's one particular lumberjack standing on the other side.

So she swings open the door thinking it'll be Frank there and gives a friendly, "Hey!" Then, after a surprised second passes, "Dr. Davis?"

"Greg." Greg Davis pulls off his trapper hat. "Call me Greg."

Penny looks past him to the porch and lake beyond. "Quick!" she says, tugging his arm. "Come inside. No one saw you head out here, did they?"

"No, I was very vigilant." He holds up a wicker basket. "And I brought you a care package. You know, as you recover here at your cabin."

"That's so nice of you," Penny says as she takes the basket. When she thumbs through it, she sees instant popcorn and a few movie DVDs.

"There's cheese and crackers, too. And a small bottle of wine." Greg looks past her toward the roaring fireplace. "I thought maybe we could toast your recuperation? Talk a little?"

After brushing through the basket, Penny considers this Greg. Greg Davis—a handsome-enough, nice-enough orthopedic surgeon. One apparently interested in her. "I'm really sorry, Greg. I actually have plans."

"You do? Going into town, somewhere?"

"Oh, no. No more town visits. I'm heading over to Gus' place."

"Gus? Is he okay?"

"Yes. But with my injury, he insisted on cooking me dinner."

"That's pretty nice of old Gus. I won't keep you, then." Greg turns toward the door, then back toward Penny. "But listen, my father's a whittler. And I saw some birch branches on the way in. A few small limbs, too, that he'd love to stockpile. Do you happen to have a pail?" Greg pauses, then puts his trapper hat back on, tugging the flaps over his ears. "Or maybe some sort of box?"

His disappointment is obvious, the way that hat got dropped on his head simultaneously with his smile dropping. So Penny offers him a friendly alternative to the declined wine-and-cheese chat. "How about this?" she asks. "There's a wagon in the shed. I'll pull the wagon along the trail ... with my *good* arm, while you fill it. Because I've been sitting for hours, and a little snow walk would do me wonders."

Greg instantly insists, with a returned smile, that it'll be a short walk as he helps her put on her parka, and as she wraps a scarf around her neck. Penny then waits on the front porch while he gets the wagon from the shed. Finally, they pick up the trail in the woods beneath the fading midafternoon light.

"Check it out," Greg says after setting a birch branch in the wagon. He points to clear footprints in the snow. "Deer tracks."

"Really?" Penny looks at the prints leading off into the trees. "How do you know?"

"White-tailed deer. Easily identified by their heart-shaped tracks."

"I never knew that," Penny says. Up ahead, the babbling brook flows beneath the rickety footbridge. She needs a clue for Suitcase Escapes, so she raises her cell phone and snaps a picture. "I'm taking a photo-clue," she explains to Greg. "So folks in town can guess where I'm snow-cationing."

"I have an idea," Greg tells her. "Why don't you put *yourself* in the clue and I'll take a shot?"

Penny tips her head, looking from Greg to the scenic view she'd snapped. "I *like* that idea," she admits, and walks onto the footbridge. There, she leans on the snow-dusted railing and looks over toward Greg framing the shot in her phone's viewfinder.

"Wait." Greg approaches her and moves a wayward strand of hair from her face, then brushes a snowflake off her cheek. "Okay, better."

Penny watches as he steps into the snow to get an angle not revealing too much scenery. "Just zoom in on the bridge, so that I can be anywhere … Vermont, or Maine even," she suggests, then gives a smile and a mittened wave.

"You're beautiful," Greg calls out after snapping a couple shots. "I mean … *it's* beautiful. What I'm trying to say is … it's a beautiful place."

Penny simply smiles and nods, then picks up the wagon handle and walks back along the trail toward her cabin. Greg catches up beside her, their feet crunching on the cold snow.

"I'm meeting my brother for pizza," he says, "so really have to get going. His wedding's next week and we've got last-minute stuff to take care of."

"Oh, a December wedding! How exquisite." Ahead, Penny sees the snow-covered pine boughs, and the illuminated cabins surrounding the lake. "All that romance, and the white, glistening snow to go with a glistening white gown. Wait …" She stops and squints at Greg beside her, trapper hat earflaps and all. "A wedding next *week*? Is your brother Wesley, by any chance? Wes the mailman?"

"He is! Marrying Jane. Jane March."

"What a small world! I work with Jane's sister—Chloe. She can't stop talking about that wedding, which sounds like it'll be very elegant. The reception's at the Addison Boathouse, right?"

Greg nods. "Great place, overlooking the Connecticut River."

"But ... oh no."

"What?"

"Please, you won't mention me to Wes, will you? I can't have word get out in town."

"Don't worry." Greg takes the wagon handle from her and begins walking again, pulling the wood-stacked wagon behind him. "Your secret's safe."

They round the side of Snowflake Lake, nearing Cardinal Cabin with its smoke curling from the chimney, and its windowpanes frosted this afternoon. When they get to the front porch, Penny turns back. "Thanks for the snow walk, Greg. It was nice."

"My pleasure." He turns toward the one-lane road on the other side of the lake. "I'll come back in a day or two to return your wagon. And to offer a complimentary house call to check on that bruised shoulder. So you don't have to come into town and risk being found out."

"You'd do that?"

Greg continues on, but turns fully and watches her as he walks backward in the waning afternoon light. "On one condition," he calls. "Save one of those Christmas movies for me. I mean, if you want some company watching them."

eight

IF THERE'S ONE THING FRANK Lombardo knows, it's this: A sure way to beat the lonely hour is to eat out. So after work on Wednesday evening, he plants himself in a booth at Luigi's Pizza. Swags of tinsel-garland drape across the ceiling, with red-glitter bells angled in each curve. On the gold-painted walls, strings of colored twinkle lights outline framed paintings of Italian garden cafés and villages, of still-life images of Tuscan tables set with wine bottles, cheese and grapes.

And all the while, the easy chatter and laughter around him, and the coats and scarves hung over chair backs, all of it fills the lonely hour, just the way he'd hoped.

So he settles in, skimming the *Addison Weekly's* holiday calendar while waiting for his pizza. He reads about the Holly Trolley's scenic routes, and the upcoming Deck the Boats Festival at the cove, until he hears his name.

"Yo, Lombardo!" Wes calls out as he walks into the restaurant with his brother, Greg. "Saw that snazzy wreath on your door today, when I delivered your bills."

"Yeah, man," Frank admits while the two Davis brothers walk over to his booth. "Finally did a little decorating."

"Looking festive there on Old Willow Road," Wes says as he hits Frank's shoulder. "That street's got to be my favorite, in all of Addison. It's where I met Jane, you know."

"Hey, Frank," Greg says as he pulls off a trapper hat.

Nodding to him, Frank asks, "And what's happening with the good doctor?"

"Weekly pizza night," Greg tells him.

"Right on schedule." Frank looks over to the take-out counter. "Except you're missing someone. Where's your dad tonight?"

"Oh, boy." Wes pulls off his gloves and sits in the booth seat across from Frank. "Cooped up in his whittling shed, finishing birchwood centerpieces for the wedding."

As Wes explains, the waitress delivers Frank's loaded pizza. She sets it front and center on the table along with a handful of napkins. "Dig in, boys," she says before breezing off.

"You dining solo?" Greg asks.

"Tonight, yeah." Frank holds up the town newspaper, noticing the Davis brothers inching closer to his meal. "When you work with your family all day, well, you know. A little peace and quiet is nice."

"Tell me about it," Wes agrees. "Father-and-son postal carriers go back three generations in my family. My dad and I cross routes all day."

Greg loops his hat on a coat hook and shoves his brother's arm as he sits in the booth beside him. "Move over, Wesley."

And before Frank knows it, his pizza slices are being lifted and devoured, which suits him just fine. One less lonely hour in the books.

"When do you want my wooden snow deer delivered to the boathouse?" Wes asks around a mouthful of pepperoni-and-sausage. "Gina told Jane not to put glitter on them. It makes a mess. So Jane painted white snow on their backs instead."

"Bring them next week." Frank slides a heavy pizza slice off the platter and drops it on his plate. "But call before you come, so I can give you a hand."

"I'll need it. They're life-sized and pretty heavy. Want one standing at either end of the head table." Wes sets down his pizza and slips out of his puffy vest. "Finally put to good use, that wood-carved buck and his doe," he says before folding back his flannel shirt cuffs and digging in for a double bite of pizza. "Especially after my first wedding fiasco."

"You never know what's right around the corner," Greg muses. He wipes a napkin across his mouth while chewing and nodding at the same time. "Take me, for instance. I actually might have a date for your nuptials, bro, after all."

"No shit." Frank hits Greg's arm across the table. "Addison's most eligible stag isn't *going* stag?"

"Maybe not. If things go my way."

"Who's the lucky lady?" Wes asks beside him while chowing down a second pizza slice.

"Too soon to announce that tidbit. Because, heck," Greg says, "I've jumped the gun two years straight now. And what happened? Derek swooped Vera from me, and you snagged Jane."

Wes doesn't miss a beat, and Frank can figure that after practically being jilted at the altar the year before, Wes has good reason to be defensive.

"Listen, Scrubs," Wes tells his brother. "You don't want your new nickname to be Sour Grapes, so stuff it. And anyway, as I can vouch from personal experience, love finds you when you least expect it."

Isn't that the truth, Frank doesn't dare say. And now he can't stop thinking of pretty Penny, and how he found her when he least expected to—in the woods, of all places.

"Sorry, bro." Greg digs into his slice and chews thoughtfully for a few seconds. "I'm happy for you two, but I still saw Jane first." With that, he gives his brother a small shove. "So anyway, I'm not going to jinx things for myself, not until I get a final answer from this woman."

"What's she like?" Frank asks.

Greg eyes Frank across the table. "Nice try, but I'm not saying anything. Except that I just got back from a winter walk with her. All that fresh air! Mmh, so invigorating!" He snags his trapper hat from the coat hook, pulls the hat on his head and sits again with a smile. "Oh yes, the promise of love."

"Be real, Scrubs." Wes elbows his brother. "The promise of a *date*. This is the third year you're looking for a Christmas *date*. So don't keep getting your hopes sky high." Wes checks his watch, then glances over his shoulder toward the take-out counter. "Keep your expectations low, like I did."

"Tread carefully," Frank warns him.

"That's right," Wes says with a nod. "No broken hearts permitted at my wedding."

And before he knows it, Frank Lombardo does it once more. For the second evening in a row, he avoids his dreaded lonely hour—this time, hanging at Luigi's with two friends having his pizza as their appetizer, before collecting their own take-out extra-large and heading into the night, just as he does.

After waving them off, Frank pulls up his jacket collar against the cold night air. He hangs a right out of Luigi's. Storefront windows glow with twinkling lights, people hurry past with shopping bags, and further down Main Street on The

Green, the grand town Christmas tree stands tall and majestic, illuminated in the dark night.

But a block before, a crowd gathers. Well, of course. They're standing in front of Suitcase Escapes' window, scrutinizing the latest photo-clue posted there.

So Frank casually walks over to have a look, too, and actually sees Penny in the blown-up photograph. He can't miss her silky copper hair cascading along her ice-blue scarf, her navy parka zippered up as she leans on the snowy railing of the little footbridge near Snowflake Lake. Her eyes twinkling, her cheeks rosy in that, wait ...

He quickly looks back at Wes and Greg carrying their pizza box and getting into Greg's car parked outside Luigi's.

Then he considers Penny bundled up in that cold, *fresh air.*

Penny, obviously not alone on her walk in the snow. A *winter* walk! Penny, looking so ... Another glance back at Greg, then at the photograph that Penny *had* to have someone take of her. Because there she stands in the peaceful hush of the woods at Snowflake Lake, looking so—to quote Greg Davis—*invigorated!*

༄

Everywhere Penny looks while clearing the dinner dishes from the table, she sees wood: wood-planked walls and floors; wood beams across the vaulted ceiling. And it's wonderful how the lamplight and flickering candles on end tables and the mantel give it such a warm hue, here in Gus' Blue Jay Bungalow.

But what strikes Penny is the one and only hint that she's in *Blue* Jay Bungalow. The wide wood trim throughout the cabin and around the paned windows is all painted the same silver-blue color of the lake nestled deep in the woods. It has to be the most beautiful shade of blue she's ever seen.

"Thank you for dinner, Gus." Penny pushes in the chairs at the dining room table. "The only other person who cooks pork chops and onions that good is my mom."

"It's the least I could do." Gus carries two steaming coffee mugs from the kitchen to another table covered with puzzle pieces. "Don't want you aggravating that shoulder. Feel bad it happened in the first place, the way that branch fell."

"I'm all right." Penny gives her shoulder a roll, her wince only slight now. "What a lovely cabin this is, Gus," she says while taking a large wicker rooster off the buffet hutch and returning it on the center of the table, now that they're done with dinner.

"I like it," he says, walking slowly across the room while carrying napkins and a miniature pewter pitcher filled with cream. "Suits me, living here at the lake. Nice place, and nice folks, too. And don't you worry, your secret is safe in these parts. The other cabin owners respect each other's privacy." Gus lifts a thin cardigan off a wall hook and puts it on before adding a log to the fireplace. "You can go out and about around the lake, or on the trails, because they actually like being a part of your traveling mystery," he says over his shoulder.

"Do you live here, permanently?"

"Yes, all year."

Penny walks to an old piano set against a side wall in the living room. Framed family photographs set on a lace runner cover the top of the piano. She picks up one picture of young children ice-skating on the lake, then another. Mixed in are photographs of an older woman who must have been Gus' wife.

"I'm a bit of a landlord here," Gus explains from where he's crouched at the fireplace, stoking the fire. Sparks fly and the wood pops and cracks.

"A landlord?" Penny asks as she walks across the creaky hardwood floor and sits down at that puzzle table set near the window overlooking Snowflake Lake. A pretty candlestick lamp on the table shines on the tiny puzzle pieces scattered there. From the box, she sees that the puzzle depicts two snowmen decorating a Christmas tree in a forest much like the one surrounding Snowflake Lake. She picks up a dark puzzle piece and sets it with a few other dark ones it might fit into.

"Used to rent out most of these cabins with my brother. We actually built them together, back in the day."

What Penny notices is that gruff Gus isn't quite as gruff when he's talking about the lake, and his family, and these little wooden cabins. His deep voice softens; his demeanor relaxes.

"Our wives named them, and the names stuck. Finch Farmhouse, Dove Dwelling, Hummingbird House, Sparrow Suite ... Tiny little getaways folks loved," Gus says from behind her. "They'd come back year after year, reserving their favorite cabin. Sit out on the porches, walk around the lake. Have a barbecue in the summertime. We'd watch the families ... newlyweds first, then with kids being born and growing up. Same folks over and over, a little older each time, but still the same."

"That sounds so nice, Gus," Penny says while fussing with the puzzle. "In a way, they must start to feel like your own family."

"They did," Gus agrees with a nod. "But we sold off most of the cabins as we got older. With some arthritis setting in, I'm not as spry as I once was. Now I only own a few. Chickadee Shanty, Cardinal Cabin."

"No!" Penny spins around in her seat toward Gus, who's standing at the fireplace buttoning his cardigan over his stocky frame. "So *you're* who I've been emailing?"

Gus throws her a small smile and shrug. "I like to keep a low profile. Don't impose on my guests. It's important to respect their privacy on getaways." He walks to the piano and picks up a framed photograph, saying, "My wife used to love tending to the guests, though. She was a good cook, and made up dinner baskets of heat-and-eat meals."

"She sounds sweet."

"Been gone five years now."

"Oh, I'm so sorry to hear that, Gus."

He brushes dust off the photograph. "Sweet as a songbird, my Betty was. She especially loved all the cardinals around here."

Penny turns back to the puzzle-in-progress spread on the table and gathers a few more edge pieces while Gus reminisces.

"Those red birds whistling and tweeting from the tree branches were her favorite. My wife would sit at the piano and sing a song, trilling just like her pretty birds."

Gus joins Penny at the table, picks up his reading glasses there and sorts through a few puzzle pieces, setting them aside in color groups. "So I kept Cardinal Cabin. Something about that little place spoke to Betty." He fits together two edge pieces and slides them her way, then adds cream to his coffee cup. "And it keeps me busy. Doing chores, renting it out."

"What about Christmas?" Penny asks. "You're not going to be alone, are you?"

"No, oh no." With a big smile, Gus sits back and sips from his mug. "My kids are all coming, with the grandkids, too. That's what the puzzle's for. Together we glue and frame a new one, every year. My grandkids have a whole wall collage of them at their home—to always remember our cabin Christmases."

When he points out the window toward the lake, Penny gives a look. The moon is rising high in the dark sky, far above the pines. Moonlight falling through the snow-covered branches casts a glow on the frozen lake. The misty scene looks magical, straight out of a winter fairy tale.

Gus picks up another puzzle piece then and tries to fit it with a few others. "Everyone knows Snowflake Lake is Santa's very first Addison stop. His reindeer get a good running start on the frozen lake."

When Penny looks over at him, Gus lowers his glasses on his nose and turns his puzzle piece as he attempts to fit it in. When he sets it down, Penny picks it up and tries it on her side of the table. The fire crackles in the fireplace behind her, and lamplight falls on the room filled with memories and shadows, both sweet and sad.

"Grandkids haven't actually seen Santa yet," his voice is saying as Gus picks up another puzzle piece beneath the glow of the lamplight. "But oh how they love to watch for him out the window, listening for those sleigh bells before turning in for the night."

nine

THE IDEA STRIKES PENNY THE next morning. A pair of white ice skates hangs on Cardinal Cabin's back door. The skates are decorative, with a gingham ribbon tied around each, sprigs of greens tucked inside them, and, her favorite, silver jingle bells knotted to the ends of the laces.

But the skates look functional, too. And about her size.

So bright and early, she bundles herself into her parka and cap, and sits on a snow-covered fallen log on the far side of Snowflake Lake. After bending over and lacing up those white skates on her feet, she turns them this way, then that. Of course, she's never skated before. Oh no, the closest she's come to skating is via her television screen, in the comfort of her cozy apartment. With a bowl of buttered popcorn in her lap, she's happy enough *watching* skaters jump, spin and spiral on a sheet of ice—as she's curled up in flannel pajamas on a soft sofa.

Which is why she thinks this travel clue, if it's staged just right, will throw off anyone who knows her. She bends down and fusses with the silver jingle bells on the laces, and sits back then. Her snowflake-patterned, cable-knit leg warmers are

69

bunched over her skinny jeans, and in the snow, her feet are crossed at the ankles to show off the white skates.

"Perfect."

Raising her cell phone, Penny frames the picture from her knees down, her warmed-and-skated feet *appearing* ready to hit the ice. And the frozen lake is close enough to be included in the background, as though she is about to pirouette and spin across it in this wintry wooded wonderland.

"Well! That's enough of a skating experience for me," she softly admits after snapping a few shots, one of which will be sent to Suitcase Escapes as soon as she's back in her cabin. These blades will never swish across the ice, at least not while on *her* unsteady feet. So it's off with the skates and back on with her snow boots.

Just in the nick of time, too! Because across the little lake, Penny sees Gus talking to someone outside Blue Jay Bungalow. Why, it must be a photographer—judging by the substantial camera he holds. And if that stranger spots her in his monster lens, her cover will surely be blown.

After a quick look left, then right, something ahead catches her eye: Gus' ice-fishing hut. The homemade wooden shelter is exactly what she needs to keep hidden from each and every roving camera angle. That hut will give her the perfect cover, if she can just get to it, pronto. Her treaded snow boots are on and laced, so while keeping an eye on that pesky photographer—who is now snapping pictures of the cabins—she inches across the edge of the lake, then further out toward that rough-hewn shanty with its door and one tiny window.

With a wary eye on the photographer, she's walking backward in tentative steps—careful to not wipe out in a slippery fall. All while hoping to blend in with the pine trees beyond the banks of the lake until she reaches her icy destination.

Finally, safety is within reach. With her feet scrambling in a mad rush, she tugs open the door, gives a last look across the lake, backs into the hut and is ... *what?*

Suddenly two strong arms reach around her and scoop her high into the air!

∽

For the second time in the past week, Frank Lombardo sees Penny and picks her up ... this time to save her from backing straight into his fishing hole, where a striper had been toying with his bait.

To stop the catastrophe, his arms reach around her and swing Penny over to the side.

"Eeep!" Penny exclaims.

"Whoa, whoa," Frank says, whisking her to safety.

"Oh my gosh, Frank!" Penny whispers as he sets her firmly down. "You scared the daylights out of me."

Frank nods to the icy floor of the hut. "You almost fell into the fishing hole."

"The what?"

Frank points to his fishing pole, with its line dangling into lake water visible through a hole carved through the thick ice. "The fishing hole. You almost took a soaker."

Holding a mittened hand to her neck and catching her breath, Penny backs up a step in the cramped quarters of this ice-fishing hut. "I'm sorry, I'm on edge because, well, there's a *photographer* out there, taking pictures. Over on the banks of the lake at Blue Jay Bungalow. I don't know if he's onto me, and my mystery location."

"Let me take a look." Frank steps over the prone fishing pole and checks out the view from the little hut window. He sees Gus beside, yes, a photographer who is snapping pictures of the lake, all while Gus chats and points out things beside him.

Suddenly in the quiet hut, Frank feels Penny sidle up behind him, putting her hand on his jacketed arm as she tries to squeeze in for a view out the window.

"Well, thanks for coming to my rescue again," she quietly says, her voice close.

After a moment, he turns slightly to her standing behind his shoulder. When he does, this pretty Penny Hart—with the copper hair and flushed cheeks—stretches up and kisses him.

Just like that.

Her mittened hand grasps his arm as she rises on her booted toes and kisses him in the tiny fishing hut.

Startled by the turn of events, Frank hesitantly kisses her—back, this time. His gloved hands hold her shoulders as she tips her face to his. But that's not all. This time, he also feels her mittened hands around his waist, *and* a smile form beneath their kiss.

Without stopping, Frank reaches behind her neck and pulls off his gloves, first, then slips off her fur-trimmed parka hood so that only her wool cap covers that silky hair. His fingers tangle in it while their kiss deepens, which warms up the little ice-fishing hut just fine.

Until Penny, if he's not mistaken, *reluctantly* pulls away. But her mittened hand gently touches his face then, when she whispers, "Frank. Something ... well, something came over me, but we really have to keep a lookout."

He glances from the window, which is now steaming up at the edges, then back to Penny, with her copper hair and soft gray eyes. Her expression is flustered, and he's not sure if it's from their kiss, or from her rush to hide out. Or is it from the forward move she kind of made on him? But she suddenly turns away and peeks out the window once more.

There's no way of really knowing. He can only watch her in her parka and leg warmers and lace-up snow boots, and wonder what it is about this woman. This woman who gets herself into ridiculous scenarios—making him all the more attracted to her. So he reels his fishing line out of the water, sets the fishing pole aside and moves behind her. With his hands lightly around her waist, he looks out the window, too.

"There!" he says. "The photographer has his lens pointed at this hut. Watch out!"

Penny moves to the side and presses her back against the wall, all while shaking her head. "How did I ever get into this mess?"

With a shrug, Frank slides a small folding chair across the ice. "Maybe have a seat and wait it out."

When Penny sits, she takes off her mittens and finally has a look around at Gus' primitive hut. Frank sees it through her eyes: the rudimentary wooden walls, the dusty shelves holding a tackle box, a battery-operated lantern, Frank's packed lunch. A hand-painted *Here Fishy Fishy* sign hangs on one wall, and the fogged window on the other gives a glimpse of the lake.

Frank sits, too. He takes a large empty pail, flips it upside down and sits on it beside the fishing hole. Since they're apparently trapped here for the time being, he also reaches for his fishing rod and angles the baited line into the carved hole, where it drops into the cold lake water.

"So this is the hut you mentioned the other day?" Penny asks.

Frank looks up from his fishing and nods. "I stop out here once a week or so, usually on Thursdays. It's the calm before the weekend storm for me."

"Storm?"

"To put it mildly." He reels in his line a little, then lets it rest. "It's a crazy time of year at the boathouse. Festive, but hectic. Like this week, for instance. Friday is the town's small-business Christmas party. Local shop owners reserve a table for themselves and their coworkers. There's great catered food, and live music, too. Then we've got a big winter wedding on Saturday. And Sunday is the holiday teddy bear tea party my sister arranged for the kids."

"Wow. Lots of happy times going on there."

"Nonstop, once tomorrow hits. So I like to come out here alone beforehand."

Penny reaches for his fishing rod then. "Can I try?"

Frank slides his pail closer beside her chair in the cramped space before giving her the fishing pole. She pulls the line up, then lets the baited hook settle deep in the lake.

"Ice-fishing's a nice quiet way to be with my thoughts. You know," Frank explains, leaning his elbows on his knees and watching the fishing hole. In a moment, he looks up at her beside him. "Until I'm distracted by someone, anyway."

"Distracted? By who?" Penny asks, her voice playful, her silky hair sweeping forward as she ice-fishes.

"Come here," he answers.

She tips her head, smiling.

"Lean close. I'll whisper, so nobody hears."

And when she does, when she leans to the side where he sits on the pail, he reaches one hand behind her neck and leaves one, just one, light kiss on her lips, then whispers her name.

❧

A few minutes later, as soon as the coast is clear and the photographer gone, Penny tells Frank she has to leave to email her latest photo-clue to Suitcase Escapes.

What she doesn't tell him is that she also has to figure out this Frank at Snowflake Lake—and his meditative ice-fishing, and lumberjack duties, and their surprising relationship shaped by random situations and, okay, passionate kisses.

Thankfully, his waterproof hiking boots have ice cleats slipped over the soles. At least someone has sure footing as they leave the comfortable little ice-fishing hut behind. Frank closes up the door and takes her hand as they slowly walk across the frozen lake. Once or twice, he keeps her from falling when her boots slip-slide beneath her.

But what Penny notices the most is this: Once they get off the ice and onto the snowy banks to retrieve her skates, Frank doesn't let go of her hand. Not once. Not when she picks up the skates, which she'd laced together earlier. Not when they turn and follow a narrow trail through the snowy woods back toward the cabins. Not during their talking and laughing about being trapped in the hut on the lake.

Through it all, his hand holds hers.

Which makes her feel better about her impulsive kiss—he apparently didn't mind it. The same way she didn't, nearly a week ago, when she fell in the snow. Still, another thought nudges that one aside. She worries that somehow her mystery location has been compromised, and that roving photographer was out here looking for evidence.

And her worry continues all the way around the lake, even with Frank walking beside her, still holding her mittened hand. It isn't until they get to Gus decorating at Blue Jay Bungalow that Frank lets go.

But as Gus turns to them while lifting a string of lights, doesn't he see it all? Penny knows simply by the way he raises an eyebrow at her. And by the way she actually blushes then.

"Catch anything in that fishing hut?" Gus asks when he shifts his gaze to Frank.

"Hmm? Oh, had a few bites."

"I'll bet." Gus returns to his twinkly-light fussing.

"Gus," Penny says as she hurries over to him at the snow-covered shrubs. "I saw that photographer here, with his big zoom lens. So I ducked in the shanty to hide. That's all it was."

Gus looks at her, squints beneath that tweed newsboy cap he wears, then untangles a bit of the lights. "He's a reporter with the *Addison Weekly*. Putting together a Christmas collage for next week's edition and wanted some nature shots. So you're still safe, Miss Hart. He wasn't onto you."

"You're sure?" Penny straightens a strand of lights as she asks.

"For good measure, I threw him way off track. Sent him to the cove to that Christmas barn. Snowflakes and Coffee Cakes, is it?"

"Oh, yes. And it's so pretty this time of year. Thank you, Gus, for covering for me."

"Least I can do," Gus tells her, "after your shoulder injury. Is it bothering you at all? Stiff?"

"Injury?" Frank asks. "What happened?"

"Just a bruise, actually," Penny explains. "A branch fell when I was filling the bird feeder the other day."

"A *branch*?" Frank looks from Penny, back to Cardinal Cabin. "I feel terrible ... first the icy patch I meant to clear, and now the branches I meant to cut. I'm so sorry, Penny. Are you okay?"

"It was nothing, really," Penny assures him. "But Gus insisted I have my shoulder checked out. He brought me into town for a quick exam at the doctor's."

"I always say," Gus adds with a waggle of his finger, "better safe than sorry."

"And Dr. Davis agreed." Penny turns to Frank then. "That's who did the exam. Greg Davis."

Gus slightly squints at Frank now. "Which would not have been necessary, had those branches been trimmed."

"They were next on my list, Gus. I *swear*."

"Hope so." Gus plugs the last strand of lights into an extension cord and suddenly the entire front of Blue Jay Bungalow is illuminated. But as he steps back to study the decorations, he first throws a glare Frank's way. "Expecting more snow this weekend. Those weak branches may come down, and they're very close to Cardinal Cabin."

"Gus," Frank says as he reaches forward and adjusts a strand of lights. "You know I've been busy puttying windows, and chopping wood."

"And I appreciate that, Frank." Gus steps closer and folds his arms across his chest. His face is rosy in the cold, and he tips up his head to eye Frank from beneath his bushy white eyebrows. "And I'd like to thank you for all your work, actually. Because Lord knows, there's only twenty-four hours in a day, and you've been practically exceeding that with your boathouse obligations and upkeep here."

"You don't have to thank me, Gus. I'm on the payroll. It's my job."

But it's as if Gus doesn't even hear him. "Why don't you come by for dinner?" he asks.

"No, Gus. That's not necessary. And it's too much work for you."

"Nonsense. It'll keep me busy." Without missing a beat, Gus turns to Penny. "You'll come, too?"

Penny somehow feels like she's caught in the middle of a secret plan—a fix-up, if she's not mistaken. A fix-up by this grandfatherly type, Gus Haynes. Which is fine by her, if Frank's the other part of the plan. She gives a finishing-touch pat to the twinkling shrubs before saying, "My schedule's open, Gus!" But as she says it, she also starts inching her way back to Cardinal Cabin. Work is work, after all, and her boss *must* be impatiently awaiting today's clue.

"And what's a good day for you, Frank?" Gus is asking as she edges toward her cabin.

"Seriously?" Frank looks from Gus, to Penny—who shrugs with an easy smile—then back to Gus. "Tuesday, I guess. Next Tuesday will work."

"Okay." Gus still stands, arms folded, eyeing them both. "We'll have a turkey dinner."

"What?" Penny asks, still backing away. "Turkey?"

Gus laughs, resettles his cap on his head fringed with white hair, and turns to his light-decorating again. "The grandkids want turkey dinner for Christmas, and I never made a turkey. My wife always cooked those big, fancy meals." He looks over his shoulder at Penny and Frank. "So you'll be my practice run."

ten

AFTER CHECKING IN WITH GINA at the boathouse later that day, Frank figures it's time to tackle his grounds-keeper duties. Especially since his procrastinating ended up hurting Penny's shoulder. Now he has two goals this afternoon: light the lakeside community Christmas tree and trim back encroaching tree branches near the cabins, particularly Cardinal Cabin. If nothing else, guilt tends to ramp up his productivity.

So for the second time this month, Frank Lombardo once again finds himself dressed in his heavy work jacket, hat and scarf, standing on a ladder and stringing lights. But this time, the ladder is wood and sunk into the snow against a tall fir tree beside Snowflake Lake.

And this time, untangling the strings of lights does not annoy him.

This time, he's not asking what it's all for, this stretching and reaching as he wraps white twinkly lights up and around the green tree with snow-dusted boughs.

This time, he might even be whistling a few bars of a Christmas carol.

When he adds the silver-glitter snowflake topper to the tree and leans back on the ladder for a better look, a neighbor from Chickadee Shanty calls out, "Nice work, Frank!"

Frank glances over at the little white-painted cabin with its dark brown front door and brown window trim. The entire front peak of the tiny cabin is strung with fresh balsam garland. The same lush greens are also draped around the doorframe. Frank waves back before straightening the tree topper, then giving it a second scrutiny.

Which is precisely when he notices a trapper hat on a tall, lanky man approaching Cardinal Cabin. When he peers around the tree from the top rung of the ladder, Frank sees that the man is pulling an empty wagon. He hopes it isn't that photographer again.

As the trapper-hat man gets closer to Penny's front porch, Frank descends the ladder—his snow boots thudding on each step—and shifts the ladder to the side of the tree for a better view. He climbs halfway up the rungs, then presses aside some of the boughs and branches. In a moment, he ducks when ... wait ... when Greg Davis glances over!

Not wanting to be seen, Frank pulls his wool cap down lower and gets busy in the boughs until Greg is actually inside Cardinal Cabin. But he's not inside for long. Quickly, Frank climbs down the ladder and shifts it to the left this time, before climbing to the top rung again. There, he lifts lights, presses down branches, and watches this new drama unfold in his day.

Except now his light-stringing is done with a heavy heart. Because seriously, how can he even compete? There's the good doctor, all assisting and helping his new patient, Penny. Together, they're picking up twigs and sweeping the snow beneath a tree in Cardinal Cabin's yard. At one point, Greg touches her shoulder, leaving his hand there for a long moment as he says something. Then, wait … Yup. Greg's actually rehanging the bird feeder as Penny points out the new branch she wants it on, no doubt within perfect view of her kitchen window.

So Frank's hunch was right, darn it. Greg's potential wedding date is with Penny Hart.

Frank studies the couple in the snow—Penny in her navy parka, her copper hair falling over her shoulders, and Greg in a long, dark wool coat. Feeling defeated, Frank descends the ladder, each boot thudding on a lower rung, then another. The heck with cutting dead tree branches today. Just forget it. He's not going back to Penny's cabin with the town's most-eligible bachelor hanging around.

Instead, Frank gives one last look to the soaring, majestic lakeside tree all illuminated in twinkly lights now. He stops for a second, closes up the ladder, then turns and heads out to the one-lane road where his pickup truck is parked.

"What's it all for, anyway?" he asks, giving one look back to Cardinal Cabin, too.

❦

"Careful," Penny warns Greg as he picks up the fallen bird feeder and trips on a branch in the snow. "That's the one that dropped from the tree and clipped my arm."

Greg walks through the snow to her. After setting down the bird feeder, he rests his gloved hand on her shoulder. "And how's that arm feeling today? Any better?"

"Much. I take it easy, but really, I'm fine. Gus was being very protective, that's all."

"And with good reason," Greg adds as he picks up a small sack of black-oil sunflower seeds and fills the feeder.

"Can you hang it over on the right?" Penny turns to gauge where her kitchen window is, then points to the branch Greg's at. "A little to the left ... Perfect! Good as new."

With the feeder hung, Greg picks up the small sack of birdseed and carries it into Cardinal Cabin.

"Here, I'll take it." Penny reaches for the paper sack and sets it on a ledge near the kitchen window. The wood on the window frame and shelf is aged, its stain faded and dried out. A little drafty air comes in where some of the glass panes need new putty. She moves over a white ceramic pitcher, and a wine bottle in a basket, and an old tin lantern before setting the seed beside a tarnished gold trinket box there.

"Now you won't have to trek out to the shed," Greg says, "to get birdseed from that big barrel. Just bring out a scoop from right here."

"Well, thank you. I really appreciate it, and Gus will be glad that you got the feeder hung again. He loves those little cardinals. And, well, so do I." Penny takes off her mittens and hat, then pulls two mugs off the open wall shelf. "Can I make you a cocoa?"

"Actually," Greg says after clearing his throat and checking his watch, "I really have to be going. Got a final tux fitting with my brother, Wes."

"Oh! Okay, that sounds nice."

"But speaking of the wedding, there's something I'd like to ask you."

Penny takes off her parka and hangs it on a chair back. "What's that?"

"The wedding is a week from Saturday. On the twenty-first. And, well, I was wondering, Penny ... What I'm saying is, would you like to be my wedding date?"

For some reason, Penny never saw that question coming. She should've, she realizes now, with Greg's impromptu visits, and the gift basket, and his helping her out with the birdseed.

But Greg hasn't been on her mind these days. Especially today. Today, she's been more preoccupied with one particular kiss. An ice kiss. Not that the kiss was icy—far from it. But it happened *on* the ice, literally. On the beautiful, frosty ice, in an isolated wood-framed hut. Her hand rises to her face as she remembers the feel of Frank's whiskered jaw.

"A nice dinner, a little dancing, some laughs," Greg is saying, holding his trapper hat in his hands now. "It'll be a good time."

"Aw, Greg, thanks so much. But I'll still be here on my mystery trip then."

"Really?" Greg spins his flapped-hat, flipping it this way and that as he clears his throat. "I thought this cabin trip was only one week?"

Penny shakes her head. "It lasts till almost Christmas. And the travel agency's really counting on me to help bring in new business with this promotion."

"Oh. Can you take a day off?"

"No, it'd blow my cover. People think I'm in Vermont, or up north in the mountains. And some think my pictures are staged to throw them off, and that I'm really on some wind-swept beach in Nantucket!"

"Okay. I understand." Greg pulls his trapper hat down over his head. "How about this, instead? Would you save one of those Christmas movies for me?"

"Movies?"

"From the care basket I brought. Take my number and call me if you feel like watching one."

Penny opens a kitchen drawer and brushes through it, looking for a pen and paper. When she can't find any, she pulls her cell phone from the parka slung over the chair and types Greg's number in her list of contacts. After all the trouble Greg's gone through, it's the least she can do. Because as much as she wishes she could say, *Oh, I'm so sorry, but I'm seeing Frank Lombardo*, she also knows that's the furthest thing from being true. A kiss here, a dinner there ... Best to keep her options open.

Now, Greg heads through the cozy living room with its fire snapping; walks past the floor vase with birch branchlets spraying from it. When he gets to the wood-planked front door, he finally stops. Stops and turns back while flipping up his wool coat collar against the cold.

"Penny. Well, listen. You just give my phone a ring, when you want to watch a crooning Bing."

eleven

FRANK LOMBARDO'S NEVER BEEN THE type to be one-upped.

Never.

Not when he was a teen, trying out for the town baseball team and hitting the ball out of the park. Not last Christmas, competing with his sister's lasagna in a family taste-test declaring his the winner. And okay, not right now, ensuring no business in Addison outshines the boathouse with Christmas lights and swags of greens.

So he's not about to throw in the towel when it comes to getting the girl.

By Friday morning, he has a plan.

A plan finding him standing on the front porch out at Cardinal Cabin. Standing and hesitating beside evergreen sprigs spilling from a vintage silver milk can.

"Okay," Frank quietly tells himself as he pulls off his wool cap, steps closer to the door and looks at the red berry wreath hanging there. "It's time to up the game. To get a little more Penny-time than the good doctor does."

And that's when he knocks. Well, he tugs the woodpecker knocker's pull-string and *rat-a-tat-tat-tats*.

When the door swings open, Penny stands there. She wears a beige V-neck sweater over cream corduroys, with a red tartan scarf looped around her neck—beneath that copper-colored hair.

"Frank?" she asks.

Frank shifts his snowy, booted feet on the porch. "Gus sent me over."

"Gus?" She looks out toward Blue Jay Bungalow. "Is everything okay?"

"Sure. He said something about extra snowshoes here. In your shed?"

"Snowshoes?"

Frank nods and glances back at the lake behind him. "The woodpile's getting low. So I need to get deeper into the woods to find fallen trees good for splitting."

And so his Friday Penny-time begins.

After she gets the key and puts on her boots, he meets her around back at the shed. They step inside the dark space, where he pulls the string from a bare-bulb fixture mounted on the ceiling.

"Is that them?" Penny walks past extra sacks of birdseed, past a pole tree-trimmer, past shovels and that wagon Frank saw yesterday. She points to the wooden snowshoes mounted on the wall. "There are two pairs."

Frank lifts one off the wall, running his hand over the laced rawhide decking. "Gus said he always keeps two pairs in his rented cabins. You know, because usually couples stay here, and they use them together."

"Oh." Penny lifts a snowshoe off the shed's back wall. Her fingers toy with the leather binding straps. "I've never actually showshoed before."

"You haven't? Well, now's your chance ..." Frank steps closer and lifts the last shoe off the wall. "They're perfect for a snow hike?"

So when Penny sits on a dusty stool in the shed, Frank helps her secure the snowshoes on her booted feet, adjusting the bindings until the fit is comfortable. She lifts her fur-lined parka hood over her head, and once outside, they round the lake and move along a forest trail. The powdery snow wafts in little clouds at their feet as they swish along, looking for fallen trees.

"There's one, further in," Franks says as he stops alongside the trail. "Wait for me."

Penny watches as he maneuvers through deeper snow, past a stand of trees, and notes the location of one that's down.

"It's an old dogwood," he calls back while pulling a compass from his pocket. "Easy to split, and burns good." After reading the compass location, he jots it in a pocket notebook and returns to the trail.

"How will you chop it there?" Penny asks with a glance over at the tree lying across the snow.

"I won't. I'll come back with a snowmobile Gus has, cut the tree into pieces and cart it to the chopping block."

When the trail widens, they walk side by side. The woods are quiet today; it's cold enough that even the birds are hushed as they sit huddled on snow-covered limbs. It's almost as though the chickadees and cardinals are eavesdropping as Frank explains the winter kayak and canoe lodging at the boathouse, and as Penny admits that this pretty Snowflake Lake is growing on her during her reluctant sojourn here.

"But no one's guessed that I'm actually right in Addison. Most think I'm far, far up north." Penny moves a wispy tree branch out of the way while rounding a curve in the trail. "My boss says that the whole town is Penny-pondering!"

"Penny ... Penny." Frank looks over at her as she lifts a snowshoed foot. "Let me guess. Short for Penelope?"

"No." Penny smiles. "Just Penny. I'm an only child, so my parents always call me their lucky Penny. My dad even mounted a copper penny in our staircase banister the year I was born, as a special commemoration. He's so sentimental, he replaced that penny with another one so he could take the original with him when he and my mom moved south a few years ago."

"South ... Florida?"

Penny shakes her head. "North Carolina. They downsized to a condominium there, near the coast. Come to find out, they *miss* the Christmas snow, so I got them a good deal from Suitcase Escapes and booked them for Christmas in Colorado this year. You know, since I'd be preoccupied here with my mystery travel engagement." She takes another snowy step and looks over at him. "Anyway, guess we've got some old-school names, Frank. Short for ... Franklin?"

Frank laughs and points to a trailside bench up ahead where they can rest. "No," he explains. "Just Frank. My parents also loved another Frank—Sinatra—and actually named me after him. Every year at this time, they'd play his Christmas album, *A Jolly Christmas from Frank Sinatra*, and dance around the Christmas tree as he crooned, as if Sinatra were singing to them, personally."

"That sounds romantic." Penny sits beside him on the wood-slatted bench.

"It was. When my sister and I were growing up, they'd shut off all the living room lights except for the tree. We'd watch them dance from the staircase. They looked like a silhouette, gliding in the dusky room, my mother in Dad's arms. It was nice." Frank reaches down to dislodge snow packed on one of his boots. "They went through many copies of that record. Wore the grooves right out."

"I'd love to hear it. Sounds very merry."

"Really?" He looks at Penny, then pulls off a glove and brushes a wisp of hair from her cheek. "I might have a copy at home. They left a lot of their things behind when they moved, including their record player."

"Oh, did they go south too, like my parents did?"

"South end of *town*, actually. Cortland Drive, in the old apple-orchard development. My sister and brother-in-law bought a house there with an in-law apartment, and when their son, Dante, was born, my parents moved right in. I bought the family house when they offered it to me at a good price."

"That's so sentimental, keeping the family home … with all its history and memories."

When Frank stands to head back then, he reaches for Penny's hand to help her up on her snowshoes.

"Where *is* your home, Frank? In town, too?"

As they swoosh along the snowy trail, alone in the woods, Frank tells her. He also slows his pace, not wanting this Penny-time to come to an end. "It's the big English Tudor on Old Willow Road." They approach the rickety footbridge, and the rustic cabins come into view ahead. "My house is past the curve, near the old covered bridge."

"The covered bridge, what a pretty spot. I'm still new to town and don't know all the landmarks, but that one can't be missed."

"I remember you mentioned moving to Addison during our grilled cheese dinner. So what actually brought you to these parts?"

"More like *who* did. It was Chloe Hough."

"Chloe." Frank tips his head while eyeing her. "Jane March's sister?"

Penny nods. "Chloe was my college roommate, and we kept in touch as we went our separate ways. Me working as a copywriter with an advertising agency in Hartford, and she starting up with the travel agency. When Chloe heard my company closed up shop and I was out of work last year, she called me with a temporary job opportunity."

"So you never planned on staying in Addison?"

"No," Penny says with a shake of her head. "I was only filling in for another travel agent, who was spending two weeks with her family in northern Vermont for the holidays. Turns out, she met the love of her life during a skiing lesson and is still schussing down the slopes with him. They opened their own ski shop, and she never came back."

"Just like that?"

"Mm-hmm. So surprise, surprise! My two-week stint turned permanent. I needed the job, so I got an apartment in the refurbished mill factory and call it home now, all while getting to know the town and sending *other* folks on amazing vacations. As for Penny Hart, local travel agent? I haven't gone anywhere since then."

"No other trips? At all?"

"Uh-uh." She gives him a smile. "Haven't set foot out of Addison."

"You mean, you're a travel agent who doesn't travel?"

"You got it, much to my boss' chagrin." Penny snowshoes off the footbridge and looks across the lake to Cardinal Cabin. "Marketing's always been my thing, and I *love* selling trips to my clients—even though I have zero travel experience. It's lots of fun planning their journeys. But me? I'm actually a complete homebody, happiest being cozy in my own place. Which is why I dragged my feet coming here for work." Walking along the snowy trail with Frank by her side, she hitches her head toward the cabin with the red berry wreath hanging on its door. "This is the farthest I've ventured from home."

⚓

As Frank rehangs the snowshoes in the shed behind Cardinal Cabin, he glances over his shoulder. "Do you need any more wood for your fireplace?"

Penny looks up from where she sits on the stool, adjusting her snow boots. She shakes her head. "I'm not really the outdoorsy type. More the thermostat type. I'm kind of used to the creature comforts. My apartment I mentioned in the old mill factory? It has a gas fireplace. So all I do is hit the switch!"

"What?" Frank shuts off the bare light bulb as Penny walks outside again. "No crackling?" he asks when he pulls the shed door shut behind them. "No pops and sparks?"

Penny laughs and waves him off.

"But that's the *ambiance*," he explains when he catches up to her. "I'll cut you a few logs before I leave."

"Going back to the boathouse?" she asks, just as Frank takes her mittened hand in his and walks her over toward his wood-chopping block.

"That's where you'll find me. The town's small-business Christmas party is there today. Dinner, drinks and assorted Christmas games."

"Ooh, you'll probably see my crew from the travel agency. Pretty sure my boss reserved a table. So what games will they play?"

"The usual. My sister, Gina, decorated a wall with employees' baby photos, and they have to guess who's who. Or there's Pin-the-Ornament, where we attach clothespins to Christmas ornaments, and guests try to pin one on someone else without that person noticing. That one gets lots of laughs. I'll be there for a few hours, then head over to a stag party for Wes Davis."

"Wes. I think that's Greg's brother, right? So you know each other?"

"Wes and I have been friends for years, graduated high school together and catch up on his mail route," Frank explains as they arrive at his chopping block. He adjusts his leather gloves and lifts a small log onto the tree stump there. "So yeah, I know Greg, too."

"He's my doctor. For my shoulder injury."

Frank merely nods as he lifts the axe over his head and in one swing, splits the log perfectly in two. "And how's that shoulder feeling? Better, now?" he asks while setting up another log.

"Definitely." Penny shifts over to the side to watch how he splits the wood. "It wasn't anything serious. Gus was just being careful."

"Good old Gus, looking out for you." Frank gives the axe another swing and the log cleanly splits, the two halves falling to the side. "These should hold you over. You call me if you're running low." He leans the axe against the tree stump. "Is your phone with you?"

"Yes! I'm always on the lookout for photo-clues to grab for Suitcase Escapes, and my phone's my camera."

"Why don't you take my number? You know, in case you need anything."

So Penny types the number into her directory, then looks over at the axe leaning against the stump. Woodchips dot the snow around them, and the smell of fresh-cut timber fills the air. "Is there a secret to splitting the logs like that?"

"It's more a science than a secret," Frank says, turning to a pile of logs behind them. "Here's a nice dry piece of maple."

When he stands it on the tree stump, Penny walks over and centers it.

"Easy," Frank tells her as he sets his hands over hers. "There, that's good."

"So maple's a good burning wood?"

"It is. It's a nice hardwood. Which means a steady, slow burn, ideal for sitting beside the fireplace all evening."

"I like the sound of that," Penny tells him. "Now what?"

Frank clears a few random pieces of wood away from the chopping block. "First, it's important to have an uncluttered workspace. Don't want to trip on anything with that axe in hand." He hitches his head for her to come closer. "Take this," he says. "It's a splitting axe. The blade is wedged, so when it drives into the wood, the wedge helps to split it right in two."

Penny hesitates before taking the axe and holding it in both hands.

"Let me show you." Frank moves behind her and reaches his arms around, placing his hands on top of hers. "One over the other, like this," he says near her ear, all while shifting her hands.

"Okay." And though he can't see, Penny drops her eyes closed for just a second, smiles, then opens and focuses.

"Now," Frank says, his voice quiet. "You want that blade to hit square in the center of that log." He slides his hands further onto the axe and lifts the axe only a few inches before lightly dropping the blade on the wood. "See?"

Penny only nods.

"And you want a solid stance, too," he says, shifting his position behind her. "To keep that swing stable when you raise the axe over your head."

"Can I try?"

Frank's arms still reach around her, holding the axe with her. "No," he whispers. "You can *lift* the axe somewhat," he adds as he steps aside then, "but don't swing it down hard. Not with your injured shoulder. Just go through the motion, slowly."

Penny looks over at him, then resets her hands on the axe handle. When he nods, she steps back and adjusts her stance at the chopping stump, raises the axe over her head, then gently brings it down to the log in a slow motion. "Like that?"

"Pretty good," he says. Then he steps behind her and again wraps his arms around her, placing his hands over hers and slightly lifting the axe before dropping the blade down on the top of the log again. "But more like this."

It's only when he stops, and silently pauses, that Penny turns her head to him. When she does, Frank shifts his position and leans around to kiss her right there. She still holds the splitting axe as he raises his gloved hands to her face and deepens the kiss, inadvertently nudging her fur-trimmed hood off at the same time. He stops only to safely remove the axe and set it against the chopping block, then tips her chin up and kisses her again. One gloved hand reaches up to her neck, while his other hand slips to her waist and pulls her against him.

"Frank," Penny whispers, her mittened hand alongside his whiskered face.

Frank takes off his gloves while still kissing her, then cradles her face before stopping to simply look at her—touching her silky hair, tucking a strand behind her ear, and kissing her again, once, twice.

"Well," Penny murmurs then, the back of her fingers running along his jaw. "I can honestly say you're the only lumberjack I've ever kissed. Do you end every wood-splitting lesson that way?"

"You're my first lesson, so ... we'll have to see." He looks past her at the split logs, the axe. "How about if I take a picture of you, splitting wood? You know, for one of your travel clues. Show the town you're stepping outside your comfort zone."

Penny turns to the axe and carefully lifts it. "That'd be fun," she says, then sets the blade on the log and adjusts her stance. "Something like this?"

"Wait, you look a little cold." Frank pulls his wool beanie off his head and tugs it over her hair, fussing with a few strands, then leaving a kiss on her cheek before she hands him her cell phone.

It's not the wool cap that does it, then, or the way he changes the position of her hands on the axe, either.

No.

What warms her right through on this chilly, woodland morning—with a silvery mist rising off the frozen lake and smoke curling from some of the cabin chimneys—is the way Frank kisses her once more, then tilts his beanie to a jaunty angle on her head before raising the phone and snapping one photo.

If the smile that won't leave her face is any indication, he got the perfect shot.

twelve

AFTER FRANK SHUTS OFF THE lights at the boat-house later that evening, he does what he always does: stops and pauses in the banquet hall's doorway. Standing there in the shadows is when he gauges how the event went. Because the space has a way of coming to life in memory when he looks into the cavernous, dimmed room. Past the shadows, and dust particles floating like stardust, he sees vague silhouettes of the guests dancing, ornament-hanging and table-hopping; hears echoes of good laughs and cheer. Though the grand Christmas tree is dark now, and the swags of garland loop unlit across the ceiling beams, only hours ago, the space brimmed with festivities. And if his guests remember what *he* remembers, then he served them well.

But for him, the festivities are just beginning as he drives through Addison. The big clock on Main Street reads five past ten. Joel's Bar and Grille is also on Main, a few blocks beyond the firehouse and a little past The Green. It's not too far from Suitcase Escapes, either. So he parks close to the travel agency. This way, he'll walk by it and get to see Penny's latest photo-clue on his way to Wes' stag at the bar.

As he approaches, a few people are stopped at the travel agency's window, prompting Frank to hover off to the side until they move past. When he has the window all to himself, he turns up his collar against the cold and walks close to the clue display. There, front and center, blown up to fill the window, is the photograph he took of Penny Hart. Wearing her blue parka, she stands at his chopping block, his wool beanie tipped on her copper-colored locks, her smile meant just for him. He lightly touches the windowpane as he reads the caption she sent along with the photo:

Split and chop. Split and chop …
Once you start here, it's hard to stop!

"Isn't that the truth," Frank says when he thinks of their kiss at the wood-chopping block. When a lone couple strolls close, he tugs his wool beanie low and heads toward Joel's. The bar is tucked into a brick building, keeping it discreet—except for those changing neon signs that management switches up in the front window. Tonight, it's the merry red neon bells, flashing this way and that.

Frank walks inside to what sounds like a raucous good time, what with the festive cheer *and* Wes' stag party taking place. He stamps the snow off his boots and shoves his gloves into his jacket pockets. Holiday nutcrackers stand sentry at either end of the bar, swags of garland are strung above it, and rocking Christmas carols play on the jukebox.

Waving to a few familiar faces sitting at the bar, Frank winds around small, square tables clustered beside a dance floor and heads to the padded red booths off to the side—where several arms are raising their beer glasses in a toast that must be for

Wes. So he leaves on his beanie, but takes off his coat, hangs it on a wall hook and makes his way over.

"Yo, there's the groom!" Frank calls when he sees Wes downing his drink.

Wes gets out of his booth and gives Frank a hearty slap on his shoulder. "Glad you could make it, Frank. Join the party, man," he says as they settle in at the booth.

In no time, Frank sees that the whole gang's here. Bob Hough, the fire marshal, high-fives him as he slides into his seat.

"Good to see you," Frank says while eyeing the melted-cheese nachos and buffalo chicken wraps set out on platters.

"Have some chow, Frank," Pete Davis says, not missing a beat with his whittling as he does. A napkin beneath his hands catches the wood shavings from a small piece he diligently carves at the table.

"Think I will." Frank reaches for one of the chicken wraps. "These look amazing," he says, then digs into the wrap over-stuffed with breaded chicken pieces, tomato, lettuce—and blue cheese dressing dribbling from the sides.

When George Carbone, notorious caterer for the boat-house, clears his throat as he lifts the beer pitcher and fills Frank's glass, Frank motions to him while still chewing his double bite.

"But not as good as your grub, Carbone," he relents, pressing the back of his hand to his mouth to catch a dressing drip. "The Main Course trumps everything."

"Good answer, Frank," George tells him. "Cheers to that."

Sitting across from him, George raises his glass to Frank, who obliges the toast, then takes another double bite of this chicken concoction. At the same time, he listens to the guys put Derek Cooper on the spot. In between the bullshitting and laughter, they relentlessly razz poor Coop.

When are you making an honest woman of Vera?

Barely see her these days. We're solid, but crazy busy.

Too busy for love?

That one brings a few hoots and hollers as Frank takes a swallow of his cold beer.

Spend a day at her shop, you'll see, Derek argues, defending Vera. *Snowflakes and Coffee Cakes is a revolving door of customers, from sunup to closing. Between that and the Christmas trees I'm strapping onto folks' cars, not to mention the snow shovels and ice melt I'm moving, hell, we're like two ships passing at night.*

At least you are passing each other.

You still living in that apartment over the hardware store?

Sure am, great digs. Easy commute, too. Work is right downstairs. Can't beat that.

Frank sees that it's Pete who says it, right as he sets down a small, whittled Labrador retriever, turns it this way, then that, before passing it along to Derek in the booth behind him.

"Shit, looks just like my Zeus," Derek tells him, "patrolling the store."

Frank finishes his chicken wrap and takes his beer glass with him as he heads over to the darts game. "Hey, Pete," he calls out. "You carve any birds?"

Pete looks up from the next block of wood he's working on. "Not lately. Got something in mind?"

"Not sure yet," Frank tells him, all while noticing Greg following him to the game area.

"Well listen, Frank," Pete says. "I updated my website for Near and Deer. There's a custom-order form there. You fill it out and I'm happy to oblige. Anything for a friend of my sons."

"A bird? Like what?" one of those sons, Greg, asks Frank as he picks up a dart to throw. "A *cardinal*, maybe?" he asks, quiet enough for only Frank to hear.

Frank looks over at him, says nothing, but spins a dart in his fingers and takes the first shot at the dartboard.

"Went by Suitcase Escapes earlier." Greg fidgets with the three darts he's now got in his hand.

Holding his next dart level with his line of vision, Frank pauses and looks over at Greg without throwing. His arm holding the dart simply stays raised.

"Seen the latest clue?" Greg asks.

"You mean from that travel agent?" Frank looks at the dartboard, brings the dart back close to his ear, then levels a second shot at the board. "Penny, I think her name is?"

"That's the one," Greg says as Frank lines up his third shot.

After Greg says it, Frank places the dart, straightening his arm in the throw and holding his fingers outstretched toward the target for a long moment.

"Someone got a good photo of her today," Greg tells him as he steps up to throw his turn.

Frank looks back at him when he's retrieving his three darts. "Wherever that Penny is, there must be staff at those resorts." He pulls out the last of his darts. "They're always happy to snap a tourist pic."

"Yeah, and how about those clues?" Greg raises his arm and follows through on a throw, the dart thudding into the dartboard. "*Split and chop. Split and chop. Once you start here, it's hard to stop.*"

"Is that right?" Frank asks, dropping his voice. "What do you suppose that means?"

"Not sure," Greg answers, flinging another dart.

One thing Frank notices as Greg throws his second dart is the way the stag-party booths seem to have quieted, the guys all watching this exchange.

"Funny," Greg says as he takes aim, his arm raised, dart clutched in his fingers. He shimmies his hand back and forth, focusing on his throw. "Looked like that Penny had your exact wool beanie on her copper locks today." *Zing*, off goes his third dart, with Greg following to retrieve them. He yanks them out slowly, one after the other.

Frank cuffs his shirtsleeve and takes his place behind the throw line, waiting for the target to clear. Before he takes aim, he pulls off his telltale hat and shoves it in his back pocket. "Speaking of women," Frank calls after him, "line up that date for your brother's wedding yet?" Raising his elbow high and level, Frank throws his dart. "We're all waiting for the big reveal."

Greg gives Frank a piercing glare as he brushes past him. "Working on it."

After a quick look back at him, Frank adjusts his firm stance, stands straight and raises his chin. Eyeing the dartboard now, he lets his second dart fly. At this point, he glances over at Wes and the others, and it unnerves him a little, the way all eyes are now riveted to the one-on-one competition. Even old Pete sets down his carving, lowers his reading glasses on his nose, and has a gander.

"If it takes *that* much work to snag the date," Frank says to Greg as he lifts and steadies his third dart, "maybe she's not that into you, after all." With that, Frank releases the dart, holding his arm extended for a long second after seeing the perfect release.

"Bull's-eye!" someone calls out from Wes' booth.

thirteen

ON THE TV SCREEN, LEO Sterling stands in front of a Connecticut weather map. It shows a wide band of snow moving into Addison, and over on the side, a computer graphic of a thermometer is pure blue, with dramatic icicles dripping from it.

"Ho! Ho! Ho!" Leo booms. "Lotsa snow is going to blow!"

Saturday morning, that's all Penny needs to hear to run to Cardinal Cabin's kitchen window, move aside the old tin lantern, lean on the sill and have a look out to her backyard. As if it hasn't snowed enough already! Everything's been blanketed in white for days. Well, white dotted with black-oil sunflower seed shells scattered beneath the bird feeder.

"Though we've had steady snowfall all month, this may be the first *major* storm of the season, folks," the meteorologist says on the TV behind her.

Which gets her panicked enough to first rush to the refrigerator to check her supplies, then to a few cabinets that she opens, scans and quickly shuts.

"Shoot!" Penny whispers with a glance at the clock, then out the window again, right as pretty white flakes begin to swirl. Pretty white flakes that will accumulate and pile up and keep her shut inside for days. Which leaves her only one option—grab her cell phone and dial.

"Gus?" she asks when he answers. "I have to get into town for some food before the storm hits. Can I pick up anything for you, too?"

"Sufferin' snowflakes, perfect timing. I need flour for my gravy. Add it to your list?"

"Gravy? You're cooking gravy in a snowstorm?"

"No, it's for our turkey dinner on Tuesday. But wait. Penny! How will you get to the store?"

"Oh, I have a ride arranged," she lies, then crosses her fingers and squeezes her eyes briefly shut. "I'll just need a snow-torcycle lift to the road."

After promising to call Gus back with a time, Penny quickly dials one more number.

"Frank?" she asks when he answers. "I really need a favor."

"Penny, name it."

"Can you somehow get me to SaveRite Grocery Store?"

By the time Frank parks at the end of the narrow one-lane road, visibility is compromised. Even worse, the snowflakes are tiny, which means the storm will be significant. He squints through the blowing snow when he hears a puttering sound, and there, coming out of the trail in the woods, is Gus on his snowtorcycle. Penny sits in the sidecar beside him, though no one would recognize her beneath those huge sunglasses covering her face, and that polka-dot kerchief around her hair. When Gus pulls alongside the truck, Frank gets out to help Penny off the snowtorcycle and into his pickup.

"You hurry safely home," he calls to Gus then. Those tiny flakes stab at his face, and he tugs his wool cap low. "The snow's coming down hard!"

Gus waves and gives the snowtorcycle a rev before taking off, puttering back down the trail toward Snowflake Lake.

The coating of fresh snow makes the roads slippery, with the truck occasionally fishtailing as Frank tries to hurry. At any traffic lights they stop at, Penny slightly ducks to avoid being seen. Finally, SaveRite is within view ... at the end of a long line of cars, blinkers on, forming a traffic jam as they wait to turn into the grocery store's packed parking lot.

"Are you sure you want to shop here?" Frank asks. He glances over and tries not to crack a smile at the getup Penny is wearing. "What if you're recognized?"

"But it'll take too long to go somewhere else now. And the roads are getting treacherous, with all this snow!"

Slowly, the vehicles inch forward. Windshield wipers are madly swishing; drivers are hunkered over steering wheels and squinting out the windows. At last, they're in. Frank maneuvers the parking lot rows, pausing for red taillights ahead of him, motioning for waiting pedestrians—furry hoods flipped up, heads down against the wind—to cross in front of him. All the while, cars snake up and down each row, veering into any space that becomes available.

"How about if you wait in the truck?" Frank offers once they pull into a parking space. He shuts off the wipers and turns to her. "You can give me your list."

Penny shakes her head beneath that polka-dot silk scarf. "No. I'm incognito, so it'll be okay. And I need Christmas cookie ingredients, too, which will be easier for me to just pick out."

"If you're sure." Frank reaches over and tucks a strand of that smooth copper hair beneath the kerchief.

"I am. Ready?" Penny opens her door and hundreds of tiny white crystals instantly blow into the truck's cab. "If you can block me," she calls over her shoulder, "we'll breeze right through!"

༄

When Leo Sterling called this storm a snow *event*, he wasn't kidding. Because once Frank finds an empty cart and squeezes into SaveRite with the masses, that's just how it feels—like he and Penny are at a packed event. Penny grips his arm as people brush against them, lists clutched in their mittened hands. Shoppers swerve in front of them for tomatoes, and carrots, and bananas. Overflowing carts stop mid-row as shoppers reach to cereals and canned peas, forcing Frank to maneuver around them while Penny forges ahead and plucks her items from the shelves.

"Psst!" Frank manically motions around a woman and her two children when Penny turns at his beckon.

"What?" Penny whispers while lowering her big sunglasses and peering at him over the top of the frame.

Frank looks past her and, left with nothing else to do, abandons their cart to hurry and nudge her close to the sacks of sugar and flour. He pulls his beanie down low and bends close to the two-pound bags, hitching his head for her to do the same.

"What are we doing?" she whispers again when her head is aligned with his, just inches from the second shelf from the bottom.

"Hiding."

Penny leans closer, picks up a flour sack and scrutinizes the label. "From who?"

"Shh." Frank barely glances behind her. "Your coworker." When Penny starts to instinctively turn to see, Frank whips his arm around her shoulders and grabs a sugar box. "Don't look! It's Chloe."

So Penny instead pushes her sunglasses up tight against her face and leans into Frank's shoulder. She points to the box he holds while keeping her back to the shoppers until the aisle is safe again.

Contrary to everyone else in the store, each step Penny and Frank take then is calculated, involving subtle turns when someone waves to Frank, and about-faces when a shopper is too familiar. Sometimes they linger, dropping decoy items into the cart when they're forced to stand and wait someone out at the frozen pancakes, or canned fruit. Frank almost feels he has a plastic mask on his face, the way his dodging and ducking must be so obvious.

Just when the coast is clear and they're in SaveRite's home-stretch, a new danger approaches.

"Oh, heck," Frank says when he grabs Penny's arm.

"What?" Penny throws a glance down the aisle while cinching her trench coat's belt even tighter.

"It's my parents! With my sister's baby, *Dante*." He spins in their direction first, then spins toward the far end of the aisle.

"Is Gina here, too?" Penny asks from behind the box of frozen pancakes she peers over.

"No. My sister is supervising another wedding at the boat-house today. Our December calendar's jam-packed. And the reception must go on, rain, sleet or snow."

"Oh, no. What are we going to do?"

Frank whips off his wool cap, shoves it in his pocket and presses the back of his hand against his forehead. His parents are on an imminent collision course with them. Again he grabs Penny's arm, but this time leans so close, he feels wisps of her soft hair alongside his cheek as he whispers harshly into her ear. "Quick! Go to the magazines." He gives her the slightest shove, then apologizes. "I'll meet you there," he assures her when she lowers her sunglasses once more and ... what? Yes, *winks* at him before dashing off.

"Frank?" his mother's voice suddenly calls out. "Frank, is that you?"

"Well, of course it is," Frank hears his father say. "Look, Dante. There's Uncle Frankie!"

With one furtive glance at the beautiful departing woman in a trench coat—a woman who steals a glimpse at *him* over her scarved shoulder—Frank strides over to his parents wheeling little Dante through the store.

After hurried hello-hugs, Frank acts completely distracted by baby Dante packed so deep into a snowsuit, hat, hood, mittens and boots that his arms and legs are partially extended and immobile. But Frank manages a couple of high-fives with his little nephew before warning his parents to hightail it right out of the grocery store and get that baby safely home.

"Gina would *kill* you if she knew you brought Dante out in this storm!"

"But it was only a flurry when we left," his mother says with a worried glance toward the store's front windows.

"And it's like a *blizzard* now." Frank glances to the windows, too, then behind him, for any sign of Penny. "Now, *out!* Out you go," he says as he turns their cart, baby and all, toward the exit.

JOANNE DeMaio

No sooner do they wave him off than Frank pivots and heads three rows over, where a glamorous, kerchiefed woman holds a magazine close to her face, seemingly engrossed in some fashion article.

But Frank knows better—she's discreetly waiting for him. He quietly approaches, double-checks both ways, and presses a kiss on her cheek. "That's enough of these charades," he whispers after Penny kisses him back. He drops his keys into her hand and closes her fingers around them. "You get out to my truck while I pay. Here," he says, wheeling their cart filled with necessities and frivolities beside her. "I'll keep you covered on the way."

Once they reach the front aisle—more trouble. At each register, anxious shoppers bundled in coats and boots wait in mile-long lines. No doubt many—if not all—are familiar with Penny Hart and her mystery travel escapade. So Penny flips her fur collar up even higher before heading straight to the exit as Frank gets their cart to the end of a line.

"Hey!" a voice calls out. It's a woman halfway through unloading her cart, dropping her orange juice carton on the checkout counter before turning and pointing as Penny rushes past. "Wait. Is that ..."

And Penny hears, too; Frank can tell by the way she ducks low and scoots around several bundled-up shoppers. Shimmying one way and twisting another, she gets herself to the doors and quickly outside. Frank leans to the side and watches through the front window as Penny slip-slides on the snowy pavement while bolting to his truck.

A few shoppers turn in unison, craning to see out the window, and suspiciously watch her go.

fourteen

IT HAPPENED SO FAST, PENNY can't believe it. The streets are covered with snow, the plows can't keep up with clearing them, and Frank's pickup truck fishtails around every curve.

"Will we make it to Cardinal Cabin okay?" she asks.

"Listen." Frank glances to her, then quickly back to the slippery road. "The roads are slick, Penny. And my home is a lot closer than the cabins. I'll stop there until the town crews get things cleared and sanded."

Penny leans forward in the truck's passenger seat and squints past the swishing windshield wipers and tiny snowflakes instantly covering the glass between every other swish. Families have turned on their Christmas lights during the storm, so that behind the swirling flakes, colors of red and green and white smudge beneath the snow. As Frank's truck inches along, they pass farmhouses with their front porches lined in lights; mailboxes decorated with garland and mini wreaths; colonials with candles glowing in their windows.

Finally, Frank pulls the truck into his long driveway, getting them safely off the treacherous roads. The brick-and-stucco

Tudor looks imposing, rising against the stormy skies. White lights twinkle on a large balsam wreath hanging on the arched door, and a tall brick chimney on the front of the home hints at a massive fireplace inside.

"Don't worry," Frank is saying as he parks near the front doorway. "The roads just aren't safe to drive on now. And no one but me will know you're here."

He wastes no time leaving the truck and rushing around to help Penny step out. Holding her close, they walk through several inches of powdery snow to the front steps, where he unlocks the door, reaches in to switch on a light, and motions for her to go in ahead of him.

Once inside, Penny hesitates in the foyer beneath the small crystal chandelier Frank had switched on. Beyond, a gold-printed rug lines the hardwood floor in a hallway leading to a turned staircase, where a grandfather clock also stands in a nook to the side.

"Come on, take off your coat in here," Frank says as he leads her down the hallway before turning beneath an arched doorway into the living room. There, paned windows adorn either side of the brick fireplace.

During the few minutes while Frank's busy bringing in the bags of groceries, Penny walks around the room. Its gold walls are framed with wide crown molding, and over those paned windows, long draperies hang to the floor, where the fabric pools on the hardwood.

There's a timeworn feel to the space, with its built-in bookshelves, and dark wood tables, and large upholstered chairs and gray sofa—especially with the wind rattling the old windows, and the blustery skies dropping crystals tap-tap-tapping at the glass. The house seems straight out of a gothic novel on this stormy day.

Until Penny turns and sees the Christmas tree beside the fireplace. The tree is tall and tucked into a corner area, and ... undecorated.

"Frank?" she calls out while slipping off her trench coat and scarf, then dropping them on the couch. "You haven't decorated your tree!" She walks to it, touching the unadorned branches.

After putting away some of the groceries, Frank comes into the room and switches on a few table lamps. "It's just an old artificial tree I dug out from the basement." He picks up her coat from the sofa and hangs it out in the hallway closet. When he returns, he's cuffing his flannel shirtsleeves and heading straight to that massive fireplace. "Been so busy at the boathouse and Gus' cabins, I haven't had much time for decorating."

"Oh," Penny quietly says, touching the tree again, then turning and spotting plastic totes against a far wall. As Frank adds logs to the fireplace and lights the kindling, she makes her way to those totes and finds just what she thought would be there. She carefully lifts out an old divided tray of vintage-looking ornaments and carries it across the living room. The ornaments are glass balls—red, green and gold—lined with strips of silver glitter. Carefully, she picks one up and hangs it on the tree.

"You don't have to do that," Frank says as the fire takes hold. He pokes the logs before joining her at the tree.

Penny lifts another ornament, this one red with glitter snowflakes on it. "I don't mind. Honestly. Actually, with my trip and all, I missed out on decorating my apartment Christmas tree." She hangs the ornament and steps back to admire the tree. "So this is nice."

Frank stands beside her, his hand to his chin, then goes to the kitchen. When he comes back, it's with two glasses of wine, one of which he silently hands to her before turning to the tote.

What happens then is something Penny had never thought she'd do this year, not while staying in her cabin hideaway. But for the next hour—between sips of wine—she and Frank lift out every ornament: glass balls and felt snowmen and crystal snowflakes. They talk softly, Frank telling family stories about the decorations while hanging a wooden red sled up high, or tucking a gingerbread man within the boughs. As they circle the tree, carefully placing each ornament, the wind blows outside the windows in nearly whiteout conditions.

Inside, the fire is crackling, the room is warm and aglow, and in no time, the tree is sparkling. But it isn't until Frank plugs in its tiny white lights that the sparkling turns grand.

When Penny crosses the room to shut off a lamp on a round pedestal table, she's distracted by an old record player on a wall shelf. A pile of albums is propped beside it. So she thumbs through the record covers, delighted to find one in particular.

"Oh, Frank. Look!" she says. "Is this the album your parents danced to?" she asks, holding it up. "*A Jolly Christmas from Frank Sinatra.*"

"That's the one." Frank crosses the living room and stands beside her.

"If you had a top hat like his," Penny says, scrutinizing him while lightly touching his whiskered jaw, "you'd look just like Sinatra."

"I don't know about *that*," Frank tells her as he takes out the album and sets it on the turntable. In a minute, there's the scratchy hiss of the needle on vinyl as the Christmas carols begin.

The funny thing is the way Penny finds herself humming along as they empty out the last tote, together. She scatters gold Christmas bells on end tables, and Frank hangs a leather strap of sleigh bells on a doorknob; she sits a glittery snowman on the hearth, and Frank tends the fire, all while Sinatra serenades them, his voice smooth and buoyant.

But when one song in particular begins, a slow song, Frank stops stoking the burning logs, sets down the wrought-iron tongs and walks to her. On the way, he shuts off both table lamps. The only sound in the room is Sinatra singing promises of home and snow.

Suddenly, as a sorrowful vibrato of violin sweeps in, time feels like it's taken on the same haunting pace as the luxuriously slow song. Frank lifts two glittered pinecones from Penny's hand, sets them on the shelf beside the record player, then turns to her, his arms open.

And Penny does it, in the hushed, golden living room of Frank's English Tudor. As Sinatra sings about being home for Christmas, she walks to Frank, and he takes her in those strong arms of his. They pause, Frank looking at her closely before pulling her near and moving a step with her. Penny smiles, and rests her head on his shoulder as they sway in the dark room, lit only by the lights of the grand tree beside the roaring fireplace.

And though the song on the record player is all about dreams of home, Penny feels like she's *living* in a dream. In the shadowy room where darkness presses against the windowpanes, the tree's twinkling lights sparkle on the ornaments, and on the evening, too. In these moments of pure warmth, and gentle touch, it's a dream Penny wishes would never end.

༄

Frank hasn't been caught up in a moment since, well, since he first kissed Penny in the snow. Now he's not only caught up as they slow-dance beside the twinkling tree, with Sinatra crooning and the snow falling outside the windows.

No, he's entangled and immersed in the romance of it all—the touches, the music, the decorations casting only faint illumination, the feel of Penny in his arms.

So when Penny lifts her head from his shoulder and looks at him, his fingers brush along her silky hair, glimmering in the low lights of the room. Finally, he cups his hand behind her neck, bends and kisses her while they dance. As he does, he feels Penny reach to his shoulder and so he drops his hands behind her back and holds her closer. Her sweater is soft, moving slightly with her every step, beneath his touch.

When Penny murmurs his name into the kiss, he pulls back and toys with her hair for a few moments.

Moments when he then bends close and rests his face alongside hers, before they continue dancing cheek to cheek.

Until this time, Penny pulls back, drags her fingers along his jaw and kisses him once more. And as the kiss lengthens, their dance goes on, but slows.

Outside the window, snow hisses against the glass. And what Frank thinks, especially with the deepening kisses of Penny in his arms that get him to lift his hands and cradle her face, is this: Their relationship is like one of those surprising snowflakes that started in a light flurry, and suddenly twists and spins into something so much more.

And yet nobody knows … Nobody knows.

It's only theirs, and theirs alone.

Which makes it just about perfect.

Feeling Penny pressed against him in the dimly lit room, Frank relishes every second of their slowing, secret dance.

A dance that stops only with Frank stroking her neck, her cheek, kissing her once, then again, before whispering her name. "Penny."

She stands in front of him, her fingers tracing along his hair, his shoulder.

"Penny," he whispers again, taking her hand in his and folding it against his chest. "Come on, let's go upstairs?"

She wastes no time—no time shaking her head no.

"No?" he asks, tipping his head.

Penny turns and looks at the roaring fireplace, the frosted windows, the sofa covered with woven and knitted throws. Then she tugs him to that sofa, still holding his hand as she sits right there in the dusky room, in the vague shadows of glimmering light.

But it isn't until her fingers delicately undo each button on his flannel shirt that Frank gets it. Gets that she doesn't want to leave this moment filled with soft light, and snow, and song. She *wants* them to be in its shadows, a part of it.

Still, it isn't until she presses his shirt off his shoulders that he places his hands on her hips. That his hands lift off her sweater, that her hands pull off his thermal tee.

And it isn't until Penny leans in and kisses him again while her hands drop to unbuckle his belt that Frank lays her on the sofa against the plush cushions.

That a different dance begins with whispers and touch as he moves on top of her. Their kisses come slow, but long. Her smile, warm. He feels the curves of her body beneath him as he brushes aside a strand of her copper hair, caresses her neck, tells her she's so beautiful, twice, their whispers blending with the hiss of snow tapping at the windowpanes, with the hiss of the needle on the record that's done, but still silently spinning, spinning.

Until afterward, when Frank drops the record-player needle at the start of the album, then pulls a knitted throw off the back of the sofa and drapes it over them as Sinatra sings another song. As the logs crackle in the fireplace. As the twinkling glow of Christmas and snowfall gleams in the dark room.

As Penny lies pressed beside him, his arm around her holding her close.

fifteen

PENNY'S NOT SURE SHE'S EVER seen a more beautiful sight. From where she lies beneath the blanket's cocoon on the couch, the dark windowpanes are frosted; the white lights of the tree and mantel garland glimmer, leaving a glow on the gold walls, on the hardwood floor, on the scrolled burgundy Oriental rug in front of the fireplace. Frank's fingertips toy with her hair, moving softly over the strands, touching her ear, her neck, her shoulder.

If they stay right where they are all night long, she couldn't be happier. An hour ticks by while they occasionally sip their wine; while Frank flips the Christmas album over to play the other side; while they slip in a few sweet, long kisses as the world is kept far, far away outside his dimly lit living room.

Until a light suddenly cuts through the soft shadows. Frank sits up on the sofa at the same time that headlights sweep past the window.

"Someone's here," he says.

Which prompts Penny to grab her jeans and get them on, then find her bra and somehow manage to hook it in her panic. But her sweater is gone. No matter where she glances—end tables, the mantel, the carpet—there's no sign of it. So Frank lifts his flannel shirt off a chair and helps her get her arms into it, then quickly pulls on his own jeans, thermal tee and socks.

When they hear a car door slam, they both freeze.

"Frank? Are you expecting somebody?" Penny asks as her fingers attempt to button his flannel shirt hanging loose on her.

"No!" He practically leaps off the couch and trots to the window, moving the partially drawn drapes. "Oh, shoot. It's my sister. Gina! What the *heck* is she doing here?"

"Should I go upstairs?"

"No time." Frank turns to Penny, cups her head and gives her a short but intense kiss, then takes her hand. "Come here."

They make their way around wineglasses and shoes and couch cushions—to the hallway where Frank first slips the chain lock into place on the front door. No sooner does he do this than a muffled foot-stamping begins on the stoop.

"Oh no!" Penny whispers. "What'll I do?"

Frank looks one way, then another, before taking her hand again and tugging her along—not that he has to tug. She's holding on to his arm for dear life, hoping for a way out of this impending mess.

When they hear the front door open, Frank stops at the coat closet and nudges Penny inside. "Shh," he whispers, his finger to her lips—just for a second. Then he kisses her once more and shuts the door.

"Frank?" Gina calls out as she presses the wooden front door against its chain lock. "What's going on?"

Penny opens the closet door a crack and sees Frank running through the living room, switching on a lamp, straightening up the couch and that sweet, warm throw—a knit throw evoking a memory that makes Penny's eyes drop closed with the pleasure of it. Until she hears Frank running back to the hallway. He's dragging both hands through his wavy, dark hair while taking a sharp breath, too.

"Frank?" Gina asks, giving the chain lock a rattle as she presses the resisting door against it. "Are you there? I'm on my way home, but just need to pick something up." Silence, then, "Frank!"

"Just a minute," he answers while buckling his belt and straightening the twisted fabric of his black thermal tee. Finally, he fiddles with the chain lock and gets it open, only to have his sister practically spill into the room.

Through the tiniest crack, Penny watches as Gina is floored by the holiday decorations. Though Frank's sister doesn't say anything, her eyes are glued to the elegant living room tastefully done up with all the old family ornaments and Christmas trinkets. In the shadows, the silvers and golds shimmer beneath twinkling lights. When Gina tears her eyes away from the perfect Christmas scene, she directs them straight to her brother. Straight to Frank, and once he's in her sights, those eyes of hers narrow to a suspicious squint.

"What's the matter?" Frank asks as he closes the front door—doing anything, Penny can see, but look at Gina until absolutely, positively necessary.

"Hmm," Gina says, stepping closer to him, then motioning to the glimmering living room. "To quote you ... *What's it all for?*"

"Eh." Frank brushes past her. "I had nothing else to do. Snowed in, you know," he calls over his shoulder as he turns on another living room lamp.

When Gina follows after him, Penny opens the closet a bit more, noticing how Frank is quickly heading to the sofa. His foot nudges something—wait, it's her *sweater*—beneath it. As his foot kicks and presses the sweater *and* an empty wineglass, he distracts his sister with questions about the boathouse.

"Listen," Frank says as he gives the living room a final once-over, "tell Joshua thanks for covering for me today. Nice of your husband, and I got a lot of new boat reservations done," he lies while his eyes dart from the sofa to the end tables.

"No prob," Gina says, sounding a little distracted. "It gave Mom and Dad some quality Dante time. They babysat all day."

"Was the snow any trouble at the reception?" Frank asks while balling up Penny's silk incognito kerchief before tucking it behind one of those flowing draperies. "Did the guests get out okay?"

"They did," Gina says from where she cautiously stands at the Christmas tree now. She's pulling off her mittens and touching an ornament or two. "Thanks to Bob Hough. His crew kept the parking lots all cleared."

But as she talks, Penny sees through the closet-door crack how Gina is doing something else. She's slowly walking around the room, noting evidence of the afternoon and evening: empty decoration boxes, the burning logs in the fireplace, the Sinatra record finished playing, but still spinning on the turntable—its needle making a repetitive, scratchy noise.

"Frank?" Gina holds up a half-empty wineglass and nods to the knitted throw hanging off the sofa. "Got a secret girlfriend thing going on today?"

"What?" He crosses the room, snatches up the blanket and nicely drapes it on the sofa back. "I had a glass of wine while I decorated, okay? And … and I took a nap. You woke me when you were at the door. Was there something you wanted?"

Gina simply tips her head and studies him.

And it's obvious Frank's had enough of her interrogation when he takes her arm and leads her toward the hallway. "Okay, well it was nice seeing you. But it's really dangerous driving out there in this storm. You better get going." He steers his sister toward the front door.

"Wait!"

Gina pulls out of his grip—and from the yank she gives, it must be no easy feat. Because Penny can see through the tiny crack in the closet door that Frank's grip was ironclad.

"I need that snowman," Gina explains. "Mom's old one, remember? The jolly tabletop snowman made out of pine-cones?" She turns around and heads down the hallway. "Mom said it's in the closet."

"I'll get it!" Frank tells her while brushing past her toward the closet where Penny is now squeezing behind the hung coats and pressing against the back wall.

"No, not there," Gina calls out. "I know right where it is."

After a moment, Penny dares a peek to see Gina opening a closet beneath the stairway alcove. She gets on her knees and digs in a box. "Got it!"

❧

"Merry criminy," Frank says under his breath.

"Dante will love this, it's so cute." Gina unzips her parka and tucks it beneath the fabric. "I don't want it getting covered with snow out there."

"All right, already." Frank opens the arched front door. "Be safe, but get out." He looks outside at the blowing snow, then back at his sister. "I mean, and well … call me when you get home so I know you made it okay." He takes her arm and helps her out the door, wondering if she notices the ever-so-slight shove. If she sees his perspiration.

Apparently so. Because before Frank has even one second to close the door behind her, Gina turns and looks back at him. Snow blows into the foyer and chills the air. "She's here, isn't she?"

"Who?"

Gina holds her coat closed over the pinecone snowman. "Your secret girlfriend."

"You have to go now."

"I *knew* it. Because you've been off all week … oddly happy, that is." She turns then, but stops after stepping into the snow and looks again at Frank, still holding the door open to see her off. "FYI, your shirt's on backward. Inside out, too."

Frank quickly looks down at the ticket on the collar, on the *front* of his thermal tee.

෴

"Frank?" Penny asks as she opens the closet door and peeks out. For all she knows, Gina will come breezing back in asking another question, or wanting another ornament.

"Close call, but all's clear," Frank says while taking her hand. As Penny gets dressed in another room, Frank leans the large sofa pillows on the floor against the couch. "I'm so sorry about that," he says when Penny walks back to the fireplace. "Once Gina gets an idea in her head, there's no changing her mind, even during a blizzard—especially if it's about her son. And she clearly wanted that snowman for Dante."

"It's okay." Penny curls up on the floor in front of the blazing fire.

"Would you like a drink?"

"Actually, some wine would be nice, Frank. My nerves are a little frayed after that fiasco."

When he returns with two glasses, he settles on the rug beside her. He also brought a plate of the cheese and crackers they picked up earlier on their grocery run.

"You know your sister's never going to let you live this down, don't you?" Penny asks as she bites into a cheesy cracker.

Frank touches Penny's hair. "I can deal with my sister's wrath as long as I don't have yours. We okay here?"

"Frank, we are more than okay," she says before leaving a breath of a kiss on his cheek.

After a few moments, Frank stands and shuts off the room lights, leaving only the mantel and Christmas tree twinkling.

And just like that, after Gina blew in like a gust of wind from the snowstorm outside, the golden glow settles on the room again. The burning logs snap, the tree seems to actually twinkle, and snow crystals outside hiss against the paned windows.

Penny gets an idea, then. So while Frank quietly watches, she grabs her cell phone from her bag to snap a photograph. A hazy image takes shape for her next Suitcase Escapes' clue—one that will keep the townsfolk wildly guessing her whereabouts.

In the soft Christmas lighting of the room, she walks to the record player and restarts the Sinatra album. A few details will give her clue the perfect finishing touch, so she moves the two glittered pinecones close beside the turntable, then adds her wineglass to the other side. Stepping back, she snaps a photograph so softly lit and evocative, people will practically hear that scratchy record playing a romantic Christmas carol.

When she sits with Frank in front of the fire again on this snowy Saturday night, he kisses the side of her head, then gently settles the knitted throw over Penny's shoulders.

"No more interruptions tonight," he tells her before tipping his wineglass to hers. "Promise."

sixteen

WHO NEEDS AN ALARM CLOCK when your cell phone keeps giving a jing-a-ling-ling of a ringie-ding-ding? Which is precisely what Penny's phone does early Monday morning back at Cardinal Cabin. First she receives a text from Ross, her boss. Lying in bed beneath her warm patchwork quilt of stitched pine trees and appliquéd red cardinals, she reads the message with disbelief. An attached image has her sit up in bed, prop the pillows and squint for a better look. It's a snapshot taken from outside the travel agency's window as swarms of people await Penny's next photo-clue.

Ross' text message reads: *Ballot box filling up with location guesses, most thinking you're in Vermont. And toy-donation box brimming!*

No sooner is Penny showered and waiting for her coffee to percolate than her phone resumes its jing-a-ling-linging. This time, Chloe's on the line.

"I'm calling to see if you lost power. We had a big snowstorm here in Addison!"

"I know," Penny says with visions of burning Yule logs crackling in the fireplace, and sips of wine by candlelight,

125

and sweet nothings murmured beneath a knitted throw. With visions of a whiskered face leaning close to kiss her, of her fingers running through wavy, dark hair.

"You *know*? How?" Chloe demands.

"Of course, well … It's … Yes, it's been all over the news here!"

"If you're in Maine, or Vermont—as everyone seems to think—you're lucky the storm missed you. It went out to sea at the Cape."

"Yes. Lucky." All Penny can think of is how she and Frank cuddled in his bed all Saturday night, and how she woke up in his arms to a fresh, hushed snowfall on Sunday morning. "I was safe and sound," she says, her voice faraway.

"Okay, good. But where's today's photo-clue of this secret snuggery you're staying at? Folks are already lined up waiting for it."

Snuggery, Penny thinks, remembering how she and Frank snuggled in the snowstorm. A perfect word.

"Penny? Are you even listening to me?"

"Oh!" With her cell to her ear, Penny pours a mug of piping-hot coffee and adds a splash of cream. "Yes, I'll get you a picture soon."

"You know," Chloe says, dropping her voice low, "people *are* starting to talk."

"What do you mean?"

"From the looks of some of your clues, they're beginning to wonder if a holiday *romance* is happening … wherever you are, especially with your last two photos. A sultry record player near a fireplace? And you on that toboggan?"

Penny has to smile with the memory of yesterday's impromptu sledding when Frank finally brought her back to

Cardinal Cabin. All that whooshing through the powdered snow, the laughs! The snow kisses. She sips her coffee, and her eyes close with the thought.

"Penny?" Chloe's silent for a moment, then softly adds, "That glow. That smile! That twinkle at whoever took your picture." She sighs, then presses Penny. "And people here are just *adoring* the possibility of a love story. Is there one? Give me a teeny-tiny hint."

"A *love* story?" Penny asks. She carries her coffee to the living room window and looks out at Snowflake Lake. A mist rises off the icy top, and the lake is fringed with snow-covered wild grasses, the blades gracefully arched beneath the weight of the powdery snow. A white-tailed deer stands outside the thicket on the far banks of the lake.

"Ooh, I want all the details," Chloe is saying. "What is your mystery man like there? Is he nice? What's he do? Because I can assure you, the crowds are exploding now that a love story is in the mix!"

But Penny doesn't reveal a thing. Keeping this new relationship as hushed as the newly fallen snow makes it feel just as special. And it's with that thought in mind that she bundles up in her navy parka—one arm at a time while Chloe's chatting—to go outside in search of a photo-clue. One that will convey that very special hush.

So she coyly bows out of her phone chat and tells Chloe she'll get the next picture to her soon.

Before she goes outside in search of it, though, she decides to send one quick text to Frank, her mystery man.

Hurrying back to the kitchen to finish her coffee too, she brings her cell phone, taps the Messages button and types in her text:

Dinner + movie night at Cardinal Cabin.
After pasta dinner ... popcorn and cocoa and cuddling?
Stop by as soon as you're out of work.

Just as she is typing that last line, a feisty red cardinal starts pecking at his reflection in her kitchen window. There's a little tap-tap-tap and a flutter of his bright red wings on the other side of the frost-edged glass. Penny looks up from her phone and laughs, lightly taps her fingertips on the window in return, and after a glance at the busy bird, hits Send.

⁓

There's nothing like the scent of simmering pasta sauce filling a house to bring pure comfort. A few hours later, Penny thinks that if she could capture that scent in a photo, it would be her next clue—especially since her earlier photo search outside was a bust. But as she finishes with the curling iron and puts on a dab of lip gloss, another idea comes to her.

Since she can't photograph the aroma in the cabin, the next best thing will have to do. So beneath the simple chandelier with white birch-bark shades, she takes a picture of her table set for two: two fringed placemats, stacked with a dish and salad bowl each. Two silver flatware settings, laid out on cloth napkins. In the center of the table, tea-light candles flicker in short crackle-glass jars. Those surround her crystal bowl spilling with pinecones and cinnamon sticks.

"Perfect," Penny whispers, snapping a few angles of her intimate table-for-two. "Absolutely *perfect*," she repeats, right as the woodpecker doorknocker *rat-a-tat-tat-tats*.

Giving the tomato sauce a quick stir first, Penny then rushes to the front door. "You made it!" she says while swinging it open.

"Penny!"

"Greg?" She looks past him toward the yard, then back at Greg Davis right as he's pulling his trapper hat off his head. "What are you doing here?"

"I know, I'm a little early. But I've been waiting for this ... Christmas movies in a cozy cabin."

"What?" Still, Penny hasn't moved. And her hand still grips the door edge, her eyes fixed on Greg.

"Your text message." Greg moves to step inside out of the cold. "I cancelled my last appointment so I wouldn't be too late. And gosh, whatever's cooking smells terrific."

"Oh, jolly jiminy!" Penny looks back into the cabin, then runs inside, calling out, "Wait just a sec!" She hears the front door close when Greg comes in, but she keeps going, straight to the kitchen, straight to the counter where her cell phone is charging. With no time to waste, she unplugs it and begins a panicked flicking through the message screens while walking back into the living room, where Greg patiently waits. He's taking in the logs burning in the fireplace, the country dining table, the throws draped over chairs and the sofa.

And is about to be unexpectedly let down. Because while skimming through her text messages, Penny's heart nearly stops and so her hand goes to her chest. It's as bad as she'd thought.

"Something wrong?" Greg asks as he pulls off his leather gloves and unbuttons his long, dark coat.

"What?" She glances up at him, then at her phone again. One more panicked check does it—has her eyes fall closed and her head drop. When she finally looks up at Greg, at his tipped, curious expression, she gives him a sympathetic smile while shaking her head.

"Uh-oh." He backs up a step. "I know that sad smile."

"Greg." Penny puts down the phone and goes to him, taking his hand. "Please let me explain."

And being true to her penny heritage, she's as honest as honest Abe—who graces every copper penny. She tells Greg of the text mix-up.

"I'm so sorry," she begins. "But you're here due to my careless mistake."

"I don't understand. Because your text message, from this morning …"

"Oh, gosh. It wasn't meant for you." Penny slowly sits in a plaid club chair. She starts to describe the little busy cardinal tapping at the window earlier, distracting her, then stops. After a second, she simply says, "I hit the wrong number. Your text message was actually meant for someone else."

"Ah, Penny Hart, you've *pierced* my hopeful heart." With that, Greg picks up his gloves and buttons his wool coat. "I guess there was no escaping it."

"What's that?"

"This is the third Christmas in a row that the girl of my dreams slips away like, well … like a melting snowflake."

Penny quickly stands and hands him the trapper hat he'd set on an end table. "Maybe you'll have a dance with a nice gal at your brother's wedding?"

Greg pulls on his hat while turning to leave. "Maybe. And some fortunate guy will have a very merry evening here." He turns back to her, takes her hands in his and gives her a light kiss on the cheek. "Hope that shoulder's okay."

Penny nods with a small smile.

"And no worries," Greg adds. "Your travel secret is still safe with me."

"Thanks, Greg," she tells him as she opens the planked door. The berry wreath hanging on the other side of it is dusted with white snow.

Greg walks past her to the small front porch. He stops, fiddles with the silver milk can on the table there, then turns back to where she still stands, her hand on the door.

"It's Frank, isn't it?" he asks. "Frank Lombardo."

With another small smile, and the slightest of nods, Penny merely turns up her hands. "But how in the world did you—"

"He's a lucky man, that Frank," Greg interrupts as he tugs the flaps on his trapper hat. "A lucky man, indeed."

༄

Busy, busy, busy. It's another tactic Frank employs to avoid the lonely hour. But on this December Monday, it looks like that hour is headed straight his way. There's no veering around it, no filling it with family. After hosting yesterday's holiday teddy bear tea party, Gina took the day off, so there's not even her fussing at the boathouse to distract him.

And thoughts of Penny don't help. After the wonderful weekend they spent together, this quiet lull only makes her absence today feel worse. Especially since he can't tell a soul about her. Sitting here alone all day long, now their relationship doesn't seem like it could possibly be real. Saturday night, together in the swirl of a snowstorm, seems like a wintry mirage.

So he sits in his office late that afternoon, doing paperwork beneath a tall table lamp. If nothing else, this solitude is good for organizing and sorting through the boat reservations for next year. Some boat owners requested new racks for their kayaks and canoes when they renewed, and he's almost caught up with those revised assignments.

As he tinkers with the reservations, his cell phone rings; no doubt, it's Wes or Jane calling him with last-minute reception details. Frank and Gina have a saying they like to toss around during wedding season: The closer the wedding, the closer you keep your phone. So when it rings now, he answers without looking at it.

"Frank?" he hears. Which gets him to drop his pen, sit back in his chair and glance at the phone's caller ID to be sure it matches the voice he *thinks* he's hearing.

"Penny?"

"Mm-hmm."

"I was just thinking about you."

"Oh, Frank. Me, too."

"Really?"

"Yes. Because I've got a table here, set for two ..."

In her brief pause, he smiles and waits for her to continue.

"Dinner and a Christmas movie? Me and you?"

seventeen

IF COZINESS COULD COME ALIVE, Frank wakes up to it Tuesday morning: lying beneath a patchwork quilt covered with rustic cabin scenes and stitched pinecones; Penny's soft hair on his shoulder; a wall clock faintly ticking, the clock shaped from a slab of raw wood. Cozy's never felt so sublime.

The only thing that would make it even better is coffee. So he quietly moves aside the blankets and gets out of bed to put on a fresh pot. He hadn't planned on staying the night, but movie-watching led to snuggling in front of the fireplace, which led to a whispered *Don't go* beneath that patchwork quilt. And so, brushing back Penny's hair, and leaving her another kiss, he didn't.

On his way through the cabin's living room now, he picks up two wineglasses and a popcorn dish with a few buttery kernels left in the bottom, and rinses them at the kitchen sink.

Finally, he brings two cups of coffee back to that sweet bed with Penny. He sets her mug on the nightstand, then climbs beneath that rustic quilt. Snow is lightly falling outside the window, red cardinals are flitting by, and he leans over and kisses the top of Penny's head.

"Good morning, beautiful." He sips his coffee and watches her easy smile. "Wish we could stay here all day."

"The only thing missing," Penny says as she sits up and reaches for her coffee, "is that Sinatra record from your house. I'd put it on right now."

"And I'd never get out of bed, then. Nothing would get done." As he drinks his steaming coffee, his cell phone rings on the bedside table. "Hello?" he says when he grabs it.

"Frank? Where *are* you?"

For the second time in twenty-four hours, he glances at the caller ID, then presses the phone back to his ear. And apparently Gina hasn't even taken a breath.

"I tried the house," she's saying, "three times. But there was no answer."

"Gina." When Frank sits up straighter, Penny reaches over and lightly strokes his arm. "Slow down. What's the matter?"

"Wes and Pete are here at the boathouse ... with Pete's life-size carved deer. And I must say, they're absolutely stunning."

Eventually Gina breathes, but it's just to wind up for her next rant.

"But they need your help," his sister says, "getting those deer onto the hand truck and wheeled into the reception room. Did you forget? Because Wes said you told him you'd be here. I'm beginning to think that your secret girlfriend actually *is* real, the way you've been behaving lately!"

Frank says nothing, and instead leans down and kisses Penny on her shoulder.

Real? he thinks. Oh, yes. *Very* real.

The problem with Gina, though Frank loves her dearly, is that there's never just one assignment being issued. After taking a quick shower at the cabin and rushing to the boathouse, he helps Wes and his father wheel the two full-size carved love deer into the reception room in time for Wes' weekend wedding. They arrange the wooden buck and doe on either end of the head table before Wes and Pete leave to get back to their mail routes. So Frank finishes up by adding a snow-blanket of tufted cotton beneath the two deer, giving them an authentic wintry look.

Right when he's making the very last adjustment to the faux snow, Gina breezes in. She's wearing a thick Fair Isle sweater over skinny jeans, leather knee-high boots, and an anxious expression that can't be missed. So Frank pulls out a chair at one of the round tables, crosses his arms and waits for whatever's coming.

"I have a kajillion things to do," Gina says with a glance at the jumbo clipboard in her hands. "Check with the caterer, *and* Wes and Jane's DJ, *then* the bakery. And I'm really sorry, Frank, but there's just no time for antlers."

"Antlers?"

∽

Yes, antlers. Antlers that find Frank, an hour later, opening the red-painted door into Addison's beloved Christmas shop, Snowflakes and Coffee Cakes. Inside the big old barn, hundreds of slow-spinning gold snowflakes hang from ceiling beams; a brightly lit Christmas train chugs around and around a loft; and everywhere, there are snowman figurines and miniature snow villages and reindeer and sleighs. He spots Vera, the shop owner, near a glittering swan carousel—the swans' necks arching gracefully with little beribboned wreaths around them.

"Hey, Vera," Frank says with a casual wave.

"Frank." Vera adjusts the sparkling carousel display, then asks over her shoulder, "How are you?"

"I'll be good if you have any antlers," he tells her while pulling off his wool beanie and shoving it in his jacket pocket. "Even better if they're painted silver."

"Decorations for another reception?"

"I need them to tuck into Wes and Jane's wedding garland, across the head table. Last-minute details."

"You know, I could actually devote part of the store to Christmas wedding décor," Vera says while plucking faux antlers out of a barrel near the checkout counter. "Winter weddings bring in lots of business here."

Frank wanders the main aisle, calling back, "Not a bad idea, Vera. My sister would love that." He browses the other barrels filled with jingle bells and boxed Christmas cards and candy canes of every size. Around him, people are selecting ornaments, holding up nutcrackers and snow globes and envisioning them in their own homes, on their hearths and mantels.

When a couple asks Vera about a display of embroidered Christmas stockings, Frank walks to the window ledge where Jingles the cat, her store mascot, is perched. He gives the cat a scratch on the head as its bushy tail flicks back and forth. All the while, the cat watches lazy-falling snowflakes spinning from the clouds outside.

"Okay!" Vera finally says when she returns to the register. She sets the necessary glittering antlers across the counter.

"I'm not sure about all the glitter." Frank picks up an antler. "It makes a mess, and Gina's really particular about keeping the banquet hall shining clean."

"No worries, Frank. Tell her to spritz the antlers with hairspray. That'll keep the glitter in place. Works like magic." She begins to carefully wrap the antlers in tissue paper. "Anything else today?"

Frank gives another quick glance at the snow flurry out the window, then asks, "How about Christmas music? Do you have any?"

"No DJ at Wes and Jane's wedding? Which Derek and I are *so* looking forward to, by the way."

"Oh, the record's for me, not the wedding." Feeling warm in the festive shop, he unzips his jacket. "I'm looking for a Christmas album."

"Albums I do have. They're making such a comeback these days. Especially since that travel agent ... Penny, is it? Ever since she posted that photograph of an old-fashioned record player. Did you see it? It was *so* suggestive, with that wineglass beside it, in low lighting. Romance at its finest."

"I *may* have seen it. Not sure."

"Apparently the whole *town* has, because now I can barely keep any albums in my inventory." She hitches her head for Frank to follow her to a bin of records on a table that also is covered with baskets spilling with red and green ornaments. He begins thumbing through the old album covers. "Have a look," Vera says, "while I help a customer who's been waiting."

So Frank does, lifting out this album, turning that one over. Most of the covers are red and depict snow scenes, or Bing Crosby in a fur-trimmed Santa hat, or old-world sleigh rides. None, though, show Sinatra in that black top hat.

"Searching for something in particular?" Vera asks when she returns.

Frank turns to her, looks at the bin, then back at Vera, waiting. "Sinatra. Have any Sinatra around? There's none in here."

"Let me see what's in the back."

Calling out for her sister, Brooke, to cover for her, Vera's off in a flash. Five minutes later, she returns—waving a single album. "I found only one," she calls to Frank while holding the album high. "*A Jolly Christmas from Frank Sinatra*. Will this do?"

"Excellent," Frank quietly says as he sets down a vintage teardrop ornament with some of its silvering now faded. He takes the album from Vera, checking it out as they head to the register together. The timing couldn't be better—he'll give this to Penny tonight, when he picks her up for Gus' turkey dinner. "Just ... excellent."

Vera rings up the decorative antlers for Wes and Jane's reception, then gives the Sinatra album a slow once-over before sliding it gently into a gift bag.

She looks at Frank then, standing there with his wallet in hand. After a scrutinizing pause, Vera tips her head with a small smile. "Playing this for someone special, Frank?"

eighteen

IF THERE'S ONE THING PENNY'S learned during her inadvertent stint as a travel agent, it's how to pack. Her clients have shared every packing tip in the book, and she's included those tips in her newsletters for novice travelers. Not to mention, Suitcase Escapes gives handouts listing the packing advice, as well.

So even though her own destination was merely a tiny rustic cabin nestled in the woods, she still followed the steadfast rules and packed a little black dress. This one, with three-quarter sleeves, is fitted and just to her knees.

"One you can dress up, or down," she tells her reflection later that evening, as though she's talking to a client. "To suit any occasion—formal or casual. Simply add a blazer for business, or a scarf for a soiree," she adds while looping a silver scarf around her neck. Certainly, Gus' formal turkey dinner will count as a soiree out here at Snowflake Lake.

And as she puts on ruby-red gemstone earrings, the same color as those cardinals flitting about in the trees beyond her bedroom window, it happens. Yes, it's the very moment she's been waiting for ... *Rat-a-tat-tat-tat!*

When she rushes out to the living room and sweeps open the door, there's Frank. His coat hangs open, and she sees he wears a black vest over his button-down, and a leather belt on his dark, cuffed jeans. The finishing touch? A tie around his neck and tucked beneath that vest. Oh, and the perfect shadow of whiskers on his face.

"You look amazing," he tells her when he steps inside along with a gust of cold wind.

"Thanks," Penny says before taking his gloved hands in hers as he bends to kiss her. "You look pretty handsome, yourself." She touches his jaw and stretches up for another kiss. "We should probably get going right away," she finally whispers while reluctantly pulling back. "I don't want to keep Gus waiting."

So after loading up Frank's arms with her warm casserole dish and a tin of Christmas cookies, she puts on her toggled camel peacoat and they walk to Blue Jay Bungalow. Outside, the evening is quiet, and their boots crunch across the snow. The lakeside Christmas tree glimmers softly, its lights throwing a glow on the frozen water. And ahead, Gus' cabin is illuminated: white lights twinkle on the shrubs and are entwined on the porch posts; swags of green garland loop beneath the porch railings; golden lamplight spills from the paned windows.

"Gus left a note," Frank says as they climb the front steps. He pulls a slip of paper off a nail beside the door. "*Be back soon*, it says. *Make yourselves at home.*"

"So we should go in?" Penny asks.

"Looks it." Frank shifts the cookies and casserole dish in his arms and opens the cabin's wood door.

There's no mistaking that Gus is expecting them, even though he's not here. It's obvious by the heavenly aroma of a turkey roasting in the oven. Frank helps Penny take off her coat, and she delivers her butternut squash casserole to the dining table. A table set with a velvet burgundy runner reaching across the aged, knotted wood. At each chair is a setting of white plates stacked on gold placemats, with tall crystal goblets and tarnished silverware beside them. Napkins folded across each top plate are anchored by large pinecones.

"I found a little to-do list, Frank, on the fridge," Penny says when she turns into the kitchen. "Maybe we can help Gus with this."

Frank reads the list over her shoulder. "Light candles, carve turkey, pour wine." He glances to the dining area. "I'll carve some of the turkey if you get the candles lit."

And so as Penny strikes a long matchstick and dips the flame to tea-light candles and pillars on the dining table's centerpiece, Frank prepares a plate of sliced meat in the kitchen, then covers it to keep it warm.

"You know, I'd never have believed it, but I'm thinking that old Gus is maybe a closet romantic," Frank says from the table when he sets the turkey platter beside the centerpiece.

When Penny turns from lighting candles in Gus' mantel-top snow village, Frank points out the sprigs of mistletoe hanging in every single doorway.

"Hmm ..." Penny muses with a smile. "Blue Jay Bungalow? Looks more like Mistletoe Chateau!"

From the kitchen doorway, Frank hitches his head with a slow grin, all while motioning her closer. And so she obliges—both him and the mistletoe—and steps into his arms.

The thing is, mistletoe or not, Penny wouldn't mind staying right there all evening. Frank kisses her once, twice, then touches her hair. "I'll pour the wine now."

When he does, Penny walks across the creaky hardwood floor to the living room. "Frank?" she asks while slowly turning beneath the beamed ceiling. "I just realized something. There's no Christmas tree. Everything else is decorated … stockings hung by the chimney, Gus' snow village on the mantel, the Christmas puzzle he's working on. But no tree!"

Bringing in two wineglasses, Frank joins her in the living room. He first stokes the fire, then walks to the puzzle table. "Maybe a tree was too much. You know, to decorate alone. It's a lot of work getting out all those ornaments."

They sit at the puzzle table and fit a few snowman pieces into place. "That's a little sad, don't you think?" Penny asks while taking a sip of the wine.

"I do, especially after we decorated my tree together. It was a wonderful night. Which," he adds after leaning over and kissing her lightly, "I'll never forget."

"Neither will I," she whispers in return.

Frank points out the window beside the puzzle table, to the community Christmas tree twinkling beside the lake. "Maybe the tree outside, over there, is enough for Gus."

Shimmering in the darkness, the grand fir rises from the snow in the cold night. Its snowflake topper glitters brightly, as though dropped down on the tree from the clouds.

But still …

Penny glances toward an empty corner near the fireplace—with thoughts of loved ones gathered round a decorated tree, all aglow in the cabin. With the memory of dancing beside Frank's tree only days ago, in a dimly lit room with a holiday record softly playing, snowflakes tapping at the windows.

Still, a home without a Christmas tree … it's just not the same.

∽

"Do you hear that?" Penny asks. She gets up from the puzzle table a few minutes later and heads to the large picture window.

"Is that the snowtorcycle?" Frank joins her at the window. Off in the distance, a headlight shines and bobs along one of the wooded trails as Gus' snowtorcycle winds its way through the trees.

"Look, Frank!" Penny points outside toward the little side-car beside Gus. He's steered his vehicle out of the trail and approaches Blue Jay Bungalow now. "A tree. He cut a tree."

Frank sees a freshly cut balsam fir strapped into the sidecar, swaying as Gus pulls up to the cabin. Wearing snow boots, a buttoned-up wool jacket and his newsboy cap, he climbs out of the vehicle. If his rosy cheeks are any indication, Gus has been out in the woods for a while.

"A cabin's just not complete without a Christmas tree." Penny takes Frank's hand. "Go help him bring it in."

Two weeks ago, Frank might have asked what it's all for.

But not anymore.

Now, Frank grabs his jacket and gloves and together, he and Gus carry in the small, fresh-cut tree. They finagle it into a stand, right near the fireplace like Penny wanted, after which Frank strings colored lights around it.

All the while, Penny and Gus set out the warm vegetable sides, stuffing and gravy, placing everything around the platter of carved turkey Frank already prepared. Finally Gus lifts a thin cardigan off a wall hook, puts it on and they sit down to his first-ever turkey dinner.

Or not.

Because sometimes, you just know when something is lies ... all lies. And from every bit of the homemade stuffing—perfectly moist—to the juicy turkey and just-right lumpy mashed potatoes, oh, Frank knows.

It's lies.

From the looks *and* taste of every dish, Gus is very obviously an expert at cooking a turkey dinner.

Making the evening more interesting—if Frank's suspicions are right—Gus is *also* an expert at matchmaking, seating Frank and Penny side by side at the table, making small talk, sipping wine.

That old Gus is a sly one. Testing out his cooking skills on Frank and Penny? Frank has to shake his head as he finishes his seconds and lifts a heaping forkful of stuffing and cranberry sauce.

"So," Gus says as he pats his napkin on his mouth and pushes back his chair. "Any input for me, kids? Have any cooking advice after eating my practice turkey?"

Frank considers Gus across the table, then looks around at the wooden walls of Blue Jay Bungalow, walls golden beneath low lamplight; sees the wide silver-blue trim around the paned windows, windows frosted at the edges; glances at Penny beside him, her copper hair glimmering in the table's candlelight.

"Well?" Gus presses them. "Turkey tender enough? Potatoes need another whisk? Stuffing satisfactory?"

Frank watches him, but only for a moment. Because regardless of the fine cuisine, he's having a hard time keeping his eyes off of Penny, actually. Off her every subtle movement in her fitted black dress beside him.

Frank finishes chewing and takes a long sip of his wine. "I wouldn't change a thing," he tells Gus as he sets down his goblet. "Not one thing."

After a quiet pause at the table, Penny looks from Frank, to Gus. "Me, neither," she softly adds.

∽

Once Gus lays into that piano in the living room, amidst all the twinkling decorations and candlelight, Penny thinks it feels just like Christmas Eve, though it's still a week away. As she and Frank wash and dry the last of the pots in the kitchen, they listen to Gus tickle the ivories, playing happy Christmas carols.

Penny hums along while wiping out the gravy pan and setting it back in the cabinet. Beside her, Frank gets the coffeepot percolating.

"Oh, star of wonder, star of light," Penny tenderly sings now. "Star with royal beauty bright." She picks up a platter and drags the dishtowel across it. "Westward leading, still proceeding," she sings with the piano, her voice a soft vibrato.

"Guide us to thy perfect light," Frank joins in—in perfect harmony, no less.

Gus looks over his shoulder at them and calls out, "It's nice to have someone to play for!" Then he switches to a simple rhythm that gets the keys jing-a-ling-linging.

And so Penny raises her eyebrow at Frank and they go at it again, singing a full-on duet now. *Dashing through the snow*—their voices intertwine—*O'er the fields we go*—as the last of the pots are dried and the coffee cups set out—*What fun it is to ride and sing a sleighing song tonight.*

But it's when Gus starts singing, too, rocking the piano keys as his deep voice blends with theirs, that the jolly good time kicks into high gear.

Jingle bells, jingle bells ...

Keeping that good time going, Gus gets the higher piano keys ring-a-linging so that they sound like festive silver sleigh bells. Still, Penny gasps when Frank takes her in his arms and two-steps her into the living room, where they dip and twirl to the lively carol, singing along as they do.

Oh what fun it is to ride in a one ... horse ... open ... sleigh!

After Gus gives a few more sleigh-bell rings on the keys, he spins around to face them, a wide smile on his face, his eyes a-twinkling just like, well, like Santa, if Penny's not mistaken, all as Frank pulls her close.

"Jingle all the way!" Frank sings while dipping Penny. Then he walks her over to the table where she'll help Gus wrap gifts for his grandkids.

"You two are just like the cardinals," Gus says as he gives the piano keys one last ching-a-ling jingle. "In most bird species, only the males sing. But the cardinals have been well documented, and the *couples* actually duet. Yup," he continues, nodding at Frank and Penny, "males and females singing together, very in tune to one another."

"That's so sweet, Gus," Penny says. "I can just picture those cheery little birds chirping together like that."

Gus joins her at the dining table, first lifting some gifts and rolls of wrapping paper from the hutch, along with scissors and tape.

It takes a few minutes for Penny to catch her breath after that impromptu dance with Frank. And her smile, well, she's sure it's permanent. She steals a glance at Frank while the coffee

146

brews in the kitchen, and while she and Gus wrap. Penny hums and tapes and trims giftwrap, as Frank arranges the wrapped presents beneath the illuminated tree.

"No decorations for your tree, Gus?" Frank asks. "Just the lights?"

"Not until Christmas Eve. My grandkids beg to unpack the old ornaments with me. They each have their favorites they like to hang. Glass balls, stitched snowmen, little red sleighs."

"That sounds nice, Gus." Frank sits on the plaid sofa, saying over his shoulder, "They must love spending Christmas here at Blue Jay Bungalow."

"Or, as I call your cabin," Penny says with a small smile, "*Mistletoe* Chateau?"

"Oh, that." Raising a bushy white eyebrow above his twinkling eyes, Gus motions to the mistletoe sprigs hanging in the doorways.

"Yes, that," Penny tells him with a wink.

So Gus explains that his grandkids are getting older, and the only way to get them to give Grandpa a kiss on the cheek is to catch them under the mistletoe. "Works like a charm," he admits before asking Penny about her travel mystery at Suitcase Escapes.

"No one suspects I'm right here, imagine? Not even my coworkers, or my boss!" As she says it, she gives Frank's arm a quick clasp when he pours her a cup of coffee at the table.

"I can assure you, Miss Hart," Gus informs her, "that you are *thee* talk of the Holly Trolley. On each of my routes, I hear everyone trying to guess your hideaway."

"Wait." Penny sets down the scissors and squints at Gus. "*You* drive the trolley? I remember seeing it toodle through town last year, thinking the driver looked a little like Santa Claus!"

"That's me. It's a nice side job. I share the routes with some other old-timers. Make some extra spending money."

"Now, Gus. Are you telling me, seriously," Frank asks while sitting with his coffee, "that people have no clue Penny's staying in their own backyard?"

"That is correct." Gus tips his head and eyes them both. "And I must confess, this is one of the most fun holiday seasons I've had in recent years. Concealing a mystery neighbor, and listening to lots of merry antics around town on that trolley. Not to mention being in cahoots with you, Penny."

"I second that," Penny says. "My time here at Snowflake Lake has brought so many surprises."

"How about a Christmas photograph, then?" Gus asks. "For my piano top." He walks to assorted framed photographs set out on a lace runner there. Gingerly picking up a candid of his wife, Betty, he smiles at it, then sets it down. "Come on, you two. Right here in the living room doorway, so I can get the tree sparkling behind you. And the frosted windowpanes, too."

When Penny stands, so does Frank. He takes her hand and walks her to the doorway, where they turn and, side by side, wait while Gus fusses with his camera.

"Nice enough," Gus says after snapping a shot. "But ..." As he says it, he points up to the mistletoe hanging above them in the doorway.

Penny smiles when Frank hesitates, like he's suddenly shy. Frank tugs the fitted vest he wears over a button-down, brushes a wrinkle from his jeans, looks from Penny to Gus—who nods slowly at him—before finally running the back of his hand across his whiskered cheek while clearing his throat.

Penny watches all this, slightly amused at her dressed-up lumberjack feeling bashful beneath the mistletoe.

Or maybe not bashful, after all.

Maybe Frank's just waiting for the right moment, as he leans down, cradles her face and kisses her.

Penny hears Gus' camera snap, but Frank keeps things going. His arms reach around her as he deepens their kiss, and when, mid-kiss, Frank slightly dips her back, holding her close in his embrace, she hears one more click and knows—without a doubt—Gus got the shot.

❧

Something about leaving Gus all alone in that festive cabin of his bothers Frank. Maybe it has to do with that lonely hour he so dreads. Okay, so it's not a lonely *dinner* hour right now. But after a meal and evening as wonderful as this, there's a loneliness to someone being left behind.

Frank tells none of this to Penny when he walks her home and kisses her goodnight. But on the way back to his truck, he swings by Blue Jay Bungalow once more and gives a knock at the door, then opens it and steps inside. "Gus?" he calls out. "How about a snowtorcycle ride back to my truck?"

But when Gus comes from the kitchen carrying *thirds* of his apple pie dessert, well, Frank eyes the pie, cuts himself a slice and joins Gus at the puzzle table, instead. Together they twist and turn a few pieces into place: a snowman's stick arm, an ornament on a snowy branch.

Finally, with a pat of the unfinished puzzle, Gus stands. "Let's get a move on, then. Got early errands in the morning."

And get a move on, they do. Gus steers and sways his sputtering snowtorcycle through the dark, wooded trail. The headlight glistens on the snow ahead, startling a white-tailed buck as it rounds the lake. With a few leaps, the buck disappears into the trees, until only long shadows fall on the snow as they pass. But in the distance, the community Christmas tree always casts a glow where it rises beside Snowflake Lake.

"Thanks for the dinner, Gus," Frank says in the parking lot near his pickup. "What a great time we had." As he says it, he climbs out of the snowtorcycle sidecar and brushes balsam needles off his jeans.

"Listen, Frank." Gus shuts off the engine while he talks. He leans close. "Don't let that be the end of it. Penny's always here, alone. And she's missing all of Addison's Christmas charm, being hidden away in that cabin."

Frank glances back through the woods, in the direction of Cardinal Cabin. "But she can't be seen. It's part of her assignment."

"Come on." Gus turns up his gloved hands in the cold night. "Smart fella like you? You ought to know, the dark of night is the perfect cover."

"What are you saying?"

"Take her out on the Christmas town! If you can't see the holiday lights *together*, what's it all for? The lights of Christmas always shined brighter with my wife, Betty, by my side." Gus looks away, then squints over at Frank in the darkness. "Be spontaneous, young man."

And there it is. Again. The whole spontaneity thing.

Which he's finally starting to get. Being spontaneous brought Penny-who-fell-in-the-snow straight into his life. Well, into his arms first. But still ...

"Okay, let's see." Frank pulls his truck keys from his pocket and jangles them. "Deck the Boats is tomorrow."

"Don't I know it. It's my shift on the Holly Trolley, and Deck the Boats night is the *slowest* of all. The whole town gathers at the cove for that illuminated boat parade, then spends hours in the Christmas barn, Snowflakes and Coffee Cakes. Shopping, refreshments ... *Everyone's* there."

Frank stops jangling his keys. His hand clutches them silently now as he steps closer to Gus. "Everyone?" he asks. "Hey, Gus ..."

"What are you cooking up now?"

"The same thing you cooked up tonight, mister—a romantic scheme. Anyway, tomorrow night, Addison will be a ghost town. Like you said, everyone will be preoccupied with Derek's boat festival, drinking cocoa and singing carols at the cove. Everyone—*except* for me and Penny. Which gives me an idea ... *if* you care to break some rules."

nineteen

N OW THIS IS SOMETHING NEW: starting the day whistling a merry tune. But by the time Frank pulls into the boathouse parking lot the next morning, that's exactly what he's up to.

Because tonight? He's going to do it. For the first time in his entire life, he'll tell someone special he's falling in love with her.

Which is exactly why he's, well, whistling like a cardinal. The lyrics run through his mind as his whistle carries the tune: *Jingle bells, jingle bells. Jingle all the way.* And he remembers the voice, too. Penny's soft voice floating through the room at Blue Jay Bungalow last night. *Oh what fun it is to ride*, he whistles while breezing through the boathouse entrance doors and down the hall to his office, *in a one-horse open sleigh.*

The building is quiet, which is always amplified in the cavernous space so that the quiet nearly echoes. But it's typical for a Wednesday morning.

Bells on bobtails ring, making spirits bright …

"Frank? Is that you?" his sister calls from her own office.

What fun it is to ride and sing—his whistling continues while turning into Gina's office and giving a slight bow—*a sleighing song tonight!*

That line alone gets him, because does he ever have a surprise planned for Penny tonight, one including riding and singing, and Christmas lights, and much merriment.

So it's with a flourish that he sets a small tray of sweet coffee cakes on Gina's desk.

"Ooh, these look good," she says. "Are they from Snowflakes and Coffee Cakes?"

"Yes, they are. Still warm, straight from the oven."

"I've really got to reach out to their baker, Brooke." Gina picks up a crumbly cake and bites right in. "Oh, heaven. Maybe she'll be interested in catering desserts here."

"Give her a call later. She's there this morning."

"Okay, I'll put it on my itinerary." Gina takes another bite of the pastry, saying around the food, "Now we can get a lot done today, Frank. Because there are no events going on here with Deck the Boats happening later. The whole town closes up to head there early and get a choice parking space at the cove."

"Just have to make a phone call first," Frank says as he hurries out. "I'll be right back to review things for Wes and Jane's wedding." When he glances over his shoulder, Gina's shoving the rest of that coffee cake in her mouth. So Frank turns, leaning on the doorjamb while watching her. "Have another pastry in the meantime, why don't you?"

Her eyes, he sees it, they scan the little cakes, lingering on the raspberry-drizzled pieces before reaching for one. But she stops, the coffee cake midway to her mouth, and looks suspiciously at Frank. "It's that secret girlfriend, isn't it?"

"What are you talking about?" he asks while unzipping his winter jacket.

"This." She motions to the goodies from Snowflakes and Coffee Cakes. "And your happy whistling. The phone call. You *must* have a secret girlfriend, and now you're calling her, aren't you?"

Frank simply waves his sister off, turns and leaves her office. When he gets halfway down the hall, on his way to the observation deck outside to have some privacy, he hears Gina call out from where she's solidly stationed at those coffee cakes.

"Am I ever going to meet her?" Quiet, then, "*Frank?*"

Once he's outside, he closes the glass door behind him and leans on the white railing. Today, the Connecticut River is crystal blue and sparkling beneath a bright December sun. To the north, Frank sees the distant Putnam Bridge spanning the flowing waters. He takes in the sweeping view for a long moment, inhales a deep breath of the chilly air, then calls Penny.

"Feeling a little cabin fever?" he asks when she answers. "Because I've got the cure, and can pick you up tonight."

"This sounds intriguing," Penny says. "Should I eat first?"

"No." He looks behind him, into the banquet room. "No, I've got dinner covered."

"Hmm, I'm not sure, though. I can't jeopardize Suitcase Escapes' mystery promotion. Will I be seen?"

"Penny Hart." Frank looks out at the river flowing past and smiles at his plan. "Just trust me."

◈

As is typical the week before Christmas, Penny's day flies by. Hours spent organizing cookie tins and double-checking cookie ingredients and preparing for Frank's secret cabin-fever excursion swirled past like snowflakes in a squall. Now, night falls like a soft blanket outside the Addison Boathouse.

Inside, white beams reach across the vaulted ceiling, and white-and-silver pendant lights hanging from the rafters softly glow. Swags of balsam garland sweep across it all. The empty banquet hall is hushed, with only the sounds of their two voices.

"This is so nice, Frank," Penny says as she bites into a club sandwich he'd set out, along with glasses of fresh cider. She can taste thin cucumber slices, and a tangy dressing, on the sandwich. Frank sits across from her at a small, round table covered with white linens. "What a beautiful view of the river you have here. And the food is amazing."

"Glad you like it," he says while checking his watch. "George Carbone over at The Main Course does the best catering. He made up these sandwiches for me earlier."

As he talks, though, Penny sees that Frank's preoccupied. He cuffs the sleeves on his crewneck sweater, twists his watch, fidgets in his seat. "Is something wrong?" she finally asks, setting down the last of her turkey club.

Frank glances back into the dimly lit room, his dark eyes sweeping across the empty tables before turning to her once more. That's when he lifts his napkin while standing, pats his mouth and pushes in his chair. "Let's go outside on the observation deck." He grabs their coats from where they dropped them on another table. "The view's even better there."

He's right, of course. Now that the sun's set below the horizon, all Penny sees is silver and gold. The boathouse is edged with twinkling lights looking gold against the night sky, and the winding ribbon of the Connecticut River glimmers silver beneath the moonlight. They walk over to the railing on this upper deck, until Frank leads her down a flight of stairs to a boardwalk winding along riverside. It's even quieter here, if that's possible. That winter hush, and the sight through the trees beside the walkway, remind Penny a little bit of Snowflake Lake—the way the moonlight now sparkles onto the river, through the tree branches.

"This is a pretty grand remedy for cabin fever," Penny tells him as they walk further on the boardwalk. "Just being beside the river like this, and seeing that water flow around the bend, it's like being on a boat, not knowing where the journey leads."

Frank nods, then checks his watch once more. But this time, he stops walking. Stops and turns her toward him as he runs his hands up and down her arms, tucks her hair behind an ear, touches the scarf looped around her neck.

"What's the matter, Frank?" she whispers, looking up to his serious face. His eyes are shadowed beneath his brow, his face whiskered. She touches his jaw. "Something's on your mind."

He only smiles, first. Smiles slightly, shifts his stance, looks beyond her, then directly at her face. "Okay, Penny. Here goes."

"Here goes?"

He nods. "Ever since that day at Cardinal Cabin when you fell in the snow, remember?"

"Of course I do."

"The thing is, well, ever since that day you fell, *I've* been falling, too." He touches her hair again, shakes his head with that smile, then runs his gloved finger beneath her chin. "Falling in love with you."

As he says it, he leans close and kisses her. Kisses her right away, she notices, before she even has a chance to answer him back—as though afraid of her response. His hand moves behind her neck, and with the stars twinkling high above them beside the river, he kisses her longer, still. But he needn't worry, because she feels the same. Her hands reach up beneath his arms and wrap around his shoulders in the perfect wintry embrace. If she had the chance to snap a picture, the moment would be one of the sweetest Christmas memories she'd ever gaze upon.

Their kiss lingers there, until Frank suddenly stops. He pulls away, glances behind him, kisses her briefly once more, then asks, "Hear that?"

"Hear what?" Penny murmurs. Left breathless by that kiss, she wasn't really paying attention to much else.

"Listen." He takes a step away from her.

Her hand tugs on Frank's jacket, then reaches to his wavy hair and toys with it for a second. "Listen?" she asks. "But I'd rather have more kissin'."

Frank obliges, but only for a second. Only until he shoves up his jacket sleeve and checks his watch again. When he does, a sound gets louder ... closer. Penny tips her head, trying to place the jingling chime ringing through the night. Before she has a chance to decipher it, Frank takes her mittened hand and they trot along the wide boardwalk, up around the corner of the boathouse toward the large parking lot. An empty parking lot where only tall streetlamps drop pools of light.

That is, until the Holly Trolley swings in.

Penny does a double take, squinting into the darkness, then to Frank as she laughs at the happy sight. The pretty green-and-gold trolley, outlined in twinkling lights, is swaying right into a nearby parking spot. A ribboned wreath hangs from the window on its rear door.

As the driver steps out, Frank inches her closer.

"Wait! Frank!" Penny says, pulling back. "I'll be seen."

"Trust me," he says before bending and kissing her briefly. "Remember?"

When she looks past him, she notices the driver—hmm, a very familiar one, at that—is a heavyset man, with bushy white eyebrows, and a fringe of white hair beneath a newsboy cap. Except his normally staid-and-serious expression is replaced with a mischievous twinkle in his eye as he removes his cap and gives a sweeping bow toward the open door of the waiting trolley.

"Good evening, folks," Gus Haynes announces. "All aboard for a private Addison holiday tour."

twenty

SWAGS OF HOLLY AND BERRIES, bells and white lights line the interior ceiling of the Holly Trolley. And the slatted wooden benches look like exact replicas from a bygone era. Penny and Frank walk down the aisle between rows of seats until Frank stops and, holding a twisted brass pole, motions for Penny to sit.

So Penny settles in beside the window and slips her arms out of her camel peacoat. Beneath it, she wears a cream turtleneck sweater over black skinny jeans. Her gold hoop earrings sparkle, and her copper hair falls in loose waves.

"Frank!" she says as Gus puts the little trolley in gear and begins the tour of the festive streets of Addison. "This is so much fun." She looks out the window, then turns to see all the empty trolley seats behind them. "But won't there be other riders? It's Christmastime, after all!"

"No," Frank says as he sits beside her and pulls off his gloves. "Deck the Boats is tonight, and the whole town turns out at the cove for it."

"I've heard so much about Deck the Boats. When I moved here last December, it had already happened, so I missed it. What's the draw? A boat festival?"

"On the cove, yeah. It's run by Derek Cooper."

"From the hardware store?"

"That's the one. It's kind of a sad event, actually. Derek's daughter, Abby, went through the ice at the cove—must be seven years ago, now." He pauses, thinking of the sad afternoon when he heard the news. "Rescuers couldn't get to her in time and she died that day."

"Oh, that's awful."

Frank nods and puts his arm around Penny's shoulder. He leans close, telling her, "So Derek arranges a parade of decorated boats out on the water each December on the anniversary, to commemorate his little girl. Puts on a Christmas show. Special, just for her. He believes her spirit is still there, and that little Abby sees all the twinkling lights on the water."

"My gosh, that's so sweet. But heartbreaking, too."

"It's something to see, which is why the whole town shows up." Frank bends in front of her to take a look out the window at the empty neighborhoods. "And according to our driver, it's the slowest night of the season on the trolley. Isn't that right, Gus?"

"What's that?" Gus calls back with a glance in the rearview mirror as he heads down Riverside Drive.

"Slow night on the trolley."

"The worst. Perfect for a romantic rendezvous, though," Gus adds before steering the trolley along Main Street.

Penny, apparently delighted with her Christmas lights tour, stretches up and gives Frank a quick kiss, then looks when he nods to the window. He points out Whole Latte Life coffee shop, all cozy with frosted windowpanes. Tufts of cotton are tucked into its window corners to look like fresh-fallen snow. And at the vintage bridal boutique, Wedding Wishes, the bride mannequin in the illuminated window wears a white fur cloak over a long white gown. At the jewelers, crystal snowflakes dangle in the display window; and at the garden nursery, statues are snowcapped, frozen in time as they await a spring thaw.

But it's when they approach Suitcase Escapes that Frank calls out for Gus to slow down so that he can see Penny's latest photo-clue in the window. It's an enlarged selfie of Penny holding what seems like a cookie tin. Her hair is in a loose topknot, silver hoops dangle from her ears, and she holds the tin beside her smiling face. The image on the tin is a snowy woodland cabin.

"What's your clue?" Frank asks while leaning to the trolley window for a better look.

"Cookies in a tin ... Might reveal where I've been ... On my mystery travelin'."

Frank squints out at the tin's cabin, seeing its resemblance to Cardinal Cabin. "Think someone will guess?" he asks, then leaves a kiss on the side of her face.

Penny shakes her head. "They'll think that snowy cabin is in New Hampshire, or somewhere up north. *Never* right here."

He gives another look over his shoulder at the photo as the trolley passes it. "Did you bake cookies today?"

"No. Tomorrow, I will. And the next day I'll put them in the wagon and deliver them to the other cabins at Snowflake Lake. A little Christmas cheer for my neighbors, especially since they've been so loyal in keeping my secret."

"I'll come with you."

"You will?" Penny reaches up and touches his face.

"I'll pull the wagon."

They snuggle close in the seat then as the happy green-and-gold trolley jingles along. It sways down Main Street, past The

Green—where balsam garland wraps up the coach-light lamp-posts topped with ribboned wreaths, and the town Christmas tree, lit in twinkling lights, soars to the sky.

"Looks straight out of a Christmas card," Penny tells him as she squeezes his hand. "It's like Addison is saying *Season's Greetings* to anyone who passes through."

And Frank knows this was the right thing to do by the way she can't take her eyes off her own, private Christmas light show. The trolley turns onto Brookside Road, heading toward the covered bridge—which is just as Frank had hoped. First comes the white-steepled chapel with a wreath on each of its double doors, followed by colonials and Cape Cods, their peaked roofs flickering with strung lights. Snow nestles on branches of evergreen shrubs, and country lampposts wear a cap of glistening white.

When the covered bridge comes into sight, Frank gets out of his seat and hurries to Gus at the front of the trolley. He bends low and talks softly to surprise Penny with his plan, and Gus listens and simply nods as he drives.

Finally, they stop just before the red covered bridge. The wooden, roofed structure is outlined with tiny white lights shimmering in the dark night. When Gus pulls the trolley off to the side of the road, Frank turns and hitches his head for Penny to follow him.

"You've got a few minutes, kids," Gus tells them. After they leave the trolley, Gus shuts off the trolley's lights so as not to draw any attention to it parked roadside.

"It's so quiet out here," Penny says as they step into the covered bridge. There is only the sound of their feet walking across the creaking planked floor.

"Believe me when I say all of Addison is watching the Deck the Boats Festival at this very moment. You're safe from any prying eyes." Frank takes her hand. "Come on."

The bridge's exposed timber and crossbeams feel like their own woodland castle, sheltering them from the world. They stop at one of the bridge's windows and lean on the sill. Out beneath them, the brook babbles along, bubbling past large stones crowned with white snow. A deer stands on the bank of the brook, taking a drink of the fresh water. But it spooks when a sudden gust of wind blows, bringing a snow squall with it. Swirling white flakes spin around outside the bridge.

"Look!" Penny says, pointing to the spinning flakes blowing over the brook and through the tree branches there. "It's so magical, like we're right inside our own snow globe!" She pulls her cell phone from her pocket and quickly snaps a picture, whispering her next clue as she does. "*I'm in a snow globe given a shake ...*" She glances up at Frank before adding, "*There's magic all around me, make no mistake.*"

Frank leans out a bit for a better view, then puts his arm around Penny when she shivers in the wind. "Cold?"

She nods and leans close into him. Her hand reaches around his waist and holds on as they stand in the old wooden bridge. "And in love, too," she tells him, then stretches up on tiptoe and kisses him lightly, so lightly, her kiss feeling like just the touch of one of those delicate swirling snowflakes. "I think this is the most special night I've had in my entire life, Mr. Lombardo."

Frank kisses her for a long moment, the snow swirling into the bridge now and reaching them, the icy flakes touching their

163

skin. But Frank feels more; he feels her smiling mouth beneath his, her hands holding him close in the night, their kiss deepening amidst the windy squall.

જે

Until a sudden *jing-a-ling* interrupts them. A *jing-a-ling* and flashing lights, then a more urgent *toot* of the trolley horn.

"Someone must be coming," Frank says. "That's our warning sign!"

Fearing being spotted by someone, they quickly run over the planked floor of the covered bridge, laughing and still running—all the way to the trolley. They barely sit breathless in their seats when Gus puts it in gear and takes off. The trolley wheels thump across the bridge and do a little burnout once they hit pavement again.

"Close call!" Gus yells over his shoulder. "Pedestrians were out sightseeing the Christmas lights. Nearly walked right in on you two."

"Thanks, Gus. What's our next stop?" Frank calls back from their trolley seat.

"The historic district," Gus announces, then gives the bells another jingle as the trolley sways along. "Olde Addison."

Now when Frank looks out at the imposing colonials with candles in each window, it all seems different. Special, as Penny leans into him, holding his hand the whole time. Outside, red ribbons flutter from balsam wreaths hung on paneled doors; garland drapes across white picket fences.

"Check it out," Frank whispers, dipping his head close to Penny's ear, feeling wisps of her soft hair. He points to a large Dutch colonial farther down the block. Its widow's walk is outlined with white twinkling lights and holds a rooftop Christmas tree, too. "That's Vera Sterling's place. She owns Snowflakes and Coffee Cakes."

But the trolley abruptly slows and they hear Gus muttering a few choice words—not particularly in the spirit of the season.

"What's happening, my man?" Frank bends low to see out the front windshield.

"We're in a bit of a sticky wicket." Gus slows the trolley further and pulls to the side of the road, then attempts a U-turn across the street.

"Gus?" Penny asks, worried now.

"Shoot!" Gus' hands cross one over the other as he struggles to turn the trolley across the street and head in the other direction.

And Frank sees why. Deck the Boats must have finished up early, and now holiday revelers line the street of historic homes. Some walk in small caroling groups, their songs rising into the night as they stop at candlelit doorways and serenade the families there.

But others are ... wait ... they're flagging down the trolley! It's obvious they want to end their night with a festive sightseeing tour on the jingling, swaying Holly Trolley.

Gus manages to get the vehicle mostly turned. He throws it in reverse, straightens it out, then puts it in drive and starts it up again, the wheels chirping on the pavement.

"Go, Gus. Go!" Frank says with a glance out the window beside Penny. Bundled in wool coats and hats and scarves, two families right there are motioning for the trolley to stop.

"Give it the *gas*, Gus!" Penny chimes in, twisting around in her seat as the small crowd is left scrambling, running into the street behind the trolley and waving wildly.

"I'm doing my best," Gus tells them. But he still has to obey the rules of traffic, and so does a tap-and-go, gliding through a stop sign, then tries to pick up speed.

But the tap-and-go was enough to draw attention. Folks taking a neighborhood stroll, admiring the house lights, flag down the trolley. With a shot of gusto to the gas pedal, Gus tries for a narrow escape.

"Step on it, Gus," Penny calls out, half lunging from her seat, then whipping around to see the strollers left in the snow-dust.

With a lurch, the green-and-gold trolley chugs along, making all the peaceful candlelit windows and gentle snow-covered lights on shrubs become one wavering blur.

Up ahead, more strollers stand at the curb, hands raised to signal they want a ride in the cold night. It's two older couples out sightseeing, as so many do around here. But in no time, their walking tours get mighty chilly and they try to hitch a ride on the trolley.

"This thing only goes twenty miles per hour," Gus yells back to Frank as he steers around a parked car and passes the two couples.

"Twenty? Well push it to *thirty*, man!" Frank shouts. He can feel the struggling trolley engine wind out as Gus puts the pedal to the metal. "Those people are actually *chasing* us!"

"Eeep!" Penny cries beside Frank. "I can't blow my cover!"

So Frank puts his arm around her and holds her close, pressing her head into his chest until they lose the chasing crowd. With a breath of relief, he finally releases her and she turns, laughing, her hand to her heart.

"Are we in the clear?" she asks between gasps.

"Almost. But hold on tight!" Gus warns while approaching another waiting family—and safely evading them. "We're rounding a corner!"

And nearly tipping over, Frank thinks as he holds Penny close again. They sway to one side, swing to the other, while approaching the covered bridge on their return trip. Once more, they've left pleading passengers behind, cold and weary and desperately waving at them.

"Oh, blinkin' Blitzen!" Frank calls out as he and Penny spin in their seat to see the forsaken family.

And for the next few minutes, twinkling lights are a-blur, trolley bells are a-jingling as the tires clatter across the bridge, then get back onto Brookside Road—where houses beneath red-and-green lights pass in a distorted, snowy haze. Frank and Penny lean this way, then that, as Gus spins the steering wheel and guides their trolley to its destination.

"Look!" Penny says as she points ahead, through the windshield. "We're almost there."

Frank leans down and scrutinizes the Addison Boathouse coming into distant view. Every single, solitary white light he'd strung on that long-and-peaked roofline glimmers in the darkness. And he couldn't be happier to see it now.

"It's so close!" Penny exclaims.

Like a beacon, the boathouse rises in the cold night.

"Gus, give it the gas!" Frank calls across the trolley while holding onto the brass pole by his seat.

Penny is in tears of laughter beside him, looking over her shoulder with him one last time, just to be sure no one's still flagging them down for a ride.

"I said *go,* Gus. Go!" Frank yells again as the trolley swings into the wide driveway of the boathouse. "*Ac-cel-er-ate!* Right through the gate!"

twenty-one

A CHILL WIND RATTLING THE windowpanes Thursday morning nudges Penny to snuggle deep beneath her cozy quilt. All she wants is a few more minutes to dream. To imagine last night's pretty Christmas lights tour on the charming Holly Trolley. To remember Frank's arm around her as they chugged along Addison's winding country roads in the dark of a winter night.

But another sudden gust of wind whistling outside that paned bedroom window has her pull the patchwork quilt halfway over her face. The window *surely* needs caulking, with the way she feels a draft of cold air breezing through the room and going right through her thermal snowflake-patterned pajamas.

"Brrr!" Penny says to herself, squeezing her eyes closed and burrowing deeper. But suddenly she sits up, fearing the cabin's thermostat is broken. She listens closely, and hears the ticking sound of warm air rising through the heaters. The problem is, the sound is constant and fast—*tick-tick-tick*—as though the heaters can't keep up with the cold air.

Wrapping the heavy quilt around her, Penny shuffles to the wall thermostat in the hallway and gives the dial a nudge, seeing that it's working fine. "Hmm," she says, contemplating the situation while still wrapped in the cocoon of her quilt. Rushing back to her bedroom, she slips into her fluffy slippers and bathrobe so she can get the fireplace started to warm up the cabin. Frank had stacked a few split logs on the hearth for her.

Except she never gets the chance to reach the fireplace.

"Oh!" she declares instead, ducking when she walks into the living room as something swoops right above her. Then again, a fluttering sound passing close to her ear. "Jolly jiminy!" she cries out upon spotting a red cardinal whooshing through the room on its way to the kitchen. So bending low with her arms crossed over her head, Penny cautiously walks beside the sofa, changes course and heads toward the kitchen, too.

"What?" she whispers then, dodging behind the doorjamb. Because right around the corner is a cardinal *calamity*. One of the kitchen windowpanes is shattered, leaving a gaping hole— the perfect entrance for all that cold air … and for hungry birds, apparently. The feisty cardinal that nearly clipped her head now pecks at shells from the open sack of sunflower seeds she left near the window. The sack lies on its side, spilled birdseed covers the countertop, and—wait!

Wait, now a black-capped chickadee has zipped inside through the shattered pane. The newest bird perches on the wire handle of an old, rusty lantern and eyes the glutton of food waiting to be pecked. Tipping its curious chickadee head this way, then that, it hops lower, to a burnished-gold trinket box. At the same time, right outside the broken window, *another* cardinal hovers, fluttering, its wings a blur as it seems to consider coming inside to this … this … this *birdie* bistro!

From the doorway, Penny cautiously reaches into the room and swipes her cell phone off the counter. While running back to her bedroom, ducking as she does, she calls Gus over at Blue Jay Bungalow.

"Gus? I have a serious problem and need your help." She looks over her shoulder before slamming her bedroom door shut and leaning against it, winded. "My cabin's gone to the birds!"

❧

By the time Gus arrives, the little chickadee has flown the coop—literally! He managed to fly outside via the broken windowpane. But the feisty red cardinal is trapped in the cabin, and losing some of his feist. He's begun crying out in short chirps and occasionally panting when he perches on a vase or table edge. So Penny and Gus devise a plan. They open several windows and doors, hoping the bird will feel the fresh air, see the sunshine and fly to freedom. The funny thing is, once the bird perches on the ledge of the open window in the dining area, he lingers there, like he doesn't really want to leave.

"I guess he likes it here at Cardinal Cabin, after all," Penny whispers to Gus.

They let the bird catch its breath, and once it calms on the sill, Gus approaches the rascally redbird while holding a blanket open, nudging the cardinal outside. As soon as it takes fluttering flight, they quickly cheer and close all the windows and doors. Finally, Gus inserts a thick piece of cardboard into the shattered windowpane.

"How did it break, Gus?" Penny asks now as she sweeps up shards of glass from the counter and kitchen floor. "I didn't hear anything over that howling wind last night."

"Those darn snowy branches did it. With that wind blowing, looks like one snapped and hit the glass. Which is precisely why I've been after Frank to get some of those trees trimmed back."

"Oh, it's okay. Don't be too hard on Frank. He does so much here. And I didn't mind the feathered fiasco." She sweeps the shards into the trash. "Not *too* much, anyway."

After a few gruff whispers that may or may not include an expletive, Gus secures the cardboard in place and leaves, telling Penny he'll send Frank by with a new window.

"ASAP," he tells her, calling over his shoulder as he walks off her front porch, "S-R-T-L."

"What?" Penny asks after him.

"*Sooner* rather than *later!*"

From those gruff whispers Penny noticed, she imagines Frank will hear them, too, once Gus calls him. But to Frank, they'll surely be more than a whisper as Gus orders him to hightail it out here to Snowflake Lake.

With Gus gone, Penny quickly changes into a cropped fisherman sweater over a blue-plaid flannel, all on top of black leggings, thick moose-print socks and duck boots. Anything to keep warm in the still-chilled cabin.

twenty-two

Two hours later, Penny hears the sputtering engine of Gus' snowtorcycle. When she looks out the window, there's Gus giving Frank *and* a new window a lift, straight to Cardinal Cabin. In moments, the *rat-a-tat-tat-tatting* woodpecker sounds at her door.

"I have a new window to install," Frank tells her when she opens the door. The wrapped window leans against the porch railing. "Luckily, Derek had one in stock at Cooper Hardware."

"Oh, thank goodness!" Penny leans out and waves to Gus as he putters away on his snowtorcycle. "Those poor cardinals don't need any more calamities."

"I have something else for you, too." Frank hands her a snowflake-covered gift bag, sealed with a gold bow. "Go ahead, open it."

"Now?" Penny asks, still standing in the doorway.

Frank nods.

"Don't you want to come in first?"

"No, my boots are all snowy, and I have to get the ladder from the shed out back."

"Well." Penny looks down at the gift bag. "Well, okay." She peels off the stick-on bow and pulls out a record album: *A Jolly Christmas from Frank Sinatra.*

"Do you like it?" Frank asks, stepping closer and dipping his head down to read her face.

The thing is, seeing that special album instantly brings tears to her eyes … tears and the sweet memory of dancing with Frank by the light of a Christmas tree, mere days ago. So she nods. "I *love* it, Frank. But I have nothing for you!" As she says it, she clutches the album close.

"A dance after dinner will do just fine," he tells her with a wink.

"It's a date."

He leans to the side and takes a look past her, inside the cabin. "What a disaster here earlier. Gus told me everything."

"Oh, yes. A disaster, but a delightful one." Penny smiles and glances back toward the kitchen. "Those pretty birds are such fun to watch … until they're in your kitchen!"

"I can get your new window installed now. But it's a two-man operation. Can you help? I'll go outside and set up the ladder. Meet me *inside* at the window?"

෨

In no time, Frank removes the old window using a small pry bar, cleans the dried-out caulk from the frame and installs a new, insulated paned window, then screws it into place. With Penny by his side, they make quick work of the job.

As he's caulking the interior of the window in her kitchen, she passes him a rag to wipe any mess. Being so busy helping him—holding the caulk gun, handing him screws—she hesitates when her cell phone rings.

"Go ahead," Frank tells her with a nod.

So she answers. "Ross the boss!" she says while brushing a piece of caulk from Frank's jaw. "Let me put you on speakerphone, Ross. My hands are full."

"Penny Hart," Ross answers over the speaker. "You are a *huge* hit!"

At which point, Frank gives her a thumbs-up, then quietly continues caulking, drawing a bead down the length of the window.

"Huge?" Penny asks.

"Sensational! And your last clue? The snowy covered bridge night scene? The votes are leaning four-to-one toward Vermont. Am I right? You in the green mountain state?"

"Now, Ross. You know I can't tell anyone—including you."

"Regardless. You are a *smash*! Suitcase Escapes is *bulging* with business." Ross' voice booms through the room. "We've got to do this again, and take you on the road."

"What?" Penny asks as Frank caps the caulk tube and wipes the window frame with the rag.

"I'm going outside to finish up," Frank whispers, slipping on his hat and red-and-black plaid jacket, grabbing the caulk gun and heading out the front door, then around back. He tromps through the snow, making his way to the ladder he'd set up earlier. As he climbs the low rungs, Penny lifts the sash all the way up from inside, leans out and gives him a kiss. But Ross gets her attention, then, and she turns back inside, the phone still on speaker, the window wide open so that Frank hears the amplified conversation.

"The travel agency's never been busier, Penny," Ross' voice says through the speaker. "You should see it here. And the donated toys, the ballot box ... overflowing! You game to keep doing this, after the New Year?"

"Well," Penny says, leaning out again and giving Frank a wink. "I'm not so sure, Ross."

Just say no, Frank thinks as he climbs higher and lines a bead of caulk along the top of the window. *I tell you I'm falling in love, and you're excited to leave now?*

Problem is, he knows Penny can't read his thoughts. She can only shrug through the window as Ross jabbers on.

"Every region of the United States is expressing interest in being a part of your mystery promotion, Miss Hart. It's gone viral, and we can hardly keep up with the media attention!"

"Wow! Nationwide? It's all gotten that big?" Penny asks. "What a surprise."

Frank draws a line of caulk down the sides of the frame, all the while keeping an ear tuned to the talk coming through the open window.

"You've got to take this show on the road, Penny. *Beyond* New England this time," Ross insists. "We've already got inns and resorts across the country wanting to host your mystery tours. I'm telling you, the phone here doesn't stop ringing!"

Even over speakerphone, Ross' enthusiasm is undeniable.

"I just can't believe it," Penny tells him. "You know, where I am, the Wi-Fi's a little spotty, so I had no idea."

And actually, Frank's glad for the distraction of installing the window. It gives him a chance to hear what Penny will decide. He finishes caulking the bottom of the window and slides his thumb along the seal.

Meanwhile, Ross can't seem to rein in his plans. "I'm thinking one year away, Penny. From the new bookings we're making with your two-week stint, I'm sure sending you away even longer will earn out, and then some. You can *blog* about it on our website, network with folks from coast to coast! Make Suitcase Escapes a household name."

As Ross blathers on, Frank is done. He gives a light rap on the window glass and motions to Penny that she can close it up and get warm now.

Never thinking that she'd press the window down as quickly as she does, thus preventing him from hearing her answer.

So Frank practically slides down the last few ladder rungs to get around the side of the cabin and back inside. Because Penny *can't* be agreeing to this ridiculous proposal. Going away for a *year*? For crying out loud, she doesn't even *like* traveling. Frank trudges through the snow, quickly rounding the corner to the side yard and dropping the caulk gun in his rush. So he backtracks to look for it. But the lost caulk gun's sunk into the powdery snow, and now he has to bend and, with his glove, brush the snow aside and dig around until he finally plucks it out.

Hopefully, Penny hasn't yet given an answer.

Hopefully, she's simply hearing Ross out.

Hopefully, Frank can get to her in time to, at the very least, shake his head. To whisper, *Don't do it! Think about things. Let's talk this through, together.* He picks up his pace, running now and nearly falling at one point, his gloved hand reaching down to the snow as he stumbles, then rights himself.

"Frank!" a voice calls out.

At first, he thinks it's the wind. Or his imagination. So he keeps going.

"Frank! Hey, Lombardo," a man's deep voice calls again.

So Frank looks over his shoulder to see Gus walking closer. He's all bundled up and has big, lace-up snow boots on, as well as leather work gloves, ready to pitch in with the window installation.

"How's it going? Need a hand?"

"Gus." Frank stops, looks toward the front porch—which is only *steps* away, as is his and Penny's fate—then back at Gus. "I'm good, Gus. The window's installed."

"Already?" Gus steps closer. "You do fast work." Gus begins heading around back. "I always knew that tree had a bothersome branch," he tells Frank. "The wind snapped it right off and it hit the window. Poor Penny was freezing in there, dodging birds all morning."

"Hey, listen," Frank bluffs as he inches toward the front porch. "I've got to warm up inside, I'll stop by your place on my way out."

And before Gus can respond, or argue, or say anything at all, Frank races around to the front of the cabin, bolts up the front porch steps, hesitates for one second—tops—in front of the red berry wreath, then tries the door. Which is locked, so he loudly raps on it with his bare knuckles, forgoing the woodpecker knocker to save a few mere seconds.

✦

With her phone still on speaker, Penny carefully wipes some extra caulk off the inside window ledge. Just on the other side of the window opening, Frank is finishing up.

Ross can't seem to rein in his plans. "We've already got inns and resorts across the country wanting to host your mystery tours … I'm thinking one year away, Penny," her boss is saying as she wipes the window ledge with a rag. "From the new bookings we're making with your two-week stint, I'm sure sending you away even longer will earn out, and then some."

As Ross relays his proposition, Frank gives a light rap on the window glass and, while climbing down the few ladder rungs, motions for her to close it now. Well, seeing how she's been cold since waking up this morning, she wastes no time shutting the window in the hope of finally getting warm. Though she tries to give Frank a little wave as he finishes up, he's already busy moving the ladder and heading around the side of the cabin.

So she turns back to her kitchen-tidying while talking on speakerphone to her boss.

"No, Ross. No, no, no. I could *never* leave long-term like that," Penny says, just as she glimpses Frank stumble in the snow outside. Her heart breaks with even the *thought* of going on the road. No, leaving Frank and this wonderful life she's finding here in Addison is simply out of the question. "And anyway, from what I've been hearing, folks are enjoying the mystery *romance* of my clues, far more than the travel destination."

"Well, *is* there a romance, Miss Hart?" Ross asks.

There's a quiet pause before Penny reveals the only possible answer. "I can't tell you yet," she explains while leaning around to see Frank outside picking up his caulk gun from the snow just as Gus walks over, chatting. "All I can say is that traveling is *not* for me. You know that, Ross. Sure, I may have fallen for this little hideaway of mine. But I'm a copywriter at heart, more interested in selling our destinations with my words and jingles. So I'm declining your offer." She leans to see Frank again, catching a glimpse of him talking to Gus at the side of the cabin. "I like being home, and I *really* like working right in Addison, with Chloe and you."

"Okay, then. So you're saying no, our travel arrangement's not a go. It was just a thought, anyway," Ross concedes over the speakerphone. "But you're probably right. The magic of Christmas, the magic of love ... it's mesmerized the entire town, and beyond! I'm not sure we could even replicate this response again. Listen, the other phones are ringing off the hook and I've got to go. Oh, and Penny? Crowds are pressing against the window, waiting for your next clue. Send a photograph—pronto!"

"Will do." Penny looks at the now-quiet cell phone. It's dead silent following her boss' click off. But still, she smiles at the vision of merry mayhem hitting the little travel agency on Main Street.

So when the phone instantly rings, she thinks it's Ross calling back and quickly answers, putting the call on speaker again as she moseys around her cabin. "Hello?"

"Hi, honey!"

"*Mom?*" Penny glances at the phone's caller ID. "Is everything okay?" As she asks, Penny gives another peek out the window to see Frank inching away from Gus, who looks like he wants to talk, talk, talk. Penny's sure he's eager to check every bit of the new window to be certain not a lick of cold air is seeping in on his tenant.

"Penny?" her mother asks. "You're echoing. This is *not* a good connection."

"Oh, let me take you off speakerphone." She hits the button and lifts the cell phone to her ear. "Better?"

"Yes! Much better. Nice and clear. Now listen, I have good news." As she's talking, Penny hears a sharp rap at the front door, so with the phone pressed close, she walks through the living room while her mother talks. "Our first Christmas away from you has Dad all torn up. We're both really missing you, and are you ready for this? We just changed our flight so we can come see you for the holidays!"

"But what about Christmas in Colorado? I booked you *there* for the holidays!"

"Colorado's canned, dear. Oh, I can't wait! We'll be having Christmas in Connecticut. With you!"

Another rap quickly comes to the door, so Penny gives a little skip and hurries there, still chatting and utterly delighted with her parents' change of plans.

♾

Frank can't believe the door's locked. It must've happened when he went to caulk the window out back. If he could only hear what Penny's saying to her boss, he'd feel somewhat better. It takes everything he's got to not give the doorknob a good rattle.

Finally, the lock clicks and Penny swings the door open, her cell phone pressed to her ear now, the speakerphone off. While talking, she steps aside as Frank walks in.

"Wow, just wow!" she's saying on the phone. "This is so exciting, I cannot wait!" All the while, she motions to Frank that she'll be a second more.

As he closes the front door, she's still gushing.

And Frank can't believe it.

What happened to Penny Hart, the reluctant travel agent? How can she be this enthused about a yearlong stint on the road for Suitcase Escapes? Staying practically in hiding as clients attempt to guess her whereabouts? As he turns around and steps into the room, he drags his hand along his jaw, then pulls off his wool cap. This season is full of surprises, isn't it?

He heads over to the mantel with a twinkling garland looped across it, listening as Penny's voice is saying *Wonderful!* and *What happy news!*

But Frank won't look at her. It's bad enough hearing how thrilled she is to plan a year of mystery destinations—and *what? Blog* about it? Who even blogs anymore?

Shot down, he looks at the wood crackling and burning in the fireplace, gives a log a poke, then finally turns toward where Penny stands at the dining table. It's been cold in the cabin, and she's bundled in a blue flannel shirt and gray fisherman sweater over her leggings.

"Okay, that sounds *perfect*," she says into the phone.

And it's enough for, well … he just can't listen to this go on and on. Not now, while she's on the phone with her boss, and not afterward—listening to whatever cockamamie reasoning she'll rattle off to him when she hangs up. To hear her excited excuses to hit the road … which will no doubt end their relationship.

So instead, Frank points to his watch and mouths, *Got to go.* Then he heads to the door, and the closer he gets to it, the faster he walks—mostly to avoid any uncomfortable situation listening to Penny justify leaving Cardinal Cabin.

Leaving Addison.

And leaving him.

"Problem at the boathouse," he quietly lies. "Gina needs me."

Though Penny nods, she holds up a finger for Frank to wait.

But he doesn't. Enough is enough, and he can't bear his happiness being deflated ... just like that. So he hurries out and closes the front door, flies down the porch steps while pulling on his cap, and nearly falls again. His hand brushes the snowy ground and he regains his balance as he hears Penny open the door behind him.

"We'll iron out all the details later, I promise," she says into the phone, then hangs up and instantly calls out to him.

Frank, halfway across the yard now, acts like he doesn't hear.

"Frank?" she calls again. "Are you coming by for dinner later?"

"No." He turns and walks a few steps backward, eyeing Penny on the stoop while trying to make, that's right, *heads or tails* of her work decision. "Wedding details to take care of," he yells to her. "For Wes and Jane." When he suddenly hears Gus' snowtorcycle start up, he trots in that direction, waving for a ride.

"But, our dance ..." From the front doorway, Penny looks back inside the cabin, Frank's sure, at his Sinatra gift-album. "Will I see you tomorrow?" she asks, cupping her hands to her mouth so that her voice carries. "You were going to deliver cookies to the cabins with me?" She steps down into the snow in her laced-up duck boots, inching closer, then wrapping her fisherman-sweater-clad arms tight around herself to keep warm. "They were going to be my Christmas gift to all the nice folks here."

At the same time, Gus steers the snowtorcycle in Frank's direction. Frank hears the approaching *put-put-put-put*, but before turning, he gives one last, long look at his Penny-who-fell-in-the-snow.

As quickly as she fell into his life, apparently she's swooping right out.

When Gus revs the engine behind him, Frank climbs into the snowtorcyle's sidecar and sits himself down. And for the second time in the past twenty-four hours, he does it.

That's right.

He says, "Give it the gas, Gus." After one glance over at Penny, he adds, "Gun it."

Except this time when Frank says the words, it's with no joy in his heart, no warmth in a genuine smile.

In fact, it's with no smile at all.

twenty-three

Ornament-shaped sugar cookies, and red velvet snowballs, and blackberry thumbprints, and Christmas tree cookies dotted with sprinkles. Peanut butter blossoms and snickerdoodles and gingersnaps. The next morning, as the sun rises in a clear December sky and as the cabin's heaters tick with rising warmth, Penny can't see her kitchen countertop or tabletop for the sweet treats spread across them. There are even cookie plates beside the old tin lantern on the wide window ledge.

As always, her kitchen holds no secrets. If you want to know what's in Penny Hart's heart, the telltale sign is in that room. Because the only way she's ever kept worries at bay is to bake. And bake. And bake. Blame it on her mother, who taught Penny to whisk away her problems by whisking batter. Cake, cookie, or brownie—no matter!

And from the looks of this sweet stash before her, her new worry is a doozy.

"Well," she says as she stacks the cookies in tins depicting sprigs of holly and candy-cane stripes and red poinsettia blossoms, "at least my pain is someone else's gain."

The problem is, it's taking a lot of time to nicely fill each tin with the fresh-baked cookies. One interruption keeps slowing her down, and that would be the living room window. The living room window overlooking Cardinal Cabin's front porch and Snowflake Lake, *and* the walkway anyone would take to come to her front door.

That living room window, all frosted at the edges, keeps her on her toes as she packs a tin, then goes to the window and looks out—leaning this way, then that—to see if anyone's stopping by this Friday morning. Sometimes she then swings by the front wood-planked door, opens it, and with a sad glimpse at the silver milk can on the small table there—and a lingering touch of the evergreen twigs fanning from it—she waits for a long moment. Hoping, and watching, to see if someone in an unmistakable lumberjack coat might round the far corner.

But no one does.

The only sight of red is the red-and-blue tartan throw folded beneath the milk can—the fringed throw perfect to snuggle under while sitting in the white rockers on the porch.

"If only," she whispers before going inside and closing the door.

After the last festive tin is packed and its cover pressed tight, Penny picks up her cell phone—her phone that's been silent all morning—and calls Frank. Because it's painfully apparent that he really will *not* be helping her deliver her Christmas cookie tins, like they had planned. When she gets his voicemail, she hesitates, then softly says, "Frank, it's me. Penny. Please call."

Since the baking's done now, she has to do something to keep her worry, and her tears, away. So she pulls her duck boots on over thick socks, zips her navy parka, flips up the fur-lined hood and goes to the shed. There, she finds her wagon, wheels it around to the cabin's front door and loads in her cookie tins. The morning is cold and quiet. Beneath a crystal-blue sky, the air is still, and so her wagon-wheeling over the snow has a lonely sound to it.

One by one, she knocks on each cabin door—from Dove Dwelling to Robin Residence to Chickadee Shanty—and slowly lightens her wagonload, one cookie tin and Christmas greeting at a time. Neighbors chat about holiday plans with family, and the fun they're having keeping her Suitcase Escapes' mystery getaway a secret. The folks keep her busy and keep her smiling, all at once. They open their cabin doors and she gets a glimpse inside their cozy lake homes with all the stone fireplaces and beamed ceilings and old, planked floors. In many of the cabins, Penny smells the pine scent of fresh-cut woodland Christmas trees, the trees decorated with glass balls and gold snowflakes and clusters of red berries.

Finally, though, her wagon is empty and she pulls it over the rutted and foot-printed snow. One more thing pressing on her mind is that it's time for another mystery photo-clue for Suitcase Escapes. Ross has texted her twice in the past hour looking for one. So it's with a heavy heart that she glances around at the scenery, reluctant to show her sadness.

But maybe she can send a message to Frank this way. He's said that he likes to check out her photo-clues in the travel agency's front window. With that in mind, when she passes a pretty wooden gazebo in Wren Den's yard, she stops and takes out her cell phone. The gazebo is set in an abandoned garden. But that lonely, snow-capped, solitary gazebo shows the longing filling her heart. And she hopes Frank will see it, too.

So she snaps the picture and sends it along to Ross, her boss, with the following clue. A clue meant for one particular lumberjack more than anyone else:

A gazebo alone in the snow ...
Has me long for someone dear I know.

By the time she returns her wagon to the shed and gets back inside Cardinal Cabin, her heavy heart is filled with dread. Because something is very, very wrong and she needs to talk to Frank. Though he never answered her voicemail, she tries his number again and is surprised when he answers.

"Look, Penny," he begins. "Maybe we both got carried away out there. It's like a wonderland at Snowflake Lake, where troubles can't find you."

Oh, but they can—and do! Penny wants to tell him. But she can't, not without tears, so she just listens, instead.

"That place is a snow fantasy," he says, "where we're cushioned from the outside world. Who knows if things would last once we got back to our everyday lives?"

"Would *last?*" Penny asks. "Fantasy? But, Frank—"

"I don't want you to have your heart broken after Christmas, so I won't beat around the bush. I think we should take a breather, Penny."

He pauses then, and the silence lengthens between them. She's too shocked at his words to even know what to say.

"Everything's been moving really fast, and we should just see how we feel once your travel mysteries are done. In the New Year, if you're even still here."

"If I'm still *here?* Frank, what do you mean?"

"Got to run."

In another pause, Penny hears a commotion there in the boathouse. A few men's voices ring out; a door slams.

"Vendors are arriving for Wes and Jane's wedding tomorrow. Flowers, music. I've got to help set up."

He holds the phone away, or maybe to his chest as he talks to a vendor. Penny hears his voice, muffled, as he gives an order before talking to her once more. "Really busy here. So ... well ... Merry Christmas, Penny."

twenty-four

THE PROBLEM NOW IS THIS: The baking's done. After Penny hangs up with Frank, she puts away the last of the cookie pans, then turns around in the cabin kitchen. The cabinets are painted a distressed burgundy and are all closed up tight. Small plates line an open shelf, each plate depicting an image of a cardinal: one on a birch tree, one on a feeder, one on a snow-covered pine branch. Standing at her new kitchen window, she thinks it's only been a single day since Frank installed it.

Since she leaned through the wall opening and kissed him as he stood on the ladder outside.

Since they laughed and planned an evening dance near the fireplace, after dinner.

And it all since fell apart.

If she could keep baking, she would. An apple pie was next on her list, but what's the use, now that Frank is gone? Let's face it; the pie was purely planned for him.

So instead of baking a pie, she chops the pie's apples into small pieces. At least this way, the cardinals can have the feast. After putting on her boots and jacket to deliver the food to the feeder, she steps out into the backyard. Right away she hears it, the *cheer, cheer!* chirp of cardinals. She gives a glance over to the nearby pine tree, one with a few low-hanging branches. And there they are, the bird couple singing their duet. The male is deep red, the female pale brown and gray—and both as happy as can be. Gus had told her that they pair for life, and are very devoted to each other.

Cheer, cheer!

She glances over again on her way to the bird feeder. Gus also saw something of the love cardinals in her and Frank, the way they sang a duet at Gus' practice turkey dinner.

Cheer, cheer!

"Oh, what's there to be cheerful about?" she demands from the birds. "Shush now!"

"Something wrong?" a voice asks from behind.

A familiar, gruff voice that has softened recently. Oh, Penny knows exactly who it is, and so she quickly swipes the tears that line her face before turning to Gus.

"Penny?" he asks, stepping closer through the snow. His tweed newsboy cap is on, and his cheeks are rosy in the cold air.

"Gus." She smiles, briefly, then empties her chopped apples onto the bird feeder tray.

"You seem sad today, Miss Hart."

She looks over her shoulder at him while she spreads the apple chunks with the black-oil sunflower seeds. With a sigh, she admits, "I think Frank broke up with me."

"What?" Gus takes off his cap and resettles it on his head, over tufts of white hair.

Penny nods. "It's true."

"Broke up with you?" Gus looks around, as though he'll see Frank there, somewhere. Fixing the window, or chopping wood. As though he'll give him a piece of his mind. "How? I mean, when?"

"Today." Beneath the feeder, she scatters in the snow the last of the apple chunks meant for an apple pie for Frank. "He said what we had out here was a ... fantasy?"

"I'm at a loss for words. *Frank* said that? Frank Lombardo?"

She can only nod once more.

"Penny, I get the feeling there's been a terrible misunderstanding. Is there anything I can do to help?"

"No, Gus. You've done so much already. It's very sad, but I guess Frank's so busy, he just has no room for love in his life."

"Oh ... humbuggery!" Gus looks back at Cardinal Cabin, then at Blue Jay Bungalow off in the distance. "You stop by my place, Penny. We'll have some of those Christmas cookies you baked, and cocoa."

"Really, I'm okay, Gus." She bends to pick up the empty bag that held her apple chunks. And to sneak in another tear-swipe.

"But I want to show you something. And anyway, cookies are meant for company, after all. You come on over for a talk."

കര

Once she's locked up her cabin, Penny joins Gus at Blue Jay Bungalow. By the time she arrives there, he's got cookies and hot cocoa waiting, and logs burning and snapping in the fireplace.

"Need help with your Christmas puzzle?" Penny asks. Taking off her parka, she walks to the puzzle table near the living room window.

"Puzzle's done and waiting for my grandkids to glue and frame it. Few more days and they'll be here," Gus says as he walks into his dining room. "Everything's done," he calls back.

Penny brushes her fingertips across the finished puzzle, feeling the tiny pieces. She has to smile at the puzzle image of snowmen decorating a Christmas tree out in the forest. Deer and brown rabbits watch from beside a snow-capped brook, and cardinals string a garland of red leaves across the tree branches. But her smile fades when she remembers sitting here with Frank just days ago, working on the puzzle ... right before he kissed her beneath the mistletoe.

So she walks to the dining room, pausing at the piano where she lightly presses a few keys to evoke another memory: her duet with Frank as they sang carols together. Her fingers slowly press some high keys, and the sound, now, is sad. Finally, she stops in the doorway to the dining room. Just like in Cardinal Cabin, the little birch-bark lampshades on the chandelier glow over the table—where her cookies are set out on a plate, and cocoa steams in two big mugs.

"For me, too," Penny says with teary eyes.

"What do you mean?" Gus dunks a cookie in his cocoa.

"Everything's done for me, too. All the special time Frank and I spent together, in this magical place ... It's done."

"Come here," Gus says, hitching his head toward her chair. "Drown your sorrows."

Penny pulls out her chair and sits, then picks up a sugar cookie and sets it on her plate. "Maybe Frank has cold feet."

"If what you're telling me is true, it's more like a cold heart," Gus tells her. "Which I'm having a hard time believing. Frank's a good guy, and practically like a son to me." Gus leans back to the sideboard and lifts a stuffed scrapbook, which he sets on the table between them. He turns it to face Penny. "My wife was an amateur bird photographer," Gus continues. "It was a real hobby of hers, and she put little notes and sayings in the margins, beside her photographs."

Penny flips to the first page, seeing a robin trilling a song from a porch railing. "So pretty," she murmurs, running her finger over the image, then reading the side note. "*Sure as announcing spring, good luck a singing robin will bring.*" Penny smiles at the rhyme.

"Betty was a bit of a poet, too."

"I can see that." Penny turns the page to a chickadee on a low-hanging branch. Its feathers are fluffed against the apparently chill air. "*When you're chipper as a chickadee, life's a jubilee.*"

But it's the next page that Penny lingers with longest. Betty placed several photos of cardinals on it, and added a few rhymes to the margins. "*When a cardinal swoops from above, your day will be filled with love,*" Penny whispers, her eyes tearing up. Because when a cardinal swooped from above when it was trapped in her cabin, her day *did* start with love—but ended so differently. "I'm not really sure about that one," she tells Gus, pointing to the rhyme and turning the scrapbook to him.

Gus puts on his reading glasses and lowers them on his nose while skimming the captions. He flips to the next page, then, and reads another rhyme. "*Cardinal, cardinal ... To my heart be true ... Bring someone special into my view.*"

"That rhyme sounds more like a wish," Penny says.

"It is. It works, too."

"How can that be possible?"

"According to Betty," Gus explains with a glance at the scrapbook, "you must recite that particular verse while watching an actual cardinal." He looks up at her. "Lots of folklore goes with those little red birds. Blessings, and comforts. Special wishes."

"Oh, Gus." Penny sips her hot chocolate. "I'm beyond dreams and wishes, especially today."

"Give them one more shot, you hear me? If you wish to see someone right when watching a cardinal, I can assure you—Betty was never wrong—your wish *will* be granted."

"I'm not sure anything will help. You should've heard Frank, Gus."

"Did you have an argument?"

"No."

"A disagreement?"

"No, but it feels like it."

Gus bites into a peanut butter blossom. He squints at Penny and quietly asks, "Could there be someone else?"

"I don't think so."

"Maybe Frank's feeling Christmas stress. Lots of people do this time of year."

"Christmas stress?"

"Sure. He's constantly busy at the boathouse, and there's upcoming holiday-table stress with the family. You know, being the one single man at the table, he might get ribbed about that," Gus ruminates. "Maybe that's all got him out of sorts?"

Penny simply shrugs, then sips her hot cocoa.

"Well, then." Gus folds his arms on the table and leans closer. "What was the *very* last thing you two talked about?"

"I'm not sure, we've been so busy—"

Gus shakes his head. "Now think, Penny! Carefully."

"Okay." Penny stands and walks to the living room doorway, looking out the big paned window across the room. "It was yesterday. We were in Cardinal Cabin. It was chaotic, after that window broke and the birds got inside! And Frank was there to fix the window."

"Go on …"

"We were fine. Having some laughs and cleaning up the mess. My boss called and since I was helping Frank install the window, I put the phone on speaker. So Frank heard the whole thing, too. Ross said my mystery destination was a smash hit." A realization slowly comes to her in snowflake-crystal clarity. "He offered me a yearlong travel opportunity that would have me constantly on the road. To become," she continues while sitting across from Gus again, "Suitcase Escapes' *traveling* travel agent."

"Which means you'd leave Addison?"

Penny nods.

"Oh, Penny … Do you plan to? Because your leaving sure would break a lot of hearts, Frank's included."

"No, Gus. I could never leave here. It's too special of a place to ever leave behind."

"And where was Frank when your boss proposed this?"

"Right there." Penny grabs a red velvet snowball and pops it in her mouth. "I was *inside* the window opening, and he was *outside*," she says around the cookie. "I remember winking at him as he listened to my work call. I turned down … my boss … Wait." She pictures Frank rushing around the side of the cabin then. "Which Frank would not have heard."

"Why not?"

"He'd finished installing the window and was talking to you out back when I told my boss no. That I wasn't interested. And then my mother called."

"Your mother?"

Again, Penny nods. "Right when Frank was talking to you, and he hurried away, remember? I'm sure now he wanted to hear my answer to Ross … Oh, no. You don't think?"

"Think what?"

"Jolly jiminy, Gus! When Frank bolted back inside the cabin, he heard me overjoyed and making plans ... with my *mother*! She called right after I'd hung up with my boss. The cell phone connection was bad, so I took it off speaker. And of all things, she and my dad surprised me with a change of Christmas plans. They're coming to Connecticut, instead of spending the holiday in Colorado, and I was *thrilled*." Penny pauses, cocoa mug cupped in her hands, thinking back. "But maybe Frank thought it was *Ross* I was still talking to. And he rushed off to hitch a ride on your snowtorcycle before I could explain."

"So perhaps there *has* been a terrible misunderstanding, after all. And Frank *thinks* you're leaving town for Suitcase Escapes."

"Golly gumdrops, I'd bet my Christmas candy cane on it!"

"Are you sure, Penny? Absolutely?"

"Well, it's either that, or ..."

"Or?" Gus interrupts.

"Or could it be that everything's happened too fast, too soon, between us? And Frank's having second thoughts about me? I just can't tell."

Gus picks up their cocoa mugs and rinses them at the sink. "Listen, I have to get to work now," he says over his shoulder. He turns then, drying his hands on a dishtowel. "I've got the evening shift driving the Holly Trolley. Do you want me to track down Frank?"

"No!" Penny stands and pushes in her chair, then grabs her parka. "Please don't. But what you *can* do is this." She pulls up her coat's zipper and flips on the fur-lined hood before leaving.

"For you two? Anything."

Penny walks to the door, already devising a plan. She turns around before stepping outside. "I need a secret ride into town tomorrow night. Can you help?"

∽

Frank gives a look back at the dark walnut bar inside Cedar Ridge Tavern. Amber pendant lights hang over it, and tabletop Christmas trees are illuminated at either end of it. He considers staying for a drink because, heck, it beats going home to his empty house. A house full of romantic memories now.

But too many guests from Wes and Jane's rehearsal dinner are lingering here. And he already did enough socializing over his chicken cutlet burger, at the long table filled with the entire wedding party and clinking glasses and silverware. With another look back, he gives one final wave goodbye to Wes and Jane. A little solitary time is in order, so he flips up his collar against the cold, walks beneath swags of green garland in the tavern's entranceway and heads outside.

A walk will do him good. "Right. A good excuse, anyway, to see Penny's latest clue," he whispers in the dark. A few Friday night holiday revelers stroll Main Street, passing windowfronts strung with white lights. More townsfolk sing Christmas carols at the towering, twinkling tree in the center of The Green.

But no one is in front of Suitcase Escapes at this late hour. He has the travel agency's window all to himself, so Frank takes a long look at Penny's most recent photo-clue. It's of a white garden gazebo, empty and seeming a little desolate. It's roof and railings are snowcapped, and around it, barren stalks of plants and bushes poke through more snow. What the sight does is hint at days gone by.

He takes a better look at the photograph, thinking that instead of being *in the gazebo*, Penny Hart will be *on the go*. And yup, he'll be guessing her every single stop on her yearlong travel stint.

"Eh," he says while shoving his hands in his coat pockets and walking away. "What's it all for, anyway?"

Up ahead at Joel's Bar and Grille, the neon Christmas bells in the front window flash and blink. A beer there will be as good as anywhere, and sure beats a lonely-hour drink at home. So Frank turns in to see silver garland and multi-colored lights strung throughout the bar. Rock-and-roll Christmas carols play on the jukebox, and the joint, well, it's jumping.

Frank finds a seat at the bar, where he hangs his coat over the back of his barstool.

"Surprised to see *you* here," a voice says.

He quickly turns to find Greg Davis nursing a drink at the stool beside his. "You, too," Frank tells him as he sits and checks his watch. "You're not still at your brother's rehearsal-dinner bash?"

"I was beat, heading home. And, well, Joel's was on the way."

"I get it." Frank motions to the bartender. "Give me a cold one."

In the quiet pause waiting for his drink, Greg asks him, "Don't you have a mystery lady to keep company? Beside a roaring fire, with a basket of holiday movies close by?"

"Afraid not." Frank cuffs his shirtsleeves. "It's not in the Christmas cards for me. Not this year."

"What?" Greg turns his stool to eye Frank directly. "You sure about that?"

Frank looks past him to the square tables surrounding the small dance floor. Every table is full, and the dance floor alive with festive foot-stamping and jolly jiving. Silver and gold ornaments hang from the garland strung above it all.

"Because I could swear Penny Hart's heart was set on you," Greg is saying.

"Not sure if that's true, Doc."

"Hey, my men," the bartender, Kevin, calls out while delivering Frank's beer. "No potential Mrs. Clauses under the mistletoe tonight?" He motions to the assorted berry sprigs hanging over the bar.

"Nope. Nobody." As he says it, Greg raises his drink in a toast.

Frank looks from Kevin, to Greg. He tips his beer to Greg's glass in agreement, something he never imagined he'd be doing these few days before Christmas.

No, what he'd imagined—a romantic holiday with Penny, cozy beside the tree in Cardinal Cabin, snowflakes drifting from the clouds outside—has faded away, somehow.

And all the while, he knows.

The lonely hours will surely be back now, once again.

twenty-five

SOMETHING ABOUT A WEDDING BRINGS out the best in people: the best happiness, hope and smiles. Frank's always observed this at the boathouse wedding receptions. It's apparent behind the tears of joy, the familiarity of toasts, the touch of dance. Maybe it has to do with the promise of marriage vows, and of a new future, too.

It's no different Saturday night when he stands against the side wall in the boathouse banquet hall. He likes this spot because it gives him a full view of the entire room—from the sparkling antlers woven through the garland arranged on the head table, all the way across the crowded dance floor, past the linen-draped guest tables to the wall of windows overlooking the outside observation deck.

Left to right, Frank takes it all in. Crystal goblets are raised in toasts, and the music kicks up a notch. He can relax, now that all the boathouse policies have been checked and enforced, including the DJ equipment set-up and the caterer's kitchen use, as well as event parking outside. Twinkling lights dangle from the exposed ductwork pipes overhead; the ceiling pendant lights are dimmed; red and gold wall lighting sets a festive mood.

And guests looking like silhouettes in the low light are dancing around the tall Christmas tree in the center of the room.

Wes and Jane's winter wedding has gone off without a hitch. Frank couldn't be happier for them as he stands in the shadows—wearing a suit and tie with his arms crossed in front of him. Silently, Frank watches the merriment. He's happy, but still, there's something bittersweet about the reception. The groom, dressed to the nines in a black tuxedo, dances with his bride in his arms now. It's a sight that Frank could've hoped for himself, *his* bride having copper-colored hair. But just days ago, his own chance at marriage came to an end as abruptly as a swing of his wood-chopping axe.

Wes, spinning Jane in her long white gown, waltzes past Frank with a nod. Beyond Wes, a few of the bridesmaids, wearing fitted silver dresses, flirt with Wes' single brother, Greg. Frank watches as one bridesmaid touches Greg's arm, laughing, and the other taps her high-heeled toe, ready to hit the dance floor—if only Greg would make a move.

Everywhere he looks today, all Frank sees is love. New love, old love, possible love. On no other day has the sight of love taunted him like it does now.

"Hey," Gina says as she rushes to him, still standing arms-crossed in the shadows. "You're not working tonight! You're a guest."

"I'm never *just* a guest, Gina. This is all on us, if anything misfires."

"Oh, relax." His sister stands beside him and takes in the view. "Aren't you so happy for Wes and Jane? And don't forget. Today's the winter solstice, too … the longest night of the year. Surely you can sneak in a few minutes for a winter dance!"

"Maybe later, Gina."

She squints over at him, then looks out at the dance floor. "Beautiful, isn't it? Love how the wall lighting glimmers up to the ceiling. Yup, we pulled off another memorable wedding reception," she says while waving to Jane twirling past. "One for the books, so join the fun."

"Eh." Frank stands straighter, crossing his arms tighter.

"Look! There's a bridesmaid sitting alone at the head table." Gina nods to the left. "She seems lonely, sipping her wine. Ask her for a dance, Frank. Be spontaneous!" As she says it, she nudges his crossed-and-unmoving arms right before her husband, Josh, sweeps her away in a line dance starting up.

And right as Frank's cell phone rings, not that he can hear it above the music and foot stomping. But he feels the vibration and answers in his dark corner.

"Frank Lombardo?" a deep—okay, and *gruff*—voice asks. "This is Gus Haynes."

Which Frank already knew. There's no mistaking that gruffness when Gus turns it on. "Gus," Frank says. And nothing more, because already, Gus continues talking, if only Frank can make out what he's saying over the music and scootin' and shakin' going on. He presses the phone close and blocks his other ear. "Wait, *wait*, Gus. Say it again."

"Fine, pay attention. In five minutes, there will be a knock at your observation deck door. You are to be there, alone, to answer it."

"What?" Frank turns toward the back of the room, where the wall of windows looks out on the deck, which is empty on this cold winter night. He bends and presses the phone tighter against his ear. "Wait! What do you mean?"

And there's no mistaking what he hears next. The clicking disconnect comes through, loud and clear. So he returns the phone to his pocket and takes a step toward the rear of the room.

"Frank!" Gina calls out as she shuffles past. "It's almost time to cut the cake. Can you check with the kitchen?" she asks while giving a saucy heel-hitch.

Frank nods, looks at his watch and waits until Gina step-slides away with Josh standing behind her, his hands on her waist. Once she's out of sight, Frank hurries along the side wall, staying in shadow as he walks to the observation deck door. Not *just* walks. No, he walks, clears his throat, drags a hand through his hair, and, once at the door, tugs and straightens the shirt cuffs beneath his suit jacket.

He's still in the shadows, off to the side, when he sees it.

Or rather, when he sees her. Sees that beautiful copper hair against a green velvet dress, over which a knit shawl is loosely draped. And in the winter solstice moonlight outside—shining on the river beyond, illuminating the bare tree branches—Penny Hart looks merely like a misty dream.

෩

But Frank knows better. With one quick look back to be sure he's safe from the prying eyes of his boot-scootin' sister, he opens the door and slips unnoticed into the night.

"Penny!" He steps closer, feeling cautious. "What are you doing here?"

"Shh!" Penny blends into the shadows over on the side, near the line of wooden oars mounted against the side railing balusters. She hooks her finger and silently motions ... *Come here.*

After one last look behind him at the couples inside—who are now slow-dancing to a sentimental love song—Frank steps closer. And with each step, he notices something new, like the way Penny's hair is twisted up in a loose chignon. Or how she wears ruby studs in her ears. And that tears glisten on her cheek. Finally, they stand within arm's reach of each other.

"Dance with me?" she whispers.

Strains of violin sweep through the outside speaker system. Frank hesitates, listening to the words of *Moon River* being sung, sentimental words about two drifters traveling the world, seeking their rainbows. In only a moment, he opens his arms and Penny moves into them, silently leaning into him in the night's darkness. Beyond, the Connecticut River glimmers like a silver ribbon winding through the snow-laced trees. Frank wordlessly waltzes with her, their fingers linked, his one hand behind her back, pressing her close.

And though her body is so near; though Frank's fingers touch her hair; though they dance silently as he listens for any of her words, something about the moment feels unreal. *Surely* he's about to bolt up in bed, waking from a dream—a mocking, teasing dream—perspiring and breathing heavily with the memory of his sweet Penny slow-dancing in his arms.

"Frank," she whispers into his ear now.

The air is cold outside, with a breeze fluttering as gently as the song's quavering strains of violin. Frank keeps dancing, his hand rising up her back, to her neck. If only this moment could go on as long as the solstice night.

But Penny pulls away then, slightly. "I think there was a misunderstanding," she says.

Not the way he sees it. Because Frank knows what he heard when he walked in on her phone conversation two days ago. There was no *misunderstanding* her happiness at traveling the country for Suitcase Escapes, and at ultimately leaving their relationship behind. So he watches her, but only shakes his head.

"Don't shut me out," Penny pleads as they slowly dance closer to the railing now. "We can still be together. It's Christmas, after all." She reaches up and strokes his face with the back of her fingers. "I want to spend it with you."

"I'm not sure that's a good idea," he says, taking her fingers in his hand and pulling back to gauge her expression. Her sad, gray eyes fill with new tears. If Frank could kiss away that sadness, he would. But that wouldn't change her decision to go on the road as a mystery traveler.

"Frank, wait—"

"Listen, I'm sorry, but I meant what I said on the phone. Everything's happened too fast, and I'm really not one to rush things. I'm actually not spontaneous at all, so it's better this way …" Then he simply touches a fallen wisp of her hair. "Penny," he whispers with regret.

And that's the last word he gets to say as the brilliant deck spotlights flash on at that precise moment. A flood of brightness shines on them, so he sweeps Penny to the side, but they're still clearly illuminated as the music fades to an end.

"Grab somebody, *anybody*," the DJ's voice announces, which they hear over the speaker system. "It's time for a romantic winter waltz in the snow. Now dash outside to the observation deck and off we go!"

Frank panics. It's the traditional evening snow dance overlooking the river that he arranges for *every* Christmastime wedding. The sight is always magical as couples slow-dance on the vast deck, swaying close, stealing a kiss. With stars above, or with snowflakes drifting from the sky, there's always a fairy-tale ambiance to the event—and he plumb forgot about it with Penny in his arms.

Now they both spin around to see the guests spilling through the doorway. To Frank, it's a blur of silver-sequined dresses and black tuxes and fur wraps and buttoned jackets, all with a hum of excitement as everyone comes out for the moonlit dance.

Penny suddenly pulls on his arm, so that he looks at her. That's when she stretches up and gives him a kiss, one she lingers with a few seconds too long, risking being seen before she turns. Turns and runs down the upper-level deck's stairs. She's holding her shawl up over her neck and partially covering her chignon as Frank helplessly watches her flee.

A new song is piped through the outdoor speakers then ... *Should old acquaintance be forgot* ... Frank spins around and starts to go after Penny. He heads toward the staircase leading to the lower level ... *and never brought to mind.*

No, no. Penny Hart will *always* be in his mind, in his heart. He grabs the stair railing, just as Wes and Jane catch up with him.

"Frank, my man!" Wes says.

Frank stops and looks over his shoulder at the groom. And takes a quick breath as he reluctantly turns around again. Jane, in her white gown, breezes to him and hugs him tightly. "Oh, Frank! This has been the best reception *ever.*"

"It has, my friend. And those wooden deer at the head table?" Wes asks.

"Bewitching," Jane tells him, her smile wide, her white gown shimmering. "Especially on the solstice."

Wes goes in for a hug, too, as he slaps Frank on the back. "You and Gina outdid yourselves," Wes tells him, turning and motioning to the guests winter-waltzing to the evocative strains of *Auld Lang Syne*.

"Wait." Jane moves to the top of the stairs and bends low, squinting. "Is someone leaving?" She looks back at Wes and Frank, and they step closer. "Who is that?" she asks while pointing at a woman in a green velvet dress, her chignon coming loose as she runs.

"Not really sure," Frank lies to Jane. "Someone you know?" he asks Wes.

Wes shakes his head and shrugs, then takes his bride in his arms for an intimate dance beneath the December moon. Frank pats their shoulders and steps aside, leaning on the railing by the staircase, arms crossed in front of him as he watches the grand outdoor gala now. Tiny lights twinkle around the roofline, moonlight shines on the river, and the guests barely sway on the deck.

We'll take a cup of kindness yet for auld lang syne.

The sentimental music suits the winter solstice as couples cling to one another, embracing on the longest night of the year. But to Frank, the night feels eternal now—with his true love having slipped out of his arms.

As the deck lights dim, and the silvery moonlight falls, many of the guests sing along, teary-eyed beneath twinkling stars.

Should old acquaintance be forgot ...

But Frank hears something else, too. The sound gets him to turn his head and glance down the staircase. Off in the distance, the *put-put-put-put* of Gus' snowtorcycle starts up.

And Frank knows just who is sitting in the sidecar, being escorted in her velvet gown back to Cardinal Cabin. He stands there, watching the bride and groom dance; watching Greg with one of the silver-dressed bridesmaids. There's Derek and Vera;

Jane's sister, Chloe, and her husband, Bob Hough; George Carbone and Amy; and even Wes' old man, Pete, swaying with Jane's mom, Lillian.

As the couples dance near him, love taunts Frank once again this night, all while that snowtorcycle sputters off. He tips his head, listening to the snorting engine and picturing the vehicle's route along the narrow one-lane road toward the little cabins, then over the winding wooded trail and alongside Snowflake Lake to Cardinal Cabin. Penny will clutch her shawl close as Gus helps her out, and she'll walk through the snow to her front porch. There, well there she might take that warm red-and-blue tartan throw off the table and sit on one of the white rocking chairs. With the wool throw over her lap, she'll look out at Snowflake Lake glistening beneath that December moon. Occasionally, she'll lift a corner of the blanket and dab at her eyes.

When the sputtering snowtorcycle engine fades and Frank can't hear it anymore, he walks inside to the banquet room, looking once over his shoulder before closing the door behind him.

twenty-six

Penny NEVER THOUGHT IT WOULD happen. But it has.

Just when her days at Cardinal Cabin were unexpectedly chock-full of happiness and laughter and bird antics and spontaneity and, well, and love—giving her photo ops at every turn—everything's changed. No more cheery toboggan rides through the powdery snow. No stolen snowshoe kisses on the rickety footbridge over the stream. No evocative record-player scenes, no wood-chopping candids.

Nothing.

Frank made that clear last night.

So by Sunday morning, Penny Hart has nothing left to photograph for a Suitcase Escapes mystery clue. After a long walk spent turning over every snowy stone here, she returns to her cabin, pulls off her cap and mittens, hangs her parka on the antler coatrack and makes a cup of hot coffee.

"Oh, who am I kidding?" she whispers when she sits at the dining table with her coffee cup. It's not the lack of photo ops getting to her. More than anything, she's frustrated that her explanation to Frank was interrupted by a swarm of festive dancers. Festive dancers who might look twice, watch her over their shoulders, recognize her and put an end to Suitcase Escapes' mystery contest. Just as she was about to tell Frank that her happiness on the phone that day was for her *mother*, not her boss, those wedding dancers spilled out onto the deck like a snowy avalanche—coming closer and closer, spinning and twirling right into them.

Now, she sees, her words wouldn't have made a difference. Frank's mind was made up, and his heart closed off, as their two-week affair led nowhere.

But they had plans, she and Frank. Penny knows that right now he's at Whole Latte Life for Wes and Jane's post-wedding café breakfast. Afterward—since Wes' brother, Greg, is on call at the hospital—Frank is driving the newlyweds to the airport for their honeymoon. Penny and Frank had thought that maybe she could've safely tagged along on the airport drive. That they'd all have a coffee as Frank and Penny revealed her whereabouts—and their *couple* status—to Wes and Jane.

But it's true—her life is the evidence. All good things *do* come to an end.

Because Frank will make the airport run alone, then hurry back to the boathouse for the Fire Department Christmas Party—better known as Addison's Ugly Sweater Contest. He'd told her it's a good time, the way the guests find the most outrageous Christmas sweaters and strut their stuff in them. His sister even brought in a temporary modeling-runway for the event.

So Frank will have not one minute to talk to her, not with that crazy schedule. And here it is, a few days before Christmas. That's why panic is setting in: Penny's true love is flitting away like one of the pretty red cardinals flitting among the snow-laced tree branches.

Which gives her an idea. She pulls on her earmuffs and duck boots, grabs her cell phone and ventures no further than her own backyard. The cardinals, bright and red like feathered ornaments, hop from the tree branches to the bird feeder to the snow beneath it, fluttering past in red flashes.

So she takes a few snowy pictures of the birds, though with the way they're twittering and swooping today, the pictures come out a little blurry, looking almost uncertain.

Just like her life.

Which is when she knows. A cardinal photo will be her very final clue. It'll almost, but not quite, reveal her holiday hideaway at Cardinal Cabin—with just the right caption.

༚

Frank knew it. He knew it all along. The thought was always there, niggling at him, somehow. And now, at the end of another day, he knows it's true. His instincts were right.

There is no escaping the lonely hour.

He'd thought they were gone, but they're not.

It's his destination. Right here.

Sitting alone at his kitchen island.

One lonely plate is set on the placemat. And one lonely fork on a solitary napkin, folded neatly in half.

He cuffs his flannel shirtsleeves, then unwraps a thick slice of leftover wedding cake and drops it on the dish. The house is dark. His grand English Tudor, with its arched doorways and soaring peaks and multi-paned windows, is in shadow tonight because he's had enough of twinkling lights, holiday cheer. Especially after standing, arms-crossed, at the side wall of the boathouse banquet room that afternoon. For hours, he watched an endless parade of gaudy sweaters being modeled: 3-D reindeer on some; silver-foil garland strung across fluorescent-green hand-knit vests; actual working Christmas bulbs blinking on red-and-white striped cable-knits. Enduring all the festive fun at the Fire Department Christmas Party, yes, he's had enough.

Enough reminders of the fun *he'd* had just days ago. Merry mayhem on the trolley, and Christmas cuddling at Cardinal Cabin, spending any spare time with his Penny-who-fell-in-the-snow.

His snowy sweetheart.

And now it's done. Reason enough to leave off the wreath lights on his front door. To forgo the twinkling lights on the mantel. To ignore the dark lights on the Christmas tree. Only one solitary lamp shines in the living room, and above the kitchen island where he sits, the pendant lights are dimmed.

Behind him, from the other room, comes a hissing, scratchy sound, over and over again. The record-player needle spins on vinyl—some bluesy album long done. Sitting on a stool in the kitchen, Frank glances over his shoulder at it, then turns to his food. He forks a hunk of frosted wedding cake and stuffs it in his mouth.

He had a taste of the good life … just a taste … but that's gone now. As he chews, he slides his cell phone closer and checks it. No messages, no Penny. Nothing. There's only that hiss of the finished remorseful record, still spinning on the turntable in the living room behind him.

After pressing his fork into the last of the cake crumbs, Frank starts to get up to lift the needle off the spinning album. Halfway to standing, he sits again, instead, and throws another glance over his shoulder at the dimly lit living room.

"Eh. What's it all for, anyway?" he asks.

twenty-seven

THERE'S NO MISTAKING WHEN SOMETHING'S on Frank Lombardo's mind: that's when he can't get himself off the treadmill. Which is precisely where he finds himself Monday morning—in his spare-bedroom-turned-workout-room. Both windows are wide open to let in the cold December air, which is the closest he can get to being outside. But the sidewalks are too slippery with snow cover. So wearing his gray track pants and black thermal top, he clocks an extra mile inside, his sneakered feet pounding the treadmill's running deck.

If he *were* running outdoors, his view would be of decorated saltbox colonials and Cape Cods and historic Federals. On this day before Christmas Eve, swags of garland would be draped across picket fences and over door pediments; candles lit in paned windows; lampposts capped in fluffy snow.

Instead his view is of memories. Every last moment he spent with Penny races through his thoughts, from when he replaced her window on Thursday, to their secret winter waltz Saturday night. If he could just pinpoint when things changed between them—and why she agreed to leave town for a year of secret getaway promotions. With each footfall on the treadmill, Frank remembers walking into Cardinal Cabin as Penny wrapped up that conversation with her boss. Her face was glowing with anticipation as she chatted on the phone.

Spending a few minutes slowing his pace and cooling down now, Frank holds the treadmill handgrips and closes his eyes. And there she is, in his memory again. Penny on the boathouse's observation deck at Wes and Jane's reception, with only the moon casting its light on her. He's sure she wanted to justify her work decision ... to explain away any hurt feelings. But she never had a chance, not with the way the wedding guests spilled outside for a winter dance and almost blew her cover.

So that's it. Another holiday season has come and gone, leaving nothing but fleeting memories.

After a shower and breakfast, Frank heads to the boathouse and goes straight to the empty banquet room. Rays of sunlight shining through the wall of windows catch tiny dust particles swirling in the air, evoking distant echoes of music and happy voices in the large room. Now, the boathouse will be empty until a New Year's Eve shindig that will surely be rocking the rafters.

And he's glad for the break. For having some quiet time to catch up on adjusting the boat-rack reservation requests. For closing out the books. For starting the New Year with a clean slate.

For being able to spend a few days at home, not here—where one glance out to the observation deck brings his own visions and echoes, of dancing with Penny beneath the moonlight Saturday. Of seeing her in that green velvet dress. Of holding her in his arms, touching her hair, her face.

After some lingering chores now, he'll be out of here. Gone, to let all the dust settle.

CARDINAL CABIN

The banquet room's round tables have been moved along-side the walls, so he lifts a few straggling chairs and flips them upside down on the tabletops. Then he grabs the push broom and sweeps the dark hardwood floor. He stops only to move the life-size carved deer still here from Wes' reception. Carefully, he slides them out of the way until Wes' father has a chance to pick them up.

Then he gets to his sweeping again. All the while, Frank keeps his back to the windows facing the outside deck. There is only the sound of his broom, rhythmically swishing over the floor. It's a lonely sound, sweeping, perfectly suited to how he's been feeling since Saturday night. Each swish of the broom is like a hand on the clock, ticking away the silent minutes of his solitary life.

So he moves across the floor, swishing and sweeping dust and crumbs and scraps, lulled by the soft brush of the broom-bristles.

Until another noise enters the room. It's quiet at first, a hum of some sorts. But as that hum grows louder, he can decipher the sound of voices. Must be Gina on her cell phone, chatting it up before Christmas, wishing someone happy greetings. So he keeps sweeping, moving away from the doorway, where it's quieter.

Except that it's not. It doesn't matter where he sweeps in the empty room. Because suddenly there's a ruckus outside of it. Lots of knocking starts up, sharp raps on the door, followed by rising voices. So Frank hurries over and opens that door to see a crowd of people dressed in their coats and hats. They surge into the banquet room, some with hands on their hips, some shaking a finger at him, all with a twinkle in their eyes or a grin on their faces.

Leading the pack is his sister, Gina.

Once Frank backs up into the room enough for everyone to crowd around him, Gina steps closer, raises her open hand over her head and pauses until the crowd goes silent.

"Where is she?" Gina demands.

"What?" Frank shifts his broom from one hand to the other.

"Where are you hiding her?" a few voices call out behind Gina.

There's a flirtatious accusation in their tones, keeping Frank on guard as he drags a hand through his hair. "What are you talking about?" he asks.

A woman's voice yells from the rear, "The picture of you and Penny Hart at Suitcase Escapes! I mean, Frank ... *ooh la la.*"

"So your secret girlfriend *does* exist," Gina tells him with a wink. "I *knew* it."

Frank looks at them all, wondering how in the world they've seen a picture of him and Penny. He meets the gaze of every single waiting face gathered in the banquet room before leaning his push broom against the wall. There's only one way to get to the bottom of this, because from the looks of this swooning crowd, engaging with them will only cause starry-eyed chaos. So he lifts his hat and jacket off one of the tables, puts them on while walking, and keeps walking—straight out of the boathouse. After being in the dimmed lighting of the banquet room for the past hour, he squints in the bright sunshine outside.

But still, he continues on. With a glance over his shoulder, he sees he's also being followed. Every single person who stormed the Addison Boathouse minutes ago is now pulling up the rear. Their boots and shoes march along, and occasionally a voice declares that they want answers. But Frank keeps walking, steady, straight down Riverside Drive before turning onto Main Street.

Oh, he knows his destination, and apparently Gina and the crowd behind him do, too. He can tell by a new noise he hears. It's quiet at first, but the voices grow louder. He slightly turns his head to hear it better. Someone starts jingling a sleigh bell as they march in step, chanting. Random voices throw in *Oh, yeahs* and *Hey, heys*, keeping a steady beat to the verse. And so a spontaneous, merry march commences.

Ho, ho, ho!
Off to Suitcase Escapes we go!

❧

Penny paces the wood floor at Cardinal Cabin. Back and forth, around the living room, across to the dining area, to the front door, then starting over again. The whole time, she fidgets with a scarf looped around her neck because she's still uncertain about her final photo-clue. A blurry cardinal shot doesn't give that *grand finale* vibe.

But no matter how hard she scrutinizes the cabin—from the stone fireplace and garland-adorned mantel, to the blanket-strewn sofa and decorative berry wreaths, to the sprigs of Scotch pine hanging from the paneled walls near the antler-shaped coatrack—she's got nothing else.

So blurry cardinals it is. Penny picks up her phone from the kitchen counter and flicks through bird images on the screen. Finally she settles on one of a solitary cardinal, mid-flight between snowy boughs of pine. It'll do, as long as she absolutely nails the clue. Slowly, she types it into her phone to email to Ross at Suitcase Escapes:

My final clue?
Cardinals are always within view.
And from me to you?
I may be, too.

She hits Send, and so her mystery journey nears its end. With only one more day here, all that's left to do now is begin packing up to go home.

Which she'll get to after she answers her suddenly ringing cell phone.

"Ross?"

"Yes, Penny. Ross your boss. Want to remind you to call meteorologist Leo Sterling at the station to let him know your precise location. He's making the big announcement on his weather forecast tomorrow morning, Christmas Eve! Folks are hanging onto every clue you send, right to this minute. You should see it here."

"Hanging onto the *cardinal* picture?" Penny walks to the kitchen window and looks out at the few red cardinals at the bird feeder.

"What? I'm not using *that* one. No way, Penny."

"Why not?"

"We're going with the photo you sent us yesterday."

"Yesterday?" Penny looks quickly at her cell phone, knowing darn well she sent nothing the day before. "I'm sure I didn't send one yesterday."

"Of course you did, you sly fox. And it's over the top! Sensational! Perfect caption, too, by the way. *One little kiss ... In a place you can't miss ... If only Connecticut you don't dismiss!* People are gobbling it up like a Christmas cookie."

"Heavens to the holiday! I wrote that? And what *picture* are you ever talking about?"

"Penny, you've got to see this to believe it. The crowds are practically breaking through the window. Tell you what. I'll brave the mobs and take a picture from outside, of the whole scene, then send it to you."

"But Ross, really, I didn't—"

She's too late. He's clicked off. So Penny sits on the couch in front of the fireplace and waits. Ross is always good for his word.

And quick, too. Minutes later, her phone dings with his text message and photograph. Penny squints at the image. Ross apparently stood behind a crowd gathered outside Suitcase Escapes. The people push together, their hats and beanies tipped up as they study the latest blown-up photo-clue hung in the travel agency's window.

So Penny looks at it, too. Then blinks rapidly and looks again. And taps her phone screen to enlarge the incriminating photo. There's no mistaking what she sees.

It makes her eyes tear up as she drops the phone in her lap and whispers, "Oh my gosh ... *Gus!*"

⁖

Frank never lets up his pace. He's getting to the bottom of whatever photo-clue got these folks all worked up. The merry march continues as he walks along Main Street, approaching Whole Latte Life with its snow-frosted café windows, and Wedding Wishes with its fur-cape-draped bridal mannequins gazing out at the Christmas commotion. He passes last-minute shoppers carrying gift-laden bags, but he stays on course, straight to Suitcase Escapes. His booted feet clomp along the snowy cobblestone sidewalk, and oddly, people smile and wave as he passes them. With a twinkle in their eye, a few even waggle a finger at him.

Finally, the travel agency is within view, and another crowd is gathered at its window. A window becoming more clear with each slowing step Frank takes. Slowing for one reason only—disbelief! Gosh darn it, it's enough to make him hike up his jacket collar and try to conceal *his* identity.

Because in Suitcase Escapes' front window, there it is: an enlarged, poster-sized photograph of a couple *very* much in love. They're dressed in fine clothes: she in a fitted black dress, he in a black vest and tie over a button-down shirt and dark, cuffed jeans. Every detail is enlarged and clear for all to see as the absolutely *smitten* couple kisses beneath a sprig of mistletoe in Gus Haynes' Blue Jay Bungalow the night of one recent turkey dinner.

The couple, well, they're actually lip-locked, *and* smiling, as Frank—yes, it's him; there's no mistaking that—mid-kiss, slightly dips a slightly breathless ... Penny Hart.

It had to be Gus who did this. Old gruff Gus, a softie at heart.

And no matter what he hears behind him as he takes in this frolicking photo, Frank can't move. But the questions, once they start, don't stop as folks slap his back, shake his hand, grab his cap and muss his hair while tossing every question his way:

Where is she? Hidden in your Tudor?
Are you in love?
Will there be a Christmas wedding?

Will you propose?
Ring shopping?
Give us a clue, Frankie boy. Any hint at all!
Where is she? Where is she! Where is she!!

The voices grow rowdy enough to get someone's attention inside the travel agency. Frank spots who he thinks must be Ross looking through the window. The man rushes to the entrance door, grabs Frank and squeezes him inside, certain to promptly lock the door behind them.

So Frank blows out a long breath he'd obviously been holding, and gives a glance out to the crowds from this vantage point. Then he sees the overstuffed ballot box filled with guesses as to where Penny is staying.

And the travel agency's phones, they don't stop ringing.

In the far corner of the office, floor-to-ceiling shelves are spilling with donated toys, wrapped and ready for delivery.

But it's those phones, still ringing, that have him shake his head.

"Frank!" Chloe exclaims when she hangs up from a call. "You *rascal!*" She folds her arms on her desk and leans closer with a wink. "We knew there was a love story in those pictures. It's with you! And close to home, apparently."

"Well, Chloe." He looks back at the poster-sized clue hanging in the window. "It's just that, I'm not ... Things kind of ..." He drags a hand along his jaw right as Ross takes his arm and pulls him along into his office, closing that door behind them, too.

Frank does the only thing he can, then. Perspiring now, he drops into a chair.

"You all right?" Ross asks. "Need a glass of water?"

"No, I'm good. Just surprised. I mean, are you *kidding* me? All that clamor," he says, motioning to the outside office, "in response to a travel agent's mystery trip?"

"Folks are responding to more than *that*, as evidenced by Penny's latest clue. Maybe a little love is in the air, too?" Squinting at Frank, Ross sits behind his desk and wheels his chair back. "Could it be *you're* the reason Miss Hart turned down our offer to be a full-time traveling travel agent?"

Frank leans forward and eyes Ross. "What?"

Ross picks up a few loose papers and drops them on his messy desk. "Turned down, with a flat-out no. Penny says it was the magic of your love story that had the whole town in the palm of our mittens, anyway."

Frank looks from Ross, to the door behind him where phones continue to ring on the other side, back to Ross still watching him.

"Declined my yearlong travel offer, and in *no* uncertain terms, too," Ross assures him then, his head tipped, his eyes sparkling.

"Wait just a minute. Back it up here." Frank takes in Ross' words for a long second, before asking, "She said *no*?"

twenty-eight

IF EVER FRANK'S FELT PANIC, it's now.

And there's only one person who'll have any answers—the same person who wants nothing more than to see Frank and Penny together.

The very same person who secretly sent Suitcase Escapes a *very* revealing photograph.

So when Frank gets back to the boathouse later that morning, a quick phone call to Gus Haynes sets him straight—and leaves Frank feeling like a heel.

"But I heard her on the phone, Gus. Penny was happy to travel the country. Thrilled—"

"That her *parents* were coming for Christmas," Gus interrupts.

"*What?* What are you talking about? Her parents?"

"You walked in on her talking to her mother, Frank."

"No, I was there when her boss called."

"Trust me on this one, son. Her parents are arriving ... on Christmas Day. It's a long story, and one you have *no* time to hear right now. Think there's another pressing matter on your hands?"

So Frank does it. He hangs up and hits every store in town looking for a Christmas gift. He drives the bustling roads, and pulls into parking spaces, and opens shop doors with a new worry. It's the day before Christmas Eve, and the shelves will surely be picked over. What if he can't find that one simple gift that might patch things with Penny?

Finally, there's nowhere left to turn; his worry played out. After scouring every shop in Addison and finding nothing, he's out of options. All he wanted was a gift to win back Penny's heart. So it's with his own heavy heart that he heads home, driving past the town green on his way to the covered bridge leading to Old Willow Road.

Right before the bridge, he passes Circa 1765 Antique Shop and looks over his shoulder as he does. There are cars parked there, so it's still open for holiday shopping. With nothing to lose, he pulls a quick U-turn and finds a parking spot near the door. Lace curtains hang in windows framed by twinkling white lights, and seeing shoppers milling on the other side of those windows, Frank decides to give it a go, too.

Inside the two-room shop, mahogany, oak and cherry antiques are displayed on a large gold-and-burgundy Oriental rug. Old painted mirrors hang on one wall, and near the checkout counter, a white snake-foot candlestand displays a framed dried-and-pressed daisy chain.

"Can I help you?" the woman at the register asks him. She's in her early forties, and a teenaged girl stands beside her, gift-wrapping purchases.

"You're my last stop," Frank says as he pulls off his wool cap. "I've been everywhere. Snowflakes and Coffee Cakes, the bookstore, the shops at Sycamore Square. I need a gift, a very special gift."

"Oh. Anything particular in mind?" the woman asks.

Frank eyes a collection of brass candlesticks atop a cherry hutch, then shakes his head. "I'm hoping I'll know when I see it."

"Well, you have a look around. My daughter and I are wrapping these last few purchases, which are going out for a final holiday delivery in my van, later today." She motions to a pile of wrapped gifts stacked on a table behind the register. "You've got ten minutes, if you'd like to include yours."

Wasting no time, Frank walks further into the store, passing other men last-minute gift-shopping for wives and girlfriends. No doubt, they're thinking they can't go wrong with something vintage or nostalgic here. And the shop is beautiful; all the brass glows, and the woods are polished to deep, liquid hues. He glances at a pair of oil paintings depicting racehorses and keeps walking. Off to the side, hanging from a slender mannequin, is an antique wedding gown with its lace train splayed over the golden oak floor. Beside that is a blue velvet settee.

None of which will work for Penny. His gift has to be something small. So as Frank passes old end tables, he picks up a trinket jar, a lamp, then sets them down. After roaming the aisles and feeling more dejected with each china plate he examines, with each ceramic pitcher he lifts, with each turn he makes, he heads out. But right before opening the door, something in the window display catches his eye. It's set in a tuft of cottony snow, within a classic snow-village exhibit. A few mantel clocks tick on a raised shelf behind it all.

Frank steps closer, feeling cautiously optimistic. Afraid to take his eyes off the potential gift—in case someone else snags it—he asks over his shoulder, "Is it too late to wrap this?" He picks it up and shows it to the woman at the register.

"It's for Penny, isn't it?" she asks while gently taking the item from his hands.

"What?"

"I recognized you when you walked in. From the photograph at Suitcase Escapes. You're Frank, aren't you?"

Frank raises and drops his hands in surrender. "That I am."

"Pleased to meet you, Frank. I'm Sara Beth," the woman says, reaching out to shake his hand. "Sara Beth Riley. You know that you're a local celebrity in these parts, don't you?"

"It's pretty surprising, actually. I had no idea, until today. And," he says with a nod to his gift, "did I ever mess things up with someone special."

Sara Beth admires the gift he chose, holding it up to the sunlight shining in through the lace curtains behind her. "This is the *perfect* gift to fix that, I'm sure." She drops her voice to a whisper, saying, "Especially for someone named *Penny*."

"You think so?" Frank steps closer, eyeing his spur-of-the-moment gift. "Really?"

"Here." Sara Beth slides him a blank holiday notecard. "You fill that out while I wrap. And don't worry," she says very quietly as she leans close, "all addresses are kept *strictly* confidential. Her whereabouts will not be revealed."

Frank looks at her for a moment, uncertain, until she gives him a pen and shoos him away, off to the side. There's something about this Sara Beth that he trusts. She's got a soul that understands love; it shows in her mannerisms, her voice. So he grabs up the card and heads to a nearby window ledge. Now's his chance to send a truly heartfelt message to Penny. To fix things. To hopefully get back his Penny-who-fell-in-the-snow. So he sets the card on the ledge and starts writing, then stops and looks over at Sara Beth with an idea.

"Something wrong?" she asks, mid-wrap, a wide red ribbon in her hand.

Frank pulls some change out of his pocket and slides a shiny copper penny across the countertop. "Can you slip this in with it, too?"

◌◌

She'd put it off as long as possible, but now? Now Penny does it. She begins packing her clothes into her few pieces of luggage. Because let's face it, after Leo Sterling announces Cardinal Cabin as her mystery location tomorrow, there'll be no more clues to write, no photos to take. Really, there's no reason for her to stay on here.

She'd hoped for one—that one reason being a handsome lumberjack who stole her heart. A lumberjack who might spend Christmas here, with her.

And that one little hope stayed nestled in her heart, but faded with each passing hour since her weekend dance with him. There's been no word from Frank. Not a phone call, not a text message. Even with that swoon-worthy photograph posted at Suitcase Escapes … nothing. Maybe he hasn't even seen it, or maybe he just doesn't care. What they had was merely a snowy affair.

Having no compelling reason to stay in this quaint cabin now, no hope for a lakeside Christmas with her one true love, Penny instead opens her suitcase on her bed. The sooner she gets back to her little apartment in the refurbished mill factory, the sooner she can resume her old life. With a sigh, she turns to her dresser and lifts out the few sweaters she'd brought along, then drops them in the suitcase.

As she does, there's an unexpected *rat-a-tat-tat-tat* at the door.

For a second, Penny freezes. It's *got* to be Frank, and so she takes a deep breath, puts her hand to her heart, and goes to find out. But when she swings the door open, there's a stranger standing there with a wrapped package in his arms and a young boy at his side. Behind them, clouds have moved in and snow has begun lightly falling, the flakes tumbling from a pale gray sky.

"Penny Hart?" the man asks.

"Yes … But how would you—"

"I'm Tom Riley. Delivery from Circa 1765." He holds up the package for her to see. "The antique shop in town?"

"Oh, yes! Of course." She smiles at the little boy peering around her into the cabin. "But I didn't order anything," she tells Tom, crossing her arms in front of her as a gust of swirling snowflakes blows in.

"No, someone else did. It's a gift, delivered to your door in time for Christmas."

"A gift?" Penny takes the package, wondering what it could possibly be, especially since so few people know she's here. Did Gus send her something for the holiday? Concerned, though, she looks past Tom to see if he'd been followed coming here. "You didn't tell anyone my whereabouts?"

"No worries, Penny. Your secret's safe," Tom assures her. "All Circa 1765 deliveries are confidential," he says with a nod.

"Thanks so much, you don't know what a relief that is!" She gives the boy a quick smile, then looks back at Tom. "Please. If you could just wait a second?"

When he agrees, she hurries inside, sets down the wrapped gift and grabs a cookie tin. Opening it on the way to the doorway, she bends low to the curious boy who looks to be about five years old.

"What's your name, little fella?" she asks.

"Owen." As he says it, Owen gets suddenly shy and looks downward while leaning into his father's leg.

"Owen," Tom says. "He's my son *and* my Christmas helper."

"Oh! Like one of Santa's elves!" Penny exclaims.

"My wife, Sara Beth, owns the antique shop." Tom sets a hand on Owen's shoulder. "We're helping out today and making the final holiday rounds."

"Just like Santa Claus. Owen, would you like a Christmas cookie? Maybe one with sprinkles on it?" She holds out the tin and he reaches in his small hand. "Pick one for your dad, too."

"Thanks, Penny," Tom tells her when Owen hands him a peanut butter cookie. "You have a merry Christmas now. We'll be tuning in to the TV tomorrow," he adds with a wink. "For Leo's Christmas Eve forecast."

Penny waves and watches the father-son team walk off in the snow, then closes the door. She eyes her wrapped gift on the dining table. Squints at it, actually, as though she might see right through that wrapping paper to what's beneath it. She brings the gift to the kitchen and sets it on the window ledge, where the cardinal had entered just days ago.

"Okay," she says. "Enough wondering."

Her fingers quickly lift off the gift card, and she pulls the note from the envelope. There's only one name she wants to see there, so her eyes drop to the only words that matter ... on the very bottom of the note ... *Love, Frank.*

"Thank goodness!" Penny says, all while ripping the wrapping paper off a gift box and pulling out a ceramic village piece.

It's a snow-laden cabin remarkably similar to Cardinal Cabin, right down to a berry wreath hanging on its front door. The ceramic cabin looks like it belongs in a snow village that could be right on Snowflake Lake, except ... She turns it over and runs her hand over the cabin's back edge.

"Why, it's a coin bank!"

Penny, smiling the whole time, gives the cabin a little shake and hears a coin rattle inside. So she opens the back of the bank and finds one single penny.

"Oh, Frank," she whispers, wiping a tear from her face as she picks up the unread note.

One quick glance at his message has her put off packing her clothes. Suddenly, she feels more like decorating, instead. Because now Penny has hope once more ... and an idea. If it doesn't work, at the very least she'll have her parents here for Christmas Day. They'll enjoy a holiday dinner at Snowflake Lake—sad as it might be, without Frank at the table. *If* her idea fails.

In the meantime, after reading Frank's heartfelt note, oh yes ... decorating is definitely in order! She'll hang red glass ornaments on the birch branches in the floor vase. Then she'll fill a basket with large pinecones and sprigs of holly berries that she found on her woodland walks. Afterward, yes, she'll get the old tin lantern from the kitchen window ledge and put a large pillar candle inside it, then set it on the hearth.

But first, she has to get to Gus Haynes.

෴

Wasting no time, Penny throws on her duck boots and parka and rushes straight across the yards toward Blue Jay Bungalow.

Gus is the only person who can help her pull this all off. Her boots crunch on the snow; her breath is misty in the cold.

And her heart? After reading Frank's note, it's so light now, she feels like she's floating. Climbing Gus's porch steps, she quickly knocks on the door.

"Penny?" Gus asks when he sees her there.

"I'm so glad I caught you, Gus!" She can't stop herself then. Her words spill out. "Is there any way I can extend my stay at Cardinal Cabin, through the holidays?"

"Really?" Gus steps back and squints at her. "Have you heard from Frank?"

Penny only nods. But she feels it, the way her eyes sparkle at the same time. And oh, Gus doesn't miss that twinkle. She knows by his next question.

"So Frank will be spending Christmas here with you?"

"I don't know ... yet," she whispers back. "But I *do* know you snuck my boss a certain revealing photograph yesterday." When Gus only raises a bushy white eyebrow at her, she waggles a finger at him. "Don't deny it, Mr. Haynes—apparently also our lakeside love liaison."

"Now, Penny. I was just—"

"I know exactly what you were doing," Penny says, her smile genuine. "And now I'm wondering if you can help me out, one more time?"

Gus steps back and eyes her closely. "Anything for you two," he finally says. "You're like the cardinals around here that my Betty loved so much. And it's just not right that you're apart." He opens the door wider and motions Penny inside the cabin. "Come on, we'll hash things out over a hot cocoa."

And do they ever. While stirring marshmallows into their mugs that afternoon, and while sipping the sweet treat, the two of them plot and plan at Gus' dining room table; they telephone contacts and make bargains with friends; they cross their fingers and finally do the only thing left: hope for the best.

∽

Once Penny is back in Cardinal Cabin that evening, she takes Frank's notecard to the sofa and sits there in front of the fireplace. Outside her window, the community Christmas tree sparkles behind snowflakes falling gently from the night sky. All Penny can do now is wait for tomorrow, Christmas Eve day, when all the pieces she and Gus planned will fall into place.

For now, in the soft quiet of Cardinal Cabin, her eyes relish every single word Frank had penned, just for her. With a flutter of anticipation, she rereads his note:

Dear Penny,

I'm so sorry I misread everything and caused you any sadness. I hope you will accept this Christmas gift with my apology. If so …

A penny for your thoughts?

I dropped a shiny penny into this snowy cabin bank. In return, if you can find it in your heart to somehow, in some small way, give me your thoughts on my one humble question …

Christmas together at Cardinal Cabin?

Love, Frank

twenty-nine

IT'S NOT LIKE FRANK TO put things off until the very last minute. But with all the distractions he's been dealing with lately—it's happened. While clocking in a couple miles on the treadmill Tuesday morning, he realizes he hasn't wrapped his Christmas gifts yet. And it's Christmas Eve day!

So stepping off the treadmill, he starts the morning in his Tudor. Doesn't shave, though—just showers, eats breakfast, cuffs his flannel shirtsleeves and gets to it. To set the mood, okay, he turns on his Christmas tree lights in the living room.

"But that's it," he says with a glance over his shoulder as he walks away.

Then he brings all his shopping bags into the kitchen, where he parks himself close to the percolating coffeepot. This is a three-cup session, at least. The kitchen table is covered with rolls and scraps of giftwrap. There are Santas and snowmen. Plaids and stripes. Candy canes and Christmas trees. He's got gifts for Gina and Josh, for his parents and little Dante. This goes in one box, that in another. Scissors and tape are lost in the merry mess.

Well, it would be merry. If only …

Because he's not only wrapping presents. He's also waiting.

Waiting to hear from Penny. More than wrapping, he's checking his phone for an email, or for a text message saying she got his gift. He goes to the living room window and looks out to see if the mail truck is rolling on by, the mailman delivering an envelope holding a secret greeting from Snowflake Lake.

In fact, Frank even listens, closely, for the sound of Gus' snowtorcycle—in case Gus might deliver Penny, personally. Because let's face it, after Gus sent Suitcase Escapes that photograph of Frank and Penny entangled in a kiss, who knows what else he might do? All Frank *does* know is that gruff Gus turns into a Christmas Cupid at the holidays.

So on his third trip to the living room window, Frank stands there beside the twinkling tree, listening. Something's off, though, outside. He sips from his steaming coffee mug and notices it. The street is very quiet, which is not typical for Old Willow Road, especially the day before Christmas when everybody's busy with preparations and errands galore. But this morning there are no people. No cars. So everyone must be at home, inside.

Of course. There's only *one* thing that would accomplish that feat: Leo Sterling's Christmas forecast—which today includes Penny Hart's long-awaited location reveal.

So Frank trots back to the kitchen and turns on the countertop TV, hoping he hasn't missed the segment. The screen flickers for a few seconds when the television comes on, and he figures the cable system is overloaded with Addison customers on this big day, filled with big announcements.

After finding the right channel, Frank sits alone at the table amidst wrapping paper, curls of ribbon, gift tags and presents. There's the plush stuffed choo-choo caboose for Dante; a manicure gift card for Gina so that Frank can have a moment's peace at work; an olive-green corduroy button-down shirt for Gina's husband, Josh.

While he waits, Frank picks up his pen and fills out each gift tag, keeping an ear tuned to the TV. Eventually, Leo Sterling, wearing his infamous snowflake necktie, comes on. So Frank keeps an eye on the screen as he folds a sheet of giftwrap over Josh's shirt box, then tapes the corners.

"Snow, snow, snow?" Leo Sterling asks, giving his necktie a shake. "All I can say is … Yes! And with a merry Ho! Ho! Ho!"

"Come on, come on," Frank whispers, urging the meteorologist through his holiday forecast. He keeps an eye on the TV while tying a ribbon around the wrapped shirt—all as Leo rattles off his wintry predictions pinpointing how much Christmas snow will arrive, practically by the hour. At one point, Frank shakes his open hands at the TV. "Hurry it up already," he mutters.

Finally, it's the moment he's been waiting for.

"To reveal the location of a mysterious Penny Hart," Leo says, introducing the traveling-travel-agent segment, "I'm happy to do my part."

"Okay, now we're talking." Sitting at the table, Frank tucks Gina's manicure gift card into a tiny box, which he quickly wraps and sets aside.

"Where in New England is Miss Hart?" Leo asks, zooming in the national map to highlight the six New England states. "The pine tree state of Maine, I will abstain."

A click of a button, and Leo zooms in closer, eliminating Maine.

"Vermont, the green mountain state?" Click, he zooms in even closer on the weather map. "That is *not* where Penny had her mystery date! Now, New Hampshire? Hmm," Leo muses, zooming the granite state off the map. "Absolutely not, now that I can assure!"

And so he continues while Frank's wrapping slows and his attention focuses purely on the small television screen. Leo eliminates Rhode Island and Massachusetts so that only Connecticut appears on his weather map. The meteorologist teases the thousands of viewers who must be yelling out their guesses as he zooms in on Connecticut now.

Frank can just imagine the nutmeg state locations being tossed at TV screens in living rooms and kitchens across town … Glastonbury, Wethersfield, Old Lyme, Litchfield! Resort hotels, beachy locales and countryside inns.

"Let's look closer now," Leo says, zooming in. "There's Stony Point Beach—not Penny's place, I can tell you each." He zooms it out of the screen. "Here's the capital city of our great state," he says. "But give a wave goodbye to Hartford. Now wait! What's *this* small area? Why … it's our very own town of Addison!"

And Frank is riveted. He's only moments away from seeing Penny on the screen, and so his giftwrapping stopped somewhere between the weather map and New England. Now Dante's soft, blue caboose is hanging loose.

Click, click, and the weather map zooms in on Snowflake Lake.

"All roads do lead home at Christmastime," Leo Sterling explains as an illustrated Santa Claus is waving happily from a tiny animated cabin on the weather map. "And now, a special appearance and the big reveal from Penny Hart, our roaming travel agent … with gratitude for all the guesses and toy donations that have been kindly sent!"

Frank stands. He stands and stops as a live broadcast comes on the screen. He just stops still at the sight of Penny sitting near the roaring fireplace in Cardinal Cabin. Lazy snowflakes fall outside the frosted windowpane beside her.

As the camera comes in closer on Penny, so does Frank— taking a few steps closer to the television set. He bends low and freezes again, squinting at the image. Penny wears a black sweater with a gold knit scarf looped around her neck. Her gold stud earrings glimmer, and her hair is swept to the side.

"Hello, everyone," Penny begins, then clears her throat. "I've been *so* thrilled with your response to my mystery getaway and won't waste any time revealing my secret location."

Frank closely watches every nuance of Penny Hart on the screen: the way her copper hair shimmers; how she fidgets with a thin ring on one of her fingers; her manner of tipping her head while talking. Her smile is slight, he notices, but also hopeful.

"And I'd like to reveal where I am," Penny says, "with one final clue." She motions to the paned window. "Cardinals are always within view … And from me to you?" Another small smile. "I always was, too." She stands then, walks to the front door and opens it to her view of the lake. "Right here in the charming Cardinal Cabin at Addison's own Snowflake Lake!"

Frank moves even closer to the television, setting his hand on top of it as Penny wraps up her announcement and thanks the town for the outpouring of Christmas cheer they brought this time of year. He squints at something he sees behind her as Penny closes the cabin door and walks through the small living room.

"The ballot box at Suitcase Escapes is brimming, the donated toys wrapped and being delivered," she informs her viewers.

Frank bends closer to the screen. Yes, right there, behind Penny. It's on the ledge of the window he replaced! It's the cabin coin bank he bought at Circa 1765. So she did receive it.

"To thank you for taking my travel adventure to … *heart*," she says now, looking directly into the camera and speaking softly, "I have a special invitation."

"Okay," Frank says, still standing and watching the TV set closely. "I'm listening."

Penny pauses, tips her head and slightly smiles once more. "I'm inviting you to Snowflake Lake for the drawing of Suitcase Escapes' very lucky winner—who will win a free weekend stay right here in this quaint cabin."

The camera pans the living room, bringing every beautiful memory back to Frank as he sees the rustic Christmas tree covered in berries and snow-capped pinecones; the tin lantern set on the stone fireplace hearth, where he showed Penny how to tend the logs; the sofa with its hooked pillows and the checked throw that they sat beneath while watching an old holiday movie; the antler coatrack where he hung his jacket.

Twinkling lights are everywhere, casting a glimmer on the cabin's wood walls, the twig wreaths, the dining table with its crystal bowl filled with pinecones and cinnamon sticks—the table where he had his first romantic grilled-cheese dinner … for two.

"Please stop by to visit this afternoon," Penny says. "And to see off Santa Claus! Santa's first official Addison stop is always at Snowflake Lake, where the reindeer get a good running start across the frozen ice," she adds with a twinkle in her eye. "There will be lakeside refreshments, ice-skating, and snowman-building for all!"

As she says it, Frank knows.

He knows with a pit in his stomach, without any holiday hesitation, that Penny and Gus used every trick in the book, and called in every favor owed them to pull off this last-minute holiday event at the lake. The two of them must have huddled closely, plotting and planning over several mugs of cocoa, just to get this done.

Frank watches as the camera zooms in on his Penny-who-fell-in-the-snow. She walks to her kitchen windowsill and touches the cabin bank he gave her, before nearly whispering, "So I hope you'll join me for a very special Christmas Eve, here at Cardinal Cabin."

When she hesitates now, Frank sees it, the way her eyes tear up right as she tucks her hair behind an ear.

"On the banks of a glistening, frosted Snowflake Lake," Penny concludes.

With the scene shifting back to Leo Sterling giving all the details from the studio, Frank shuts off the TV and slowly sinks into his kitchen chair. He glances at the wrapping mess on the table, then at the quiet TV screen. If he could watch Penny's segment again, he would—checking for hints in her smile, her mannerisms. Because he's just not sure.

Was Penny giving an open invitation to the entire town?

Or was her personal Christmas invitation really meant … just for him?

thirty

SNOWMEN OF EVERY SIZE AND shape stand around Snowflake Lake. Short and squat to tall and tottering. There are jumbo-jovials with wide smiles made of coal. Then the saucy ones have top hats tipped just so on their snowy heads. One snowman lies down, his stick-arms making a faux snow-angel. Beside another, there is a snow-dog with a sprig of spruce for a tail, and two smaller sprigs for the pointed ears.

Nearly all of Addison showed up for Penny's Christmas Eve lakeside gathering. The afternoon's been a blur of activity as she took pictures with residents, surprisingly signed autographs for children, and mingled among the merriment. Even after she drew the winning name for a weekend stay at Cardinal Cabin, courtesy of Suitcase Escapes, families lingered.

And she can see why. Wouldn't this sight make a perfect jigsaw puzzle holiday image, all cozy and enchanted? A puzzle that her partner in crime here, Gus, would likely choose for his grandchildren. From where Penny later stands on Cardinal Cabin's front porch, her view is unobstructed straight to the frozen Snowflake Lake. There, picnic tables have been cleared of snow and now hold Christmas cookies, paper plates and cups. A toboggan set atop two stools becomes a makeshift cocoa station.

Townsfolk and families still mill about in the snow. Penny can't miss their colorful coats and puffy parkas, their wool beanies and pom-pom caps. It all looks like a wave of color, undulating as people build more snowmen, cup hot chocolate in their mittened hands, and take snow walks near a portable fire pit for a bit of warmth.

But those snowmen … everywhere! Crystallized at the lake's edge; one cupping a mug at the cocoa station; a frosty couple holding stick-hands, right on the icy lake; one wearing skis on the trail, his snowman body leaning to the side as though he's schussing along.

She looks beyond them, where the community lakeside tree is twinkling as the sky darkens to twilight. On the frozen lake, people ice-skate—bent at the waist, their scarves flying behind them. All around, the other cabins glimmer with candles in the windows and lights strung around doorways. Wren Den, Robin Residence, Chickadee Shanty … each one snug beneath rooftops blanketed in white snow. And now, as though custom-ordered for this special afternoon, more gentle white flakes spin down from the gray sky.

With the afternoon waning, folks are preparing to leave for services at the town's little white chapel with the living nativity set up beside it. Or to begin their holiday dinners with families. Taking the clue that it's time for her closing remarks, Penny steps off her porch and hurries to the temporary platform set up for this event. White lights twinkle around its perimeter.

"Can I have your attention?" she asks into the microphone while motioning the people close. "Gather round!" Turning up the collar of her camel peacoat, she can't miss the familiar faces in the crowd: her boss, Ross; Chloe and her husband, Bob; Sara Beth and Tom Riley from the antique shop, along with their children; Gus and his entire family, eager grandkids included. Everyone huddles in front of the platform as the afternoon turns cold with the sun setting and flurries beginning.

"Before you leave, I want to thank you for coming along on my holiday journey this year. What I've learned about the wonder of traveling is that you can go so far and see so much, all in a simple venture out to your own backyard." Just then, she notices the way Gus listens with a knowing nod. "You see," Penny continues, "the magic of travel isn't always about how far you roam. It's about keeping your curiosity and sense of adventure, even while close to home. Life can then take you in new and surprising directions."

She pauses while rubbing her mittened hands together to stay warm. But more than that, she's scanning the milling people, looking for even a glimpse of Frank Lombardo. Of his lumberjack coat, or his wool beanie over his wavy hair.

"But the *true* beauty and magic here on Snowflake Lake, for me," Penny continues, "was seeing so many cardinals during the Christmas season. Each one looked like a pretty red ornament on the soft, snow-laden pines."

Thinking of snow-laden branches, and the one that broke her window, makes her feel sad, though. If there were only a hint of Frank's red-and-black plaid coat, of Frank himself— looking scruffy with his unshaven face, his dark hair—the memory might make her smile, instead. She scans the crowd once more, with still no sign of him. A smile is not to be hers today.

"Making the birds even more special, folklore has it that cardinals grant wishes," Penny explains. "My neighbor and very dear friend here, Gus Haynes, told me that when you see a cardinal, make a wish. But ... here's the important part. After making the wish, close your eyes. Tight," she orders, raising her mittened hand to her eyes. "If the cardinal is still there when you open your eyes, legend has it your wish *will* come true."

Something happens, then. Penny sees it. More people gather and press close at her speaking platform. They're hushed and watching her intently. Some have a sympathetic smile on their faces, as if they know she *really* needs a special wish of her own granted.

So Penny clears her throat and sets her sights on a cardinal sitting on a distant birch tree branch. "Something like this will do," she says. "Cardinal, cardinal ... To my heart be true ... Bring someone special into my view."

And when Penny squeezes her eyes shut, no one would know that, more than anything else, it's to stop her stinging tears. To prevent them from spilling over onto her cold cheeks as she misses Frank Lombardo being right here with her.

Or maybe they do know. Because when she finally opens her eyes, Penny sees that everyone in the crowd squeezed their eyes shut with her. Some with a smile, some with fingers crossed— making her simple wish a town-wide group wish. Some might have also wished for family members dearly missed. Others for loved ones to join them at their holiday tables. Children, Penny's certain, wished for a view of Santa.

And good golly, Gus will *not* disappoint the children!

Because it's a jingling sound that then gets everyone to open their eyes—looking first from Penny, then to Gus and his grandkids dispensing silver bells on the crowd's outskirts.

"The jolly man is on his way!" Gus calls out as the crowd murmurs with excitement.

"Jingle bells are complimentary, from our favorite local Christmas barn, Snowflakes and Coffee Cakes," Penny announces at the microphone. "Please take a bell to welcome Santa Claus upon his arrival here. Thank you, and I'm wishing you all a very merry Christmas!"

With a wide wave, Penny steps off the temporary stage and walks back to her front porch at Cardinal Cabin. From there, she watches the townsfolk separate into two long, lakeside lines, their hands raised and jingling silver bells. The sound is so magical in the snowy forest as the merry ringing rises to the tree branches.

Moments pass. The happy jingling grows louder beside the lake, jing-a-ling-linging until Santa and Mrs. Claus arrive. They ride along on a horse-drawn sleigh between the two lines of families, neighbors and friends.

Penny gives a friendly wave to Derek Cooper and Vera Sterling, who were game to play the parts of Santa and his wife today. Dressed in white-trimmed, red-velvet costumes, they toss mini candy canes into the crowd while giving a hearty *Ho, ho, ho!* Sleigh bells ring on the trotting horse as it pulls the red sleigh over the snow, the horse prancing its legs high in a merry step. Derek steers the sleigh along a wide path around the snowy lake, then heads toward the footbridge in the woods, where he and Vera eventually disappear into the trails among the trees.

৩৯

All day long, Frank wasn't sure. Not absolutely. Was Penny's invitation that morning meant for the entire town of Addison, which she dearly loves?

Or was it meant for him?

And so he arrived late at Snowflake Lake, remembering what Gus suggested a few days ago when Frank took Penny on a Christmas tour of twinkling Addison: hide beneath the cover of night.

Frank took Gus' words to heart and for the past forty-five minutes, he hid among the snowy pines, in the shadows beside the lake, beneath the cover of dusk.

Hid, and worried. Worried enough that he's feeling too warm in his lumberjack coat.

But hearing Penny's cardinal wish now, given in front of practically the entire town, Frank knows.

Her invitation was meant solely for him.

He'd given her a penny for her thoughts in that cabin bank, and she just now obliged with a private, heartfelt wish to see him. Her words were filled with doubt, and hope. He can tell by the way she closed her beautiful eyes after making the wish. By the way she stood there in her toggled camel peacoat, her copper hair showing beneath her beanie, her mittened fingers squeezed tight.

With the crowd thinning after Santa's departure, Frank is left behind, watching and waiting for the path to clear. As soon as it does, he steps out from the trees, crosses the snowy footbridge and walks on the path toward Cardinal Cabin, heading slowly to the front porch. Slowly, in case he was somehow wrong about Penny's words being meant special for him.

But he's not wrong. It's obvious when Penny spots him and instantly swipes at her eyes. Oh, he totally gets that. Because he's got a tear or two of his own he's struggling with, along with a lump in his throat. She steps down the porch stairs into the snow, walks a little faster, then picks up speed to an easy trot—for only a few seconds—until she's in an all-out run.

Okay, so one thing's for certain—Frank can't mistake her happiness. Her hat falling off behind her, Penny rushes across the snowy trail, straight to him in such a way that he finally laughs, sweeps her off her feet and swings her around and around in the snow. The powdery flakes swirl and spin with them, sparkling and falling from the sky.

So for the third time in so many weeks, Frank Lombardo finds his Penny and picks her up.

And this time, she doesn't let go. Penny embraces him tightly while Frank brushes aside her silky hair and whispers into her ear, "Merry Christmas, Penny." When she pulls away, smiling, they kiss right there in the snow, in clear view of any lingering merrymakers. And he hears it, the applause that breaks out when their kiss is publicly witnessed.

So now Frank kisses Penny's mittened hand, and together they walk toward Cardinal Cabin.

Leaning into him, Penny softly says, "About last week ... I can explain—"

"No need to, Penny. Good ol' Gus filled me in," Frank assures her as he gives her hand a squeeze while they continue on.

The glow of the surrounding cabins' Christmas lights, as well as that of the twinkling community tree, all reflect on the frozen surface of the lake. Big, lazy snowflakes drop from the sky, and smoke curls from the cabins' chimneys.

But after only a few steps, Penny stops.

"What's that?" she asks while tipping her head and turning around toward the distant footbridge. It's lined with people wearing long capes and furry hats and hand muffs. Candlelit lanterns are set along the bridge.

"Carolers," Frank says, turning with her. "Out for a starlight serenade. They visit every nook and cranny in Addison, on every Christmas Eve."

He and Penny stand and listen to the singing voices rising in the dusky, winter night. The sound is soft, spiritual, until the carolers eventually turn and leave along the woodsy trail. They sing as they go, their chorus fading in the evening until all is silent once more. So Frank puts his arm around Penny's shoulders and they walk side by side to her cabin. Their boots crunch in the snow, the pine branches around them rustle in a wintry breeze, and all of Snowflake Lake hushes now.

As they climb the porch steps, a familiar deep voice calls out, "Merry Christmas!" So he and Penny turn and wave to Gus on his own front porch. Frank swears that even from here, he can see the mischievous twinkle in the old man's eyes as he waves back to them, then herds his grandchildren inside to Blue Jay Bungalow. Without a doubt, Frank's sure that old Gus will sneak in one or two mistletoe pecks on the cheek from those kids … before they unwrap their favorite ornaments and hang them on Gus' undecorated Christmas tree.

When Penny then walks toward her front door with its berry wreath and silver milk can filled with fresh pine branchlets, Frank stops her. He takes her arm and gently turns her around, to him.

"Wait," he says. That's it. Just one word. His hands rise to her neck and he cradles her face, brushing his thumb along her jaw, her cheek. "Penny Hart," he whispers then, "you so have my heart." Before giving her a chance to get in a word, he leans close and, still cradling her face, kisses her. Really, he could stay on that porch all evening, kissing and holding her. He gets the feeling she could, too, with the way she stretches up, leans in and kisses him even deeper. Maybe later, they'll sit out on the porch rocking chairs beneath that fringed throw and look out at the illuminated Snowflake Lake.

"I love you, Frank," she murmurs into the kiss. When Penny pulls away, she touches his face lightly before looking to his eyes. "Merry Christmas."

Now she opens the door to Cardinal Cabin. Once inside, Frank hangs his jacket on the antler coatrack, then turns to the living room. Two logs burn and snap in the fireplace, and beside it, lights twinkle on Penny's woodland Christmas tree adorned with pinecones and red berries.

What it all is, Frank thinks, is perfection. Or magic. Or, yes, after picking up his fallen Penny a few weeks ago … maybe it's the pure luck that came into his life.

Penny takes off her coat and mittens, crosses the room, and goes to a record player set up on a small table in the corner. There she sets the needle on the Sinatra album he'd given her. When she turns to him, her hair falls in waves over her gold scarf; her smile fills the room. Soft Christmas carols begin to play, and so Frank pulls off his wool cap and sets it down.

As he walks across the room—seeing the wood walls glowing beneath low lamplight and flickering lantern light, seeing the twig wreaths on those walls, the floor vase filled with white birch branches—he remembers how he wondered what it's all for … the holiday ornaments, the twinkling lights, the garland.

The fuss, the busyness.

So many times during the past few weeks, he'd still ask himself that question: *What's it all for?*

Penny walks to the dining table then. A table set with fresh-cut fragrant greens, and candles, and vintage plates, and crystal goblets. Candlelight flickers on the silver and glasses set around two—yes, *two*—gently tended, carefully arranged place settings.

Two plates, two silverware settings on two linen napkins.

And Frank knows, somehow, that the lonely hour was never his alone.

He takes another step into the room, and his eyes tear up when Penny pulls out a chair ... then motions for him to sit, with her, at the table.

Outside Cardinal Cabin's windows, snow falls heavier, but silently. Inside, sprigs of pine hang on the wood-planked walls. Burning logs snap in the fireplace. Mason jars etched with delicate cardinal motifs sit on end tables. The aroma of cooking food fills the air.

And in the low light, assorted candles glimmer on the table beside their dishes.

What's it all for?

The answer's been in front of him all along.

With a smile and shake of his head, he knows now.

What's it all for? he thinks again.

Frank sits in the chair across from the sweet Penny he loves. This. Simply this.

KEEP READING FOR A SPECIAL EXCERPT FROM

SNOW DEER AND COCOA CHEER

Another wintry novel from

New York Times bestselling author

JOANNE DEMAIO

Wes and Jane's snowy love story begins . . .

An Excerpt from
Joanne DeMaio's

SNOW DEER
AND
COCOA CHEER

Chapter One

FRESH SNOWFALL GLISTENS ON THE old maple tree beside the red barn. A soft layer of it clings to the tree's outstretched branches reaching skyward. Someone once told Jane March there's something special about New England snow; it's different from other snow. So she looks closely at the painted planks of the barn walls, at the snowcapped roof and pale gray clouds above. It's true; there's no denying it. Maybe it's the hush of it all, or the gentleness to those twirling, spinning snowflakes that seem to waltz in a wintry breeze. As they fall in front of the red barn, it becomes perfectly clear. A simple balsam wreath hung over the barn doors would do it, would say Christmas in that quintessential style that stirs the heart.

She sits back for a moment before touching her brush bristles into the green paint and adding a wreath shape onto the barn wall. Overlaying a drop of water gives the delicate pine needles a slight sense of motion in the wind. Later, when the paint dries, she'll speckle white snow on the wreath and finish it with a burgundy bow.

"Done." Jane gets up carefully, still favoring her newly broken left wrist. She adjusts the sling around her neck and walks to the windows. At least it's her left wrist that's broken, leaving her free, somewhat, to continue her designing. Her mother set up a temporary office space in the farmhouse's sunroom, with its wall of paned windows overlooking the carriage house and field beyond. It's a spot where the deer often graze, where they blend in with the sweeping brown and green wild grasses of autumn.

Outside, the scene that meets her eyes is a far cry from the December image she just painted for her latest greeting card. This window view is one of her favorites, though, this palette of gold and red and yellow October foliage, the copper weather vane on the carriage house glinting in the sunshine.

But autumn views won't help her artwork. If she's going to hold onto her job, she has got to find a way to channel *Christmas* during these brief weeks recuperating at her childhood home in Addison. It would really help if the vintage holiday cards she ordered would arrive. Their charm and whimsy from years gone by might inspire her to capture the spirit of the season, with a Jane March modern-day twist. Not needing a repeat of yesterday's front-door incident, she hurries back to the large table covered with her computer and paints and images, and grabs a blank sheet of paper. In a friendly cursive, she jots *Hello!* to the mailman, then asks if he might bring the mail up to the front stoop and leave it on the milk can there.

Hoping it's not too much to ask, Jane folds the note in half and heads to the door. With her good arm, she drags a brass umbrella stand over and props it in the doorway to stop the front door from locking shut behind her. Maybe those vintage cards will finally arrive today. She walks to the mailbox at the curb and tucks the note inside. Halfway back to the house, she looks over her shoulder, returns to the mailbox and flips the red flag up.

∽

Something about the country music playing on the radio suits him just fine. The way the singer's voice slides, it gives a sort of woeful rhythm to his stops, to the opening squeak and closing snap of the mailboxes. Until a car is idled, parked right in front of the next house and interrupting the sadness he's been channeling in song. Must be someone talking on their cell phone, pulled over to the curb oblivious to the necessary, and anticipated, approach of the letter carrier. Wes gives his mail truck horn a toot to move the driver along, then steers over to the curbside mailbox. He lifts a few letters from the side tray and tosses them in, giving the mailbox's loose door a good slam when it flops open as he puts the truck in gear.

Further down the road, the truck tires thump across the wooden planks of the covered bridge. Wouldn't he love to pause right there and look out on the babbling brook beneath it? Instead, he finishes delivering envelopes and sale flyers to the Brookside Road rustic Cape Cods and gabled-roof colonials, before turning onto Old Willow Road.

First stop there? Beautifully suited to the historic ship captain's house at the end of a long driveway is a shiny black mailbox mounted on an elaborate white post with a scrolled-metal vine displaying the house number. But the second box on the street is bungee-corded together, the cord wrapped around and around the box and post. Really, would it be too much to replace these shabby boxes barely attached to their dilapidated roadside posts? He opens it with a sigh, and the door wobbles on one hinge as he puts a padded envelope in the mailbox, then aligns the door and presses it shut before pulling away from the curb. All while some lonely cowboy wails about his heart, singing words he might as well have borrowed from Wes.

The air is cooler here in Olde Addison, which is closer to the water. The Connecticut River snakes off in the distance, a silver ribbon winding around the curves of the river valley, beyond the red and gold trees. He maneuvers past a weeping willow with branches cascading alongside the curb. At the March house, the flag is up on the blue-painted mailbox, and he's surprised to find that the note is for him. Surprised at first, then annoyed. Another delay interrupting the rhythm he and the country crooner have pieced together, Wes slamming mailboxes in beat to the song's bleeding heart.

So he flips up his non-postal-approved bomber jacket collar, checks his reflection in the rearview mirror to be sure he doesn't look too haggard, not having shaved for two days now, and slides the truck door open. A brisk wind flaps his regulation side-striped trousers, so he quickly walks along the stone path, up the stairs to the matching blue-painted porch, and sets the March mail on the milk can.

Right when he starts to turn, a gust of that October wind lifts one of the envelopes and flips it onto the floor, so he picks it up and knocks at the door with a few sharp raps. When no one answers, he glances around and sees an empty clay flowerpot perched on the porch railing. That'll have to do, because he can't waste any more of his meticulously scheduled time waiting to hand-deliver to finicky families on windy days. He drops the envelope on the milk can, sets the dusty flowerpot on top of it, turns and dashes down the porch steps, pushing up his leather jacket sleeve to check his watch as he goes.

"Wait!"

Oh, the thought crosses Wes' mind, so briefly, to keep hurrying to his truck and his now-behind-schedule mail delivery. The way her voice gets lost in the wind, she might think he missed hearing it. But instead he stops halfway down the walkway and turns back. He does a slight double take, expecting to see an apologetic Lillian March standing on the farmhouse porch, maybe waving an envelope she's hoping he can take. Not expecting to see who he believes might be her daughter, wearing a knitted shawl over jeans and leaning out from the doorway, sandy blonde hair swinging over her shoulder. He squints a moment, satisfied it is the daughter—Jane, he thinks her name is—and heads toward her.

"Did you have something to mail?" Wes asks.

"Wes?" Her right hand shields her eyes from the glare of sunshine as she stands in the open doorway. "Wes Davis? Is that you?"

"Guilty as charged."

"Well, how nice to see you. It's been so long."

"It has, Jane. It's Jane, right? How've you been?"

"Okay!" she says, nodding. "I'm doing okay. You're the ... mailman?"

As she says it, he sees it: the wide grin and slight tip of her head that he can't really read. "Just got my ten-year pin." Without thinking, he lifts the lapel of his non-regulation bomber and flashes the official pin on his shirt collar, before hiking up the leather jacket around his neck again.

"How do you like that! Very nice, and so is this valet mail service. Thank you."

He notices that Jane doesn't leave the house, but rather leans against the wood-paneled door, half in and half out. "No problem today. But it's a one-time deal, I'm on a schedule. Only the package companies do regular door delivery." His mail truck idles at the curb; it's where he itches to be, listening to that lonely heart singing his sad calamity—twang and all. And the way Jane's standing, still partially inside the house, it's clear she doesn't want to chat about mail routes, or the way packages are sequentially lined up in the rear of the truck. "Plus it's a busy road. Too much traffic to be parking the truck curbside."

Jane looks down to the—wouldn't you know it?—now-quiet country road. "It's just that my mother has the only key. She must have misplaced the extra, what with the past year she had," she explains. "And yesterday? Gosh, what a fiasco! I got locked out when this temperamental door closed behind me when I went to get the mail. Sat stranded on the porch all morning."

Wes checks his watch. "Sorry to hear that, but you're all set now." He turns to leave, and when she starts to ask something about handing her the mail from the milk can, he waves his hand without looking back. Seriously? She can't take a step outside for her mail? "Nice seeing you, Jane," he calls. As he trots down the blue-painted porch steps and along the stone walkway, he hears her dragging something across the floor. When he approaches his truck, he glances her way and sees an umbrella stand propped in front of that temperamental wooden door. As Jane steps out and bends for the mail, her shawl swings to the side—and he also catches sight of her left arm in a sling, leaving him feeling pretty much like a complete heel.

END OF EXCERPT.

CONTINUE READING IN...
JOANNE DEMAIO'S
SNOW DEER AND COCOA CHEER

Also by

JOANNE DEMAIO

Wintry Novels
Snow Deer and Cocoa Cheer
Snowflakes and Coffee Cakes

The Seaside Saga
The Beach Inn
Beach Breeze
Beach Blues
The Denim Blue Sea
Blue Jeans and Coffee Beans

Countryside New England Novels
True Blend
Whole Latte Life

For a complete list of books by *New York Times*
bestselling author Joanne DeMaio, visit:

www.joannedemaio.com

About the Author

JOANNE DEMAIO is a *New York Times* and *USA Today* bestselling author of contemporary fiction. She enjoys writing about friendship, family, love and choices, while setting her stories in New England towns or by the sea. Joanne lives with her family in Connecticut and is currently at work on her next novel.

For a complete list of books and for news on upcoming releases, please visit Joanne's website. She also enjoys hearing from readers on Facebook.

Author Website:
www.joannedemaio.com

Facebook:
www.facebook.com/JoanneDeMaioAuthor

Made in the USA
Middletown, DE
30 October 2017